I0652935

Reruns

Selina Rosen

YARD DOG PRESS

This is a work of fiction. All the characters and events portrayed in this book are fictitious, and any resemblance to real people is purely coincidental.

ISBN 978-1-945941-08-5

First Edition Copyright © 2004 by Selina Rosen
Second Edition Copyright © 2017 by Selina Rosen

All rights reserved, including the right to reproduce this book or portions thereof in any form, including electronic format, except for purposes of review.

Yard Dog Press
710 W. Redbud Lane
Alma, AR 72921-7247

http://www.yarddogpress.com

Edited by Tania Mears
Copy Editor Leonard Bishop
Technical Editor Lynn Stranathan
Cover art by Sherri Dean

First Edition June 1, 2004
Second Edition June 1, 2017
Printed in the United States of America
0 9 8 7 6 5 4 3 2 1

For everyone who ever wanted to be a Super Hero.

Chapter 1

"What the hell are you?" Tricordious demanded from where his tattered body was pinned against a brick wall by an iron-strong hand.

"What do you think I am?" the masked, raven-haired beauty countered.

"A demon manufactured in hell," he croaked out in gasps, his face quickly turning blue under the applied pressure of her hand on his throat

"You're wrong, Tricordious. *I* am a champion of justice, *you're* the demon manufactured in hell." She slung him to the ground, then dragged him over and handcuffed his unconscious body to a light pole. She lifted her wrist adorned by a huge, boxy-looking contraption to her mouth and spoke, "Captain Johnson, you'll find Tricordious gift-wrapped and waiting at the corner of Sixth and Main."

She turned and started to walk towards the sleek, black motorbike. "Who... who is this?" a man's voice asked.

She didn't raise the communicator back to her lips, just whispered into the darkness, "I am *Dark Avenger*, the Guardian of the Night. I am the Darkness."

She got on the bike and drove away just as police cars arrived on the scene.

"Fucking beautiful." Terry pressed the rewind button as she took a long drink from the beer bottle she held.

That's my fucking superpower. She thought without humor. *Beware evildoers! She can actually operate a remote and drink beer at the same time. Tremble in fear as she walks while chewing gum! She is Multi-Tasking woman.*

When the tape had finished rewinding she turned it back on. She watched the opening credits ten times in a row, watching then rewinding and watching them again. *I was something. Look at me; I really look the part, really looked invincible. The camera can make the impossible look real. A video can take you back to a time when you actually were someone.*

There was one scene where she was running around the corner full tilt. She wasn't even in the costume, but she looked... Well, the way she wished she looked now. That was the problem – having something like that to live up to. *Dark Avenger* was a woman on a mission, and no one was going to stop her reaching her final destination.

Terry felt like she'd reached her final destination, and now she was just going to lie here drinking beer and getting fatter. Her mission was apparently to see how miserable she could become, and she was off to a fantastic start.

I've never done anything since that has even mattered to me. I'm a friggin' tabloid joke, but I used to be Dark Avenger. I used to be her.

The show had come to an end twelve years ago. After a great seven-year run, the network had decided the ratings weren't high enough. A cable channel wanted to buy it, but the producers insisted on too much money and that was it. The end of an era, and in Terry's opinion, the end of her life.

Unlike most actors who feared typecasting, she would have been happy playing *Dark Avenger* or *Dark Avenger*-type characters for the rest of her life.

Terry had only really felt whole when she was playing that part. It was like the character was more her than she was. The problem was that, at least for the time being, Hollywood and America had lost their love of superheroes. It went in spurts. One week every other channel had a superhero show, and all the major filmmakers were flinging superhero movies out like popcorn. The next it was worn out and tired and there were none.

Her single mother had stuck Terry in front of a camera when she was two, successfully making Terry the "breadwinner" in the family. Terry had done a long string of minor roles, commercials, and lots of modeling jobs, until she got her "big break." It was as if the part had been custom made for her, and she knew the minute she tested for the part that she had it.

Her cold, controlling, money-grubbing stage mother died in a car accident four weeks into shooting the first season, and Terry felt like she had been reborn. Between her new role and finally being free of her mother, life had become perfect.

The show had been unbelievably successful, and she had been propelled onto the A-list. She was invited everywhere, and she saw and did anything and anyone she wanted to.

Mostly she just wanted to be *Dark Avenger*. It wasn't hard to get her to show up for public appearances in her costume, so the fans loved her.

It just hadn't dawned on her that it would ever – *could ever* – end, so when it did she was completely unprepared.

It was like someone reached up and shut off her life, and suddenly – as quickly as it had come – it was all, every bit of it, gone.

She watched the credits over and over till her bottle was dry, and then she shut the VCR off and went to get another beer. She didn't have to go far because the travel trailer she lived in just wasn't that big.

She reached in her refrigerator and pulled out one of the last three beers.

"Oh cruel fate," she cried out to the emptiness of the trailer.

The tapes were starting to show signs of age. She wished she had one of those DVD players they were always advertising on TV. The whole series was now available on DVD, and in fact she had been given a set as part of her royalties, but she couldn't afford the damn player.

She flopped back down on the tattered remains of her recliner and stared at the blank screen. People never understood how movie and TV stars who had made so much money could wind up destitute, but Terry could have told them exactly how.

It didn't matter how much money you had made; you still wanted to work. You didn't want to disappear. You wanted to stay on top, and the only way to ensure that you wouldn't become yesterday's news was to stay in the game. It cost a hell of a lot of money to stay in the Hollywood game. You had staff, and staff cost money. You were expected to be certain places and do certain things and have a certain lifestyle, and all of those things cost money. Meanwhile you got a few jobs making guest appearances on shows, and maybe you got some bit parts in some TV movies, but sometimes – most of the time – that perfect-for-you role only came around once in a lifetime. Eventually you found yourself lucky to be asked to sit in on this or that game show until even those jobs petered out.

She couldn't remember the last time she'd been found big enough to be on the Hollywood Squares. It hurt when you were a has-been among has-beens.

Eventually the only people who seemed to care about her

or even remember who she was were the hard-core sci-fi fans, but in the last few years even the sci-fi conventions were calling less often. They would, in fact, rather have someone who'd done a walk-in on a current show than have you.

So, you laid off the staff a little at a time till you didn't have one, and you sold off stuff till you were living in your old set trailer in the middle of a twenty-acre piece of ground seventy miles from any major city, because it was the only thing you hadn't managed to lose over the years trying to stay in the game.

Or at least that was how it had worked for her.

She sighed and guzzled the beer. It took the edge off, and put the weight on. She remembered a time when drinking a single beer would have put her mind to work on what she *wasn't* going to eat the next day. When she had counted every calorie that entered her body and worked out an hour a day just to make sure she looked... Well, like she did in the opening credits.

Several developers had tried to buy her land over the years, but she promised herself she'd turn her electric off and eat bugs first. She made enough money from royalties – thank God for reruns – to exist even in California.

And that was what she had decided to do, to exist. A year ago she'd quit trying to stay in the game, admitted that it was all over, and just slumped down out here in the woods to exist. She went into town two or three nights a week, got shit-faced drunk and woke up in the morning with one total stranger or another, with no idea how she'd gotten there or what had happened to the pocketful of money she'd had when she'd gone to the club.

It wasn't fair. They had given her something and then taken it away.

Fickle. That was the problem; the public was fickle. She had watched every *Dark Avenger* over and over again from the beginning to the end. The show hadn't lost any quality; in fact, she herself willingly admitted that she was a much better actress by the last season than she had been in the first. She had grown into the character, and the show had grown, too. It had, in her opinion and the opinion of most of the show's hard-core fans, gotten better over the years.

But somewhere along the line the general audience had gotten bored with *Dark Avenger* and moved on to the new sensation. Nighttime soaps if she remembered correctly.

The show left the air to be seen only in reruns. The dolls left the shelves, and three years later it wasn't unusual to hear a kid at a convention whisper back to their parent, "Who's *Dark Avenger?*" as they walked past a table where she was supposed to be signing autographs, but where there was no line.

It sucked. Reality sucked, and she longed to put on the uniform and transform herself into *Dark Avenger* again.

Of course there was no part of her that would fit into that suit right now. She knew because she had recently tried.

The suit didn't fit her, and she didn't fit into the real world.

She was just screwed.

"Terry, you have got to stop this shit, dry your ass out and come back to the real world," Janey pleaded.

Terry sighed. She had avoided this lunch date for three months because she didn't want anyone to see her as she was, and because she knew exactly what Janey was going to say.

"You know, Janey... You just have no idea what it's like. I couldn't get a job playing a rocket if I had fire coming out of my ass."

Janey laughed in spite of herself. "You know, Terry, you're funny, you're one of the most beautiful women in the world..." Terry stopped her with a simple look down her flabby frame. "That's not you. In fact, Terry, none of this is you."

"Janey, you just don't get it. The show ended, and you right away landed a part in a movie. You wind up winning an Oscar for your – excuse me for saying it – chickenshit role, and the rest is history. You go from playing second banana on a superhero TV show to being one of the most sought-after actresses in Hollywood, doing feature films. If even *you* can't get me work – and you can't – then what makes you think there are any parts for me? I suppose I could give up beer and pizza, go back to working out an hour a day, and get back into shape. And I realize I should if for no other than health reasons, but I just can't make myself give a shit about anything. Least of all my health. I go to sleep most nights hoping that I don't get up in the morning. Don't think I don't appreciate your friendship, because I do. I know it would be easy for you to just turn your back on me the way everyone else has. I know how busy you are," Terry sighed. "Why do you waste your time trying to save me?"

"Because I'd like to have my friend back."

Terry shrugged. "Then tell them to bring the show back."

"You know what the problem is, has always been? You don't want to be an actress. You want to be *Dark Avenger*. Well, you can't be, Terry, so why don't you just get over it and try to have some semblance of a life?"

Terry just shrugged and smiled as the waiter approached the table. "You paying for lunch?"

"Yes," Janey said with a sigh.

"Good, then I can get something that's like food. Don't worry about me, Janey. I'm just in a funk, it'll pass."

"Yeah, but is it going to take five more years?"

The waiter hit their table and they ordered.

"You can't go on like this, Terry," Janey said sadly.

"I don't want to go on at all. I can't *just go on*, because there is nowhere for me to go. Put yourself in my shoes, Janey. What if the show ended and you never had another decent role again? That show... being *Dark Avenger*, being Rita Clay, was all I was ever really good at. I need a reason to change my life, and I don't see people throwing one my way any time soon."

"Maybe it's time you quit waiting for answers to fall out of the sky into your lap and actually got off your ass and went looking for them."

"See now, that just sounds like an awful lot of work. First there's the getting up off my ass, and then there is all the looking around. No thanks. I'll just wallow in my self-pity. It's a damn sight easier."

"But it's not better," Janey said.

"See, Janey, that's the thing, you just don't know that for sure. I might get off my ass, look around for something to tack my life to that's going to steer me in the right direction, and find out that I already am right where I'm going to be. In which case, why make the effort? If I try again and fail again, I'm just going to feel even worse. Since I've fallen about as far as I can afford to fall, I just don't want to take the chance."

Chapter 2

Terry woke up with a pounding in her head. She didn't remember drinking that much. In fact, she was pretty sure that having spent all her money for the month she was still at home. She opened an eye slowly to see and realized she *was* at home at the same time she realized the pounding in her head was actually someone knocking on her door.

She got up, threw a stained terrycloth robe over her naked body, grabbed a cigarette and yelled, "Hold onto your shorts!" as she stumbled over the rubble to the front door. She swung it open and yelled, "What!" making the five foot four inch man standing there jump.

"God dammit, Terry." He stepped into the trailer, which she hadn't even bothered to level, and stepped around the litter, clothes and dishes that covered the floor. "I might have been an axe murderer for all you know."

"Axe murderer, worthless agent, it's all the same to me."

"Dammit all, look at yourself. You must have put on another twenty pounds."

"Twenty-five, but whose countin'?" She lit her cigarette and blew smoke in his general direction. "Close the door, the heater broke about a month ago."

"When did you start smoking?"

"Hello! Broken heater," Terry answered with a smile.

"Look at this fucking mess, and what is that smell?"

"I think it might actually be me," she sniffed at her armpits in turn. "Yep."

"Why do you insist on doing this to me?"

"Oh yeah, Dan, all this is just ruining your fucking life." She turned and went to the counter looking for the coffee and once finding it dumping some grounds into a pot, filling it with water, and setting it on the stove.

"I want to help you, I really do. I want to get you work, but you keep making it damn near impossible."

"I wasn't always fat, drunk, or smoking."

"No, but the series hadn't been shut down a whole year

when you announced to the world that you were queer."

"Yeah... well Ellen did it."

"Yes, and look at what it did for her career. She's just now come back into her own."

Terry shrugged. "They were saying being a lesbian was chic, I thought coming out would guarantee me some work. *You* sure hadn't gotten me anything worthwhile since the show ended. How was I supposed to know that everyone was lying about how cool everyone thought it was? I told everyone I was just kidding that I was really straight."

"No, what you did was insist that you weren't the woman in the video that your gold-digging ex-girlfriend made a fortune off of when she posted it on the web," Dan said, trying to remain calm.

"Same thing," Terry said with a shrug.

"If you weren't such a talented little shit, and if you hadn't once made me a shitload of money, I'd have washed my hands of you a long time ago, so you listen and listen good because I'm only going to say this once. They are talking about doing a *Dark Avenger* movie..."

"You're shitting me!"

"No I'm not. Now it's all speculation right now. Which is good, because if you have any chance of getting the role you are going to have to get yourself back into shape, and..."

"Done." Terry pulled the cigarette out of her mouth and crushed it out in the sink. Then she opened the refrigerator and took the twelve pack of beer out. She started opening them and pouring them down the sink one at a time. "All I needed was a good reason."

No gym would give her credit; her old trainer reminded her she still owed him money from five years ago, and her old dietician told her basically the same thing. So she bought herself some "healthy" food and topped off her tank and she was completely out of money till the next month – and it was only the fifteenth.

After having a mostly unproductive day she drove home in what was left of her Kia Sephia. The car rattled up the rutted dirt driveway, no doubt a large part of why it was in such shitty shape. She parked and looked at her place. Trash littered the ground. The trailer tilted at an angle so sharp she rolled into the corner every night. She'd had all sorts of plans when she'd first had to move up here. Coming to the woods was going to change her life, but it hadn't. She'd had the septic system hooked up, brought in water and electric, and had the phone hooked up. After she bought a few hand tools she'd been completely broke.

Realizing that she didn't have the money to do any of the things she'd planned, like build a home, she'd half-assed parked the lot trailer she'd been given when the show ended, and which had been in storage ever since. She'd only about half blocked it so that it didn't roll off down the hill. It did, however, rock. Then she'd settled back into a life of excess.

There didn't seem to be any way for her to catch a break.

The tools lay under the trailer, unused and collecting dust.

It had been easier to give up. It was too much work to try to change things without any money and without any help. People talked and talked and said they wanted to help, but they never actually *did* anything but give her advice that she couldn't take because she no longer had the money or the connections to "make things happen."

It seemed to Terry like someone was always throwing road-blocks in her way, keeping her from actually getting any-where, when all she really wanted was to get back to where she had been. Like today... she'd paid those shitheads a small fortune to basically stand there and watch her work out and tell her what to eat. Would it have killed either of them to have given her a break? There had been a time when any gym would have practically paid her to work out in their health club. Now she couldn't even afford any workout equipment, and she no longer had anything even approaching credit.

It was a phenomenon that baffled the imagination. As long as you were on the A-list – which meant you had more money than God – everything was given to you for free. The minute you slipped from the A-list and could actually use the free shit there was none to be found.

Now Rita Clay, she would find a way, Terry thought. *Dark Avenger was unstoppable. That's why I loved that character so much. She didn't put up with shit, and she never allowed herself to give up. If I want to be Rita Clay again, I have got to look like Rita Clay again. What would Dark Avenger do?*

The answer was clear. Rita Clay didn't need people to watch her work out and tell her what to eat. She was self-assured and self-reliant. A loner. She'd find a way to get what she needed without anyone's help.

Dark Avenger wouldn't live in such filth, in a torn up trailer that wasn't even level. She sure as hell wouldn't spend every penny she made in clubs getting drunk and screwing around with cheap women. *And not just because the character was straight, but because she would know that wasn't going to get her where she wanted to be. Dark Avenger would make the best of what she had and find a way to make her life better. Then, in success, she would bring her enemies to their knees.*

Rita Clay's enemy was Terry North and the apathy she'd let herself slip into.

She got out of her car and started picking up the trash. She'd just realized how she was going to get into shape.

She shoveled her trailer out and cleaned it till it shone inside and out. Then she took the cheap-assed jack from her car and used it to level the trailer. She gathered rocks in her wheelbarrow and stacked them around the bottom of the trailer like the old stacked-rock walls she'd seen when they'd shot some footage in Oklahoma. She slammed the rocks into place with a hammer till the trailer no longer rocked.

By the end of the third day every muscle in her body hurt, but she made herself get up at six, eat two eggs, drink a black cup of coffee, and get right to work again.

Next she worked on gathering rocks and filling the holes in her driveway.

Three weeks later, when that task was completed, she'd lost fifteen pounds and was already starting to get toned, and she also had a nice, smooth driveway. So she decided to clear some brush from around the trailer. All she had was an axe and a machete, so it was quite a workout.

She worked from early in the morning till it was dark all day, every day.

Clearing wasn't going to be enough, though. Terry wanted it to look good, but didn't really know how to do that. Now *Dark Avenger* had Marilyn Sims, the college librarian and computer genius, to do her research. Unfortunately, in real life Marilyn was actually Jayne Williams, a very successful actress, so Terry had to do the research herself. In the evenings she drove down to the county library and checked out books on gardening, landscaping, and building. She even downloaded plans she liked off the Internet.

Of course she couldn't remember everything she read because she didn't have Rita Clay's total recall, but she could make notes with the best of them.

When the area around the trailer had been cleared, she grabbed a shovel and started digging up flowerbeds. She laid a stone floor on the side of the trailer that had the door and circled the flowerbeds with stones. Then she bought plants and planted all the beds, mulching them with pine needles.

Since she had managed to stay away from the clubs and had quit drinking, she actually had money, so she had the supplies delivered to cover the trailer and build a room over the stone floor she had laid.

She built the entire project herself from plans she'd found on the Internet, modifying them for her needs, and she didn't think it looked half bad. She used rough-sawn boards on the exterior and interior walls with a layer of insulation between them. She took the door off the trailer and hung it for a front door in the addition and took the windows from that side of the trailer and put them in the walls. She knew they weren't exactly level, but they were close enough.

She thought she was about out of projects, but then she discovered cement. It was cheap and easy to use, and she had a never-ending supply of rocks.

She rocked up the trailer to the new roof so that she now had what appeared to be a very rustic stone and wood cabin. She filled in the cracks in her stone floor with concrete and built a stone chimney, because by then she had saved enough money for a wood stove. Which gave her a whole new project – dragging in deadfall, chopping it up, and stacking it for firewood.

She bought a weight set and put it in her addition, though she wondered why she had even bothered. She had never been this physically healthy in her life. Still, it couldn't hurt to get really pumped.

She felt good. She'd seen or talked to nearly no one in almost a year, yet she felt like she had found purpose. Dan called periodically to tell her that he hadn't heard anything solid on the movie, but something told her it was a done deal. They were going to make the *Dark Avenger* movie, and when they did, how could they not use her? She *was Dark Avenger*.

Terry had put her old *Dark Avenger* suit on, and the only

place it was tight was on her arms, because she was just in that good of shape.

She was ready.

I never would have guessed I was spending so much money at those damn clubs. I'm caught up on all my bills, I've done all the work here, and I was able to buy that new couch and chair, a DVD player, recliner and car in just one year."

Janey watched as her friend threw wood into the stove. "You know, Terry, I'm really proud of the way you have turned your life around. I mean, I would never want to live the whole wild-woods girl thing, but it seems to suit you."

"I did all this because I couldn't afford a trainer or a gym," Terry said with a laugh.

"What? I mean I'm glad you've come back to the land of the living, but you want to tell me exactly what the motivation was? I'm sure it wasn't my pep talk as much as I'd love to take credit."

"Dan told me they were talking about making a *Dark Avenger* movie. I knew I had to get in shape if I was going to get the role." She closed the door to the stove and turned to face her friend. "I'm just waiting for him to get in touch with me now."

Janey had been afraid of that. Dan had warned her that was Terry's only real motivation for her sudden transformation, but Janey had held on to some shred of hope that it wasn't true.

"What?" Terry asked suspiciously as she stood up.

"Nothing..."

"Don't fucking nothing me, what the hell is wrong?"

Janey took a deep breath. "All right, but you aren't going to like it. Dan sent me up here to talk to you."

"Dan did? What the hell's going on, Janey?"

"They... Well, they didn't want to use you at all. Didn't even want to talk about it with Dan. He went to the mat for you, Terry. They said they'd let you test..."

"Test!" Terry flopped into her new chair. "They're going to make me audition for my own role? That fucking sucks on ice. What about you?"

"I told them I wouldn't do the role unless you played *Dark Avenger*. I told them I could see no reason for me to be there if you weren't. I don't want to play that role against anyone but you."

"What did they say?"

"They said that was my option, but that they doubt they will be using you, so they'll be testing for my role as well."

"You didn't have to do that," Terry said.

"Yes I did. You heard me. I'm not doing this movie without you. I don't want to, and I sure as fuck don't need the work or the money. That role never meant to me what your role meant to you."

"I just naturally thought I was a shoe-in," Terry said.

"You probably are. I mean look at you, you're as gorgeous as ever, and I actually think you have more muscle."

"I did all this for nothing..."

"Hello! Earth to Terry," Janey said with a laugh. "Look at what you've accomplished in the last year, and you're happy – aren't you happier?"

"I was happy because I thought I had a chance to play *Dark Avenger* again. I was working towards something, I had a goal."

"Terry for God's own sake, this is why Dan didn't want to tell you himself. You have got to stop this shit. You aren't Rita Clay, you're Terry North and that isn't such a bad person to be. Just look at what you've done here. You built a house for Christ's sake, and you haven't lost yet. When they see you they've just got to cave. You'll knock their socks off."

Terry nodded silently.

They made her wait with fifty other girls, and they made her take a number.

"Hey, aren't you Terry North?" asked one of the girls, a woman with hair as short and as dark as hers and eyes just as blue, and who was maybe twenty.

"Yeah," Terry said.

The girl giggled. "My name's Mary Bright. I guess the rest of us might as well go home. I loved you so much in *Dark Avenger*. That's why I wanted to try out for this part. Such a great character."

Terry looked around the room realizing that they could have all been clones of her and all were at least ten years younger.

She read as she had never read before. She knew that she'd done the best performance of her life, and yet just as she had known that she was going to get the part that first time, she knew she wasn't going to get it this time.

They had made up their mind that they wanted someone younger in the role, and no matter how good she looked or how well she acted they just weren't going to give her the part. Maybe they were afraid of the whole queer thing, after all the Republicans were in office.

She was at Janey's to make sure that she'd be close if they wanted her to test again or just needed to talk to her, when she got the call from Dan.

"I'm really sorry kid," Dan said.

"Who got the part?"

"Mary Bright."

"So... it didn't even take them to the end of the day to decide they didn't want me. It's all right, Dan. You did your best, and I appreciate it."

"Listen kid, you stay in shape. I'll find you work. You look fabulous, and your reading... they were crazy for not using you."

"Thanks, I'll let you go, Dan."

"Don't do anything stupid, kid. You've come too far to go back now."

"Goodbye," she hung up.

Janey just looked at her, obviously afraid to say anything. "They gave it to Mary Bright."

"A girl whose name defies explanation since she's got to be the dullest crayon in the box."

"Yeah... Well, guess I'd better get home. It's a long drive.

"I really think you should stay with Tom and I tonight. We'll go out or something. I know how much this meant to you, Terry, and I don't think you should be alone."

"I won't be. Thanks for everything, Janey, but I don't want to be a very depressing fifth wheel. I mean you and Tom are actually together like maybe five times a year, and I'm not going to be fit company for anyone."

"We'd like you to stay," Tom said, walking into the room. "Please, Terry, we'd rather not have to worry about you."

"Don't. I don't drink and drive. I'll just go to a club, get sloshed, and some girl will take me home." She forced a smile. "Don't look at it like I'm falling off the wagon, just look at it like I'm getting my life back. It's the only life I seem to be fit for."

"Terry, it's just a fucking *part*. It's not your life. Don't do this shit to yourself," Janey begged, but Terry was already out the door and halfway to her car.

Tom grabbed Janey's arm at the door. "Let her go, Janey. She's hurting, probably needs a good cry, and you know she isn't going to do that in front of us,"

Janey turned and hugged him, crying on his shoulder. "It's just not fair. I have everything. We started out in the same place, and now I have everything and what does Terry have? It's just not right. Those fucking bastards."

"Would it make you feel better to call them immediately and tell them to stuff the part they want you to do up their collective tight asses?" Tom asked gently.

"Yes, I think it would."

And so she did for about ten minutes.

Terry drove till she came to the nearest gay club and then she parked her car and started for the door. Suddenly she stopped; what the hell was she doing? Janey was right; she'd come too far to just go back to what her life was like before.

She really *was* happier. It wasn't a heavenly life, but it beat the living hell out of what her life had been like before. She looked good, she felt good. So her life basically sucked. It didn't suck as bad as it had when she'd been living in squalor, filthy, barely able to walk without getting winded, with creditors on her back, letting scags she wouldn't look at sober have their way with her and basically roll her for all her money.

She hadn't been laid in the last year, but big deal, she didn't really remember getting laid the three years before that.

Right next to the bar was a Jujitsu school and class was in session. She'd trained in martial arts when she'd been working on the *Dark Avenger* set, but she hadn't done it in years.

She had the money. Maybe she'd walk right in and sign up.

Next thing she knew she was standing in gi pants and shirt working out with the rest of the class.

As she was driving home she called Janey.

"Hello."

"Hello, Janey, this is Terry. I thought you'd want to know..." and she told her what she'd done. "You're right, I can't go back to that. I have to try to persevere. Make things happen. If I never work away from the house again, who cares, right?"

"Exactly. I'm so glad you called. Just keep the good attitude, Terry. Things are about to turn around for you. I read it in your horoscope."

That night as Terry lay down to go to bed she wasn't happy, but she did feel as if she'd won a battle.

Chapter 3

Six months later Terry had already earned her black belt and was teaching a class of beginners three nights a week. It didn't pay much, but it was something to do, and it meant her own lessons were free.

At the end of the class one of the students who had just started that night walked up to her rubbing her wrist, which wasn't unusual for a beginner. She was a beautiful little Asian woman, about five-four, with a well-sculptured body you could have bounced quarters off of. She wore her long black hair in a braid that reached to the middle of her back, and her black eyes sparkled with life. So yeah, Terry had noticed her.

"Aren't you the same Terry North that used to play *Dark Avenger?*"

A year and a half ago it had been rare that anyone recognized her, but in the last few months it was happening more and more. People would walk up with their kids and ask for autographs, it felt good. "That would be me," Terry said, wiping her face on a towel.

"My name's Natalie Stein. My friends just call me Nat. I just got a job playing a bit part on *Monster Killer*. I've got to do a bunch of fighting scenes, so I thought I'd better take some classes, especially since I sort of told the producer I already knew martial arts. Since I'm Asian he just naturally assumed I was telling the truth, because of course all Asian people are gifted in the martial arts. I mean you can't look at me and tell I was raised in Beverly Hills by a middle aged Jewish couple. I can cant the section of Torah I did at my Bat mitzvah and speak fluent Hebrew, but I don't know shit about martial arts."

"Stereotypes can be so weird can't they? I sort of guessed it was your first time. Don't worry you've got a lot of natural ability, so you'll catch on quick. Hell, I told one producer that I was an expert on classical literature, and at the time the most classical thing I'd read were old X-men comics," Terry said with a laugh.

"Terry, you work out with me now," the sensai said with a

sly smile.

"Hang out if you'd like to see me get my ass kicked, might make you feel better about that twisted wrist."

"I just might learn something," Natalie said with a nod and a smile.

Chang did stomp her ass, but Terry noticed with pride that he had to work harder at it every time.

Natalie had obviously showered and changed her clothes but was still hanging out. "So," she acted a little nervous, which surprised Terry more than a little. "You want to maybe go get some coffee?"

"Sure, just let me get cleaned up." Terry didn't for a minute think that the younger woman was hitting on her, though that would have been nice. Most probably she wanted to pick Terry's brain about jujitsu, acting, or both. She showered quickly and changed.

"There's a place I noticed around the corner," Natalie said.

Terry nodded – she'd seen it before – and followed.

"I must have watched every *Dark Avenger* adventure about fifty times."

So the topic was to be acting.

"Me, too," Terry said feigning surprise. Natalie laughed.

They walked into the coffee house and took a corner booth. Terry preferred these to the ones where you had to wait in line. If she was going to spend two bucks for a cup of coffee, the least they could do was to bring it to her.

"Why didn't you want to do the movie?"

Terry took a deep breath, counted to ten, and let it out.

"Sore subject?" Natalie guessed.

"I wanted the part more than I wanted to live. I even tested for it, which I thought was crap. I just didn't get it. I don't know exactly why. I did a kick-ass reading, best one I'd ever done. The age thing, or the gay thing, maybe the video tape of me boffing some trollop, or maybe all three. They just didn't want me. They never wanted me for the role. So yeah, I'm more or less permanently pissed about the whole thing."

Natalie nodded silently, and Terry would have known from the expression on her face even if she hadn't said, "I've decided to stay in the closet. At least for now."

"That's probably for the best as long as the Republicans are in office," Terry said with a smile.

"The part I have... it's not a big one, but they say it might grow. I want to do a good job. I'm not looking to get in a relationship right now. I just want to work on my career, devote all my effort to acting. So I see no reason to open myself up to the kind of crap you've been through. They keep saying society's open and it's not a big deal, but every time an actress comes out she winds up getting bit parts if she gets any work at all."

I just want to be friends, so you stay on your side of the table and I'll stay on mine. I just want to talk to another gay actress, I don't want to start a thing. OK, kid. I get it. It sucks, but I get it.

They talked for a long time – till Terry had the shakes from drinking way too much coffee – about everything and nothing. Then Natalie looked at her watch and said, "It's late and I've got an early casting call. Thanks for listening to my crap."

"Thanks for listening to mine. So I'll see you Thursday night?"

"Yeah, till I either get good enough to keep them fooled or they figure me out and fire me."

Three times a week for six weeks she and Natalie met, worked out together at the school, and then had coffee and talked. They became good friends, and Terry never tried to make it anything more though she very badly wanted to. In fact, it was *because* she wanted so much to pursue Natalie that she kept her distance. She'd never had this good a connection with anyone, and she just didn't want to risk screwing it up.

It was nice just to have a friend she had so much in common with. Terry had a vivid imagination and she didn't mind at all pretending that their relationship was more intimate than it was when she was all alone in her own bed.

Of course just when she was sure their relationship was about to make that most important jump soon, they started shooting the season in earnest and Natalie had no time for either classes or coffee. She called occasionally when she just needed to vent, but other than that Terry didn't hear from her.

Terry continued to make the hour-long drive to the school three nights a week to teach classes and get her ass kicked by Chang. It had taken the place of getting drunk and clubbing, which she decided was at least physically healthier although sometimes when she had an exceptionally large bruise she wondered.

By day she kept busy working on her place. After a neighbor's dogs dismantled her flowerbeds and she had to start over again from scratch, she decided to fence her property. Fencing twenty acres with a dog-proof fence turned out to be a bigger project than she would have thought. First you had to clear a path to put the fence up, so she bought a chain saw and started cutting and a month later she had enough firewood for five years but still hadn't finished clearing the line.

When she walked in from a hard day of cutting timber the phone was ringing and she picked it up.

"Hello," she said, trying to catch her breath.

"Hello, Terry, this is Dan."

"Well I'm guessing from the tone of your voice that you didn't call to tell me you've found me a huge role just right for me."

"Brian York called today."

Terry knew who he was – the producer for the *Dark Avenger* movie. "What the fuck does he want from me?"

"He... Well, he says you are no longer certified to appear in public in the *Dark Avenger* suit."

"Fuck him..."

"He's threatening to bring a lawsuit, Terry. The movie's coming out in two months and they want to make sure that people start to see Mary Bright as *Dark Avenger*..."

"But she's not and she never will be."

"I know that, Terry, but..."

"I won't wear the damn costume. Fine. I've got like what maybe two Sci-Fi conventions to do all year? I didn't wear it for all the years I couldn't, and I won't wear it now."

"I'm sorry, Terry."

"Don't be sorry, Dan, it isn't your fault. I'm thirty-two years old and I'm a has-been. I live off royalties from the series I shot in my youth and I work three nights a week training rich people's brats and bored housewives how to fight. It's a life. It ain't a good one, but it's mine."

She hung up, and when the phone rang a few minutes later she fully expected it to be either Janey or Dan checking to make sure she hadn't slit her wrists, so she answered the phone with a hardy...

"Hang on, I ain't done bleedin', no need to call 911 yet."

"Terry... are you all right?" Natalie asked.

Terry realized then that she'd been crying and worked at controlling herself. "I'm fine," she answered after a long pause.

"Well you don't sound fine," Natalie said, concern edging into her voice.

"Well I am, just let it drop. What's up with you?"

"Nothing important, now what the fuck's wrong?"

"You'll just think it's some stupid shit,"

"Tell me anyway. I call to whine to you three times a week. I think maybe it's my turn to listen to your stupid shit. It will sort of even the playing field,"

Terry told her what had just happened. "...I know it's crazy, but asking me not to wear that damn suit is like telling me to leave my skin at home. I haven't worn the damn thing in public for years, so I don't know why it's bothering me so much, but it is,"

"It's a really chickenshit thing for them to do. I mean you were *Dark Avenger* for what six years?"

"Seven, but whose counting?"

"And this bimbo has been the character for like fifteen minutes."

"Exactly." She suddenly felt better. She realized why Natalie called her so much. It helped to have someone on your side. It made you feel better knowing that not everyone thought you were nuts about the petty little shit that bothered you about the business Natalie was part of, and that she had once been part of.

"You know, Terry, any time you need to talk all you have to do is pick up the phone."

"Thanks, I will. I... I miss hanging out at the coffee shop just talking and drinking way too much coffee,"

"Yeah me, too. Maybe we should get together sometime."

But they didn't. They just called each other every time they needed to bitch, which still made it the best relationship Terry had ever had.

The movie had been released a month earlier and everyone at the convention found it necessary to tell her that Mary Bright would never be *Dark Avenger*, and how much they hated the movie, which was good because she needed to hear it. Of course the information was tainted because if they had been truly loyal they wouldn't have gone to the fucking movie in the first place, and as it was her "loyal fans" had made the movie an instant box office smash. Thus ensuring that Mary Bright would forever more be *Dark Avenger*.

Terry made a point of telling every group she spoke to how the producers had dissed her and told her she couldn't even wear the suit.

She felt somewhat vindicated.

Terry didn't have anyone to come between her and the fans. She couldn't afford it. So she just mingled with them, and – aside from the occasional weirdo – enjoyed them. The other minor stars in attendance had large entourages and pictures to sell. She sat at the autograph table and signed memorabilia the fans brought her, napkins, and program books.

She was a total loser, but they all thought she was still a hero.

She sat in the dealer's room with five other "stars" at the first of three mass signings she was to do during the weekend.

She looked up and saw someone's rather large entourage approaching. It was so big in fact that she couldn't see who the star was. No doubt it was the headliner. She had no idea who that was – she never even bothered to look at the program book till she was home anymore. At one time she had tried to meet the other movie and TV stars at these things, but then seeing her as a has-been, they had started to snub her, and that was just too much. So she just went, and if the others talked to her great, and if they didn't that was all right, too.

Suddenly she saw movement at the entourage's back. She looked up at the guy whose program book she was signing. "Excuse me." She stood up and walked quickly around the table. She <u>wasn't</u> seeing things. She ran, grabbing a sword off a dealer's table as she went, ignoring his screams and ran towards the entourage. "Look out!" she screamed, and the idiots parted like a wave, allowing the maniac with a sword to head straight for the star they'd been shielding.

The blade was screaming through the air, and then she was there between them catching the blade on the one she held. She kicked out, hitting the guy in the stomach and sending him flying through the air to land against a dealer's table, which fell with a clatter. She jumped across the expanse and stepped on the guy's hand where it held the sword. She rested the tip of the sword she held against the thug's throat and said, "If you move I'll cut your head off."

The guy started screaming in pain, "Get off my hand you crazy bitch!"

"How's, NO! grab ya?" Terry screamed back.

Security ran in. One of them asked Terry for her sword, and she handed it to him, just barely aware that she'd done so. Her blood was pumping; she felt empowered. *Bring on another bad guy – I ain't even worked up a sweat.*

"My God, Terry, you're hurt," she heard Natalie's voice saying.

She looked down at Natalie's face, and the blood on her arm, and spat out in one breath – as you can only do when you're adrenalin is doing the talking. "Hey Nat, it's great to see you. What are you doing here with the rest of us peons?"

"Terry... you just. You just saved my life," Natalie said. Terry was a little hurt by the tone of disbelief in Nat's voice; after all she was a fucking superhero. "Terry's hurt, can we get some help over here?" Natalie yelled.

EMTs seemed to appear from thin air. They sat Terry in a chair and started to administer first aid to her arm. "Miss North, you're going to need a couple of stitches," one of them said.

"Really? It doesn't even hurt," Terry said.

"You could have gotten yourself killed!" Natalie screamed at her, and Terry smiled up at her.

"Ah, Nat, I didn't know that you cared," Terry said jokingly.

"It's not funny, Terry, he might have cut your fool butch head off."

"Miss Stein, if she hadn't appeared when she did, you might have been killed," some miscellaneous fan boy said.

"I'm a bad-ass mother fucker, oh yeah," Terry said as they were laying her on the stretcher. Then she was out.

She came to a few seconds later as they were putting her in the ambulance, feeling considerably less butch than she had before she passed out.

"Ms. North, can you hear me?"

"Yes, did I lose that much blood?"

"No, just a combination of all the adrenalin and the pain of the injury. You lay down and blacked out for a second is all. It happens all the time."

"I kicked that guy's ass."

"Yes you did. You're a hero, but then you are *Dark Avenger*."

"Accept no fucking imitation!" she yelled out the back of the ambulance. She saw Natalie being dragged away by security and heard police sirens coming in.

They closed the doors to the ambulance. She felt high. The feeling remained all the way to the hospital and as she watched them putting the six stitches in her arm. Even when she was answering the police officer's questions about the attack, she felt great. The whole time she had to fight the desire to crow. When the police drove her back to the hotel she started to come down, then remembered what a bad ass she was and felt pumped right back up again. As she walked in people started clapping. She bowed flamboyantly, and then she did let out a crow.

She momentarily wondered where Natalie had gone then walked straight back to the dealer's room and sat down at the autograph table as if nothing had happened. Immediately a huge line formed, much bigger than it had been before, and she started signing autographs, talking to each person. The guy whose sword she'd taken showed up with the sheath for the sword and asked her to sign it.

"You want me to sign the sword?" Terry asked.

"Can't, they took it for evidence. They said I can probably have it back later."

"So," she said signing the scabbard. "Did that guy pick up a sword here, too?"

"No, bastard smuggled it in under his shirt, but you know it will cause the sword dealers no end of grief. By the way, I'm sorry I yelled at you. I didn't know who you were. You were so fast I just thought someone was stealing a sword."

"Do we know why he went after Natalie?"

"Rumor is he's the guy that's been stalking her. Sending threatening letters and such. They're saying he fell in love with her character and then got upset when Lang Su started banging James on the show. He thought he was like killing a cheating girlfriend. Real weirdo."

Not the sort of thing you expected to hear from a guy with six piercings on his face and tattoos covering both arms.

"Yeah, no doubt," Terry said.

He walked away, and the next one walked up. She looked up and saw Natalie heading her way, now flanked by two security guards as well as her entourage.

She left them behind in spite of their protests and squeezed in behind the table with Terry. She knelt down and asked in an angry whisper, "What in hell's name are you doing?"

"Saving young girls in distress, taking down bad guys, later I'm thinking of leaping a tall building in a single bound," Terry said with a smile as she signed the program book she was handed.

"You know what I mean. Why aren't you in the hospital?"

"Because it's not much more than a scratch," Terry said with a shrug, "and when you're me you have to savor any attention you can get."

"A scratch doesn't need stitches. You should at least be in your room resting. That's what *I* was trying to do when my people told me you were on the floor again."

"You know, if you keep bitching at me," Terry said in a whisper, "people are going to think we're an item."

Natalie turned a little red.

"Now *I* have a reason to be pissed off. Why didn't you tell me you had a stalker?"

Natalie managed a smile then as if suddenly finding her sense of humor again. "I didn't want you to be jealous." Then she added on a more sober note. "The police had been handling it. But it was just letters, and I personally thought he was just a harmless crank. Shows what I get for thinking. Frankly I'm scared shitless, aren't you even scared a little bit?"

"No." She never stopped signing autographs. "Maybe the reality of it will kick in later but right now I just feel like I could kick the world's ass."

"You saved my life, Terry. I don't know how I'm ever going to thank you for that."

"Don't sweat it – I didn't even know it was you."

Then her brain kicked in and she thought. *Shit, sexy woman I've got a crush on gives me a line like that, and I tell her I didn't even know it was her. I am soooo losing my touch with the ladies.*

She tired to think of a save, but couldn't. The moment was gone forever. So she just continued in the same vein she had been going in. As the TV cameras and news crews showed up she was actually practically screaming, "For *Dark Avenger* fights injustice and corruption no matter who is at peril. Friend or stranger – it matters not."

They spent most of the next two hours being interviewed by this reporter or that one, and the whole time Terry kept thinking. *That'll teach them not to give me the part, not to let me wear the suit. You stupid fuckers. You hired some chicken-shit baby actress when you could have hired the real Dark Avenger.*

Terry had to take a bath when she preferred to shower – that was about as much annoyance as the wound was caus-ing her. She swore it didn't hurt. She was just getting out of the tub when there was a knock on the door.

"One moment!" She dried off and threw on her robe. She looked out the peek hole, saw it was Natalie and opened the door. Natalie came in and Terry made a point of looking out the door. "Where is everyone?"

"Asleep like my – and apparently your – good sense," Natalie answered smiling.

Terry closed and locked the door. She looked at the clock. It was after midnight. "So what are you doing out in the middle of the night, little girl?"

"I couldn't sleep. You know part of me is so thankful that you saved me, and another part is so angry that you would risk your life like that, and I guess that's why I can't sleep."

"Huh?" Terry asked with a confused smile.

"I never wanted to care this much about you Terry. Not this way, and not now. My career is just getting started. I just wanted to focus on that, not this, not with you. I mean, you're mostly a nut job. I've tried staying away, but I wind up calling all the time, and not just because I need to vent. I make up excuses to call because I just want to hear your voice. And today... I knew you were going to be here, but you didn't know I was going to be here, did you?"

"No," Terry answered honestly. "I just go where I'm told to go. I never check the guest list."

"My agent told me not to do this convention, that I'm too big for it, if you can believe that shit."

Terry nodded, "When you're on a popular show that's still running, hell you can be an occasional guest star and be too big for some of these conventions."

"The point is that I took it anyway to have an excuse to see you. I won't meet you for coffee fifteen minutes from my house because I'm afraid something will happen or someone will see us together. But I'll travel halfway across the country, where we'd both be working and nothing would be likely to happen, and I could just be close to you and see you, and... My God, Terry, playing my stupid game I almost got us both killed. I don't know what I'd do if anything happened to you. I can't go on like this, wondering if you might feel the same way, and if you do I don't want to play this game anymore. I just want us to be together."

Terry slapped herself in the face – hard.

"What the hell?" Natalie stepped back startled.

"I'm just having such a great day I had to check to make sure I was awake." She closed the distance between them and took Natalie in her arms and kissed her. She didn't get slapped again, so she was pretty sure she *was* dreaming.

Terry woke up the next morning and turned slowly in the bed, half afraid she was going to find that she was alone or with some old hide. She wasn't. She kissed Natalie's bare shoulder then moved up against her back and wrapped herself around her.

She felt Natalie wrap her fingers up with hers and smiled. "So, are you sorry you're here?" Terry asked carefully.

"Not at all," Natalie snuggled back into her. "What about *you*? Are you sorry I'm here?"

"You know I'm not," Terry said.

"How's your arm?" Natalie asked.

"It itches. It still doesn't hurt."

Natalie stretched and yawned then let go of Terry's hand and rolled in her arms to face her. Then she was jerking away and crawling across the bed. "My fucking God!"

"Is my breath that bad?" Terry asked with a laugh.

"I just saw the clock. It's 11:00 I'm supposed to give a talk at 12:00. If Sarah goes to wake me up..."

"You'd better get back to your room," Terry said, her disappointment evident in her voice as she watched Natalie throw her clothes on.

Nat ran over and kissed Terry quickly on the lips. "Tonight?"

"Yeah."

And she was gone.

Terry frowned and pulled herself out of bed. She should really check her itinerary and see what she was supposed to be doing and when.

She stood in the middle of the room, oblivious to her nakedness and smiled. Yep, yesterday was definitely worth writing down.

Superhero saves the day and gets the girl.

Her itinerary said she didn't have anything to do till 1:00, so she flopped back on the bed and turned on the tube, just reveling in the moment.

She looked at the dressing on her arm. *Oh yeah, I'm it. I know, I'll get dressed go down, work out and show up at my talk in my gym clothes all sweaty. Show people that I don't let a little thing like a sword cut stop me. No-siree-Bob.*

She took another bath, reluctant to wash Natalie's DNA from her body, but wanting to feel fresh before she went and got all sweaty. After her bath she dressed in tank top – to show off her wound - and sweat pants and headed for the gym.

The gym was disappointingly empty. Since there was actually no one to impress with her incredible butchness, when her arm started to throb – actually hurting for the first time since she'd gotten the injury – she quit and started back for her room, deciding being sweaty wasn't nearly as cool as she thought it was going to be.

Someone fell in behind her and she gave him a quick look. Just some fan boy, nothing to worry about.

Well at least nothing for me to worry about. He steps out of line and I'll...

"Terry?"

She turned to face the guy. He was familiar.

"Terry North?"

She smiled broadly as recognition flooded in. "Paul Aderly, you old dog." She walked up to him and hugged him. "Damn, I haven't seen you since..."

"They canceled our show," he said, an edge of bitterness to his voice.

Paul Aderly was the creative genius behind *Dark Avenger*, and from what she understood the new movie had screwed him at least as badly as they had her. The producers had apparently used a clause in his original contract to basically steal the entire *Dark Avenger* universe away from him. He hadn't been called back to write for the new movie, and had in fact been told that he had sold all his rights, and therefore wouldn't be making a dime off the movie rights. They could do whatever they wanted with the character and the universe he had created.

"I have to say I'm a little surprised. They had told me... I heard you'd... well, let yourself go. You look great, better than ever."

"Thanks, but in all honesty I did let myself go. I got as big as a fucking house. Then... well I thought I was going to get to play *Dark Avenger* again if I could only get back in shape so... I did, and they basically screwed me the same way they did you, without the Vaseline."

"Yes, well at least you didn't bend over and ask for it. I take a closer look at anything I sign these days," Paul smiled. "So... I heard about yesterday." He pointed at the bandage on her arm and smiled. "Did you forget you weren't her for a minute?"

"No. For a minute I just flat *was* her." Terry laughed. "It was so incredibly cool... I mean not that someone was trying to kill Natalie, that's not cool, but the way my instincts just seemed to kick right in. I've actually gotten my black belt in jujitsu. I've been training with a master, but I never would have guessed how my body would just react with my brain just going along for the ride."

Paul nodded. "Give you impenetrable skin and photographic memory and you'd be ready to go fight crime?"

"I'd need a cool suit. They won't let me wear the *Dark Avenger* suit any more you know."

"I'd heard that. It's a real load of crap isn't it? I mean, I made the character up, you brought it to life, and now we're on the outside looking in as they destroy what took us years to build. Everyone's going to see the movie, but no one I've talked to likes it, and while they might tell *you* that just because of who you are... Well, no one ever knows who the fuck the writer is, do they?"

"They made me test, which already pissed me off, but then... I get there and they have all these twenty-year-old bimbos. Well, I know then what they're going to do. They're going to go back to the very beginning and redo the origins of

Dark Avenger. The problem being that all the hard-core fans have already watched that about a billion times in episode one."

Paul nodded. "Then the dumb bastards, figuring that's the case, change the story, which fucks with what our fans know is true and so they hate it. Unfortunately all the new fans have no idea what or who *Dark Avenger* is supposed to be."

Terry nodded. "What time is it?"

"12:30."

"Damn, I've got to get cleaned up and changed. I'll talk to you later, maybe we could meet for dinner."

He nodded and she started to walk away.

"Hey, North!" She stopped and turned around. "For my money, no one else could ever be Rita Clay."

"You know Paul, most days I still wish I *was* Rita Clay." She laughed. "And yesterday for a split second, I was."

They asked mostly stupid questions that she'd answered hundreds of times before, and some brand new ones.

"What do you think the big difference is between the series and the movie?"

"Well, in all honesty I haven't seen the movie..."

"It's pure crap!" one of the fans screamed.

"Well, that would be one of the differences. Listen, they dissed me, and they dissed Paul Aderly. He created the entire *Dark Avenger* universe, so how can the movie be anything like the series without Paul writing it? Without him at least having some creative input? I met Mary Bright during the screen tests. She's a nice kid, but she ain't no Rita Clay, and she certainly isn't *Dark Avenger.* You have to play both parts well or it just doesn't work.

"Rita Clay is smart, too smart to fit into the real world, to have a normal life. *Dark Avenger* is driven by passion, a creature that moves with animal-like instincts and attacks the same way. The whole story is about the conflict between this character's very different sides. How she learns to deal with both her incredible intellect and her animal instincts.

"I don't know if they've captured that duality in the movie. I personally doubt it, because Mary Bright seemed like a pretty one-dimensional person. Next question."

"If you could pick your next role, what would it be?"

Damn, how many times had she been asked that over the last ten years? But today she had a slightly different answer. She smiled. "Well, after the events of yesterday I can honestly say that if I could choose I wouldn't play a role anymore, I'd just BE *Dark Avenger*. If I could be anything I wanted to be, I'd be a superhero. Janey always said that about me, and yesterday I realized she was right."

She had hoped that Natalie would meet her outside the door but knew that probably wasn't going to happen. She was glad to see Paul.

"Paul." She hugged him.

"So... eat in the bar?"

"Yeah, that'd be great. I'm starved. I haven't eaten since last night sometime."

He led her towards the bar. "I caught most of your Q and A session. So you really want to be *Dark Avenger*?"

"Shit yes, who wouldn't?" Terry laughed. "Without the aversion to sunlight, of course, because that would just suck. But I'd love to just run around kicking bad guy's asses. It would be way cool."

They sat in a corner booth, and a waiter seemed to appear from thin air. "Beer?" Paul asked.

"One, a lite," Terry said.

"I love you," the waiter gushed.

Terry smiled. "Thanks."

"I'll have a lite beer, too."

"We have Miller, Busch, and Budweiser."

"Busch," they both answered.

"We'd like menus, too," Paul said.

"I got it." The waiter left.

"So... what have you been doing with yourself since they canceled the show?" Terry asked.

"Working for the government in textiles actually, till about six months ago. They decided my methods were too unorthodox and nixed my program."

"Yeah, I remember you said you had some degree in biochemistry."

"That's right," Paul smiled. "And do you remember why I said I created the *Dark Avenger* universe?"

She didn't even have to think about it. "To cope with what happened to your family." Of course she remembered, how could she forget? Paul had been sixteen. He'd come home from Boy Scout camp to find his mother, father and two sisters brutally murdered. They had been a lower middle-class family living in a lower-class neighborhood, and no one had heard or seen anything. No one had bothered to ask why his father hadn't showed up for work. No one had bothered to ask *anything*, and Paul had come home to find their bloated, stinking at least one week old – because of the lack of air-conditioning in the home they had no real idea how long they'd been dead – mutilated corpses. There was no apparent motive. Nothing had been stolen, but everything had been smashed. Paul's family had been one of the only white families in the neighborhood, so the police suspected a local black gang, but no one was ever charged. The killers went free, and Paul wound up in an institution for children with nowhere else to go. He had escaped all that had happened to him by creating an alternate universe, a place in which at least one person stood against the darkness and helped those for whom there was no justice. A character who was judge, jury, and executioner when the crime warranted it.

"I don't think any of those bastards even knew, and if they did they didn't bother to remember. *Dark Avenger* got me through a really hard time, and I always hoped that it helped other people get through some hard times, too. It was important to me."

"It was important to all of us, Paul, and they took it away," Terry said bitterly. "That's the way this stinking business is, handing you the world on a silver platter and then ripping it away from you as soon as you get used to it."

"People need hope, Terry. They need something, someone to believe in."

"In a time when justice is blind, and serves only the rich and powerful, when the innocent cry out in pain, only one champion will split the darkness," Terry quoted the opening sequence for the show.

The waiter brought their beers and the menus then waited while they ordered. When he left Paul took a long drink of his beer, then started talking again.

"When the show ended I didn't want to write anything else. I'm a scientist, an inventor, not really a writer at all."

"Paul, you're a great writer," Terry protested.

"No I'm not, Terry. I told one story very well. Everyone's got at least one story in them. Mine was *Dark Avenger* and we both know that I stupidly farted around and lost all the rights to it. So I went to work for this textile company, which does a lot of stuff for the military. I was there for four years then... well they decided everything I was doing was," he changed to a high pitched nasal whine, "too expensive and over the top," he took his real voice back again, "I had some real ideas. Different ones, they of course wanted to make something cheap and deadly that they could put in the hand of every soldier boy on the front, side or back lines. I had something a little more complex but smaller scale in mind. After what happened to me with *Dark Avenger* I wasn't about to let someone take my hard work pervert it and cut me out. Like I said I read contracts a lot more carefully these days."

"No one can blame you for that. So... what are you doing now?" Terry asked.

"Well... I don't want to brag but I took all the money I made on *Dark Avenger* and put it in Microsoft stocks before all the hubbub and sold before the crap started. So I've basically got more money than God. I've been just sort of hanging out working on my projects getting closer to my goal."

"Now what would that be?" Terry asked with a smile.

Paul smiled back and shook his head. "Let me tell you a little phrase I learned when I was working for Biological Technologies... I'm not at liberty to say."

"Understood," Terry had finished her beer and was fighting the impulse to have another one. When the waiter walked by she asked him to bring her a bottle of water.

"What kind," he asked, "we have..."

"Something in a pretty bottle."

He nodded and walked away.

"So what have you been up to?" Paul asked her.

"Well you knew about my whole coming out thing?"

"Yes."

"And the video tape."

"Yes."

"Well, boom!" She flung her hands out for effect. "No career. I kept trying to buy my way back into the game and wound up having to sell almost everything to pay my debts."

"Almost everything?"

"I got to keep my lot trailer and twenty acres I'd bought just outside of Big Sur." She smiled. "I bought it because I wanted to build *Dark Avenger*s woodland hideout, and yes, I know that's crazy, but it's a good thing I did because otherwise I wouldn't have had anywhere to stick my trailer. Well I'll never have the money to do that, but I've sort of made my own hideout. To tell the truth I mostly lay around drunk, eating pizza, and screwing any woman who would take me home, till about a year and a half ago, when I got in shape so I could get the *Dark Avenger* role. I almost went back to the beer, pussy, and pizza diet after I didn't get the part."

"I'll bet."

They ate their dinner and Paul had another couple of beers and started talking about shit she didn't really understand about spider DNA and milking goats and making bulletproof vests, but it was pretty obvious that he was a lot smarter than she'd given him credit for and a hell of a lot smarter than she was.

How intelligent someone is, is directly related to how little you understand what they're saying. Terry thought with a smile.

A woman walked up to Terry she coughed.

"Ms. North I hate to bother you when you're eating dinner. I'm..." she looked nervously at Paul and then leaned down to whisper in Terry's ear. "I'm Nat's personal assistant, she wanted me to ask you for your room key, she said to tell you she'd be waiting for you." The woman straightened looking around and in the process making herself much more conspicuous than she otherwise would have been.

Terry smiled, nodded, reached in her front pocket, extracted the card and handed it to the woman. Who took it quickly, nodded, shoved it in her pocket and took off.

Across the table Paul gave her a knowing smile. "She wasn't bad looking."

"No, but she isn't my girlfriend." *Girlfriend,* she thought about that for a minute, was Natalie her girlfriend, or where they just having a fling over the weekend? It didn't matter. She wanted Natalie to be her girlfriend so she would call her that.

Paul nodded. "Natalie Stein?"

"Now how did you know that?" Terry asked in a low angry whisper.

"It made sense. Why else would you risk your life for her? How you'd know to watch for the stalker?"

"Actually, smart ass... I didn't even know Nat was going to

be here. I didn't know it was her that I was saving. And I didn't know about the stalker, she never told me. It was weird, Paul. Like I told you this morning it was like for a second I was her. I just saw a guy with a sword and I acted – I didn't think. I was running on pure instinct and adrenalin just like *Dark Avenger*." She put down her fork and shook a finger at him. "By God, Paul, you better not tell anyone about me and Nat. I don't want her to end up like me."

"Hey, chick, remember who you're talking to. I was out of ye old closet long before you were. I would never out some-one, it ain't cool. And she'd be doing good to end up like you. You're smart, you're funny and how many people in this world would put their life on the line without even knowing who the target was? That's what makes you a hero, Terry. That was what you brought to the part that Mary Bright never could."

"Thanks, Paul," she smiled feeling smug.

She ate the rest of her dinner too fast. "Paul, do you mind..."

"Picking up the tab."

She stood up and took her wallet out of her hip pocket. "I can pay for my own meal. I was just going to say do you mind if I hurry off? It's been fun, but..."

"Say no more, Terry, if I were you I'd be rushing back to my room, too. Let me get dinner, like I said..."

"More money than God."

"Yeah," Paul answered. He stood up and they hugged. She kissed him on the cheek and they parted.

"It was great seeing you again, Paul."

"Yeah, hey I live in Marina del Rey – that's not too far from where you live. Maybe we could get together sometime."

"I'd really like that, got a piece of paper?"

"Don't need it." He pointed at his head.

She gave him her number, then said good-bye and headed for her room. She knocked on the door and waited. It didn't open right away, so she knocked again. The door opened a crack; a hand reached out, grabbed her wrist, and tugged her into the room as the door slammed shut behind her.

A naked Asian woman shoved her against the door, stand-ing on her tiptoes to kiss Terry as she slid the security latch closed. Terry was by no means complaining. She let her hands slide over Natalie's bare back, relishing in the warm smooth-ness of her skin.

"So... did you miss me?" Natalie whispered in her ear.

"Yes," Terry answered when she could find her voice. She watched as Natalie undid the buttons on her shirt and then the clasp on the front of her bra. "I'd ask if you missed me, but it would seem a little redundant right now."

Natalie was lying with her head resting in the middle of Terry's chest, which meant she was mostly laying all over her.

Terry didn't mind. She had her arms wrapped around Natalie and was holding her tight. She didn't ever want to let go. She kissed the top of Natalie's head.

She swallowed hard, before she spoke. "So... is it too soon to say...

"I love you, Terry."

"So, I'm guessing no," Terry said. Natalie moved, sitting up so she could look at Terry. Terry knew why. "I love you, too. I don't know how or when, but I do."

"I knew the minute I saw you."

"That would explain your lovely little 'I don't want to get involved' speech, and here I thought all this time it was just because you could see the wanton lust in my eyes."

"It's not funny, Terry." She got up and started pacing back and forth across the room. Terry decided it was a good view, a view she wanted to get used to. "I had plans, big plans. All I ever wanted to do was be a successful actress, and now I finally get what I thought I wanted and I'm going to screw all that up because all I really want is you, and..."

"Baby, you're ruining our big tender moment," Terry said with a smile. "Come lay back down." Natalie walked over and lay down reluctantly on the bed. Terry covered her up and then wrapped herself around her. "Listen carefully." She took a deep breath. "I used to screw every willing trollop in tinsel town..."

"Now see, I don't think I wanted to know that, Terry." Natalie said pulling a face.

"Just listen, that's not the point, this is. No one ever said I was queer, except the tabloids, which no one ever listens to. Till I came out it was like people were willingly blind, and let's face it, you are a much more believable straight woman than I am. When I came out and there was no more speculation then it caused me nothing but trouble, but as long as they were wondering 'is she? isn't she?' it actually helped my career. When people ask you, then you say things like 'That's really no one's business.' Or, 'do I look gay?' In Hollywood there are so many closet queers that everyone covers for everyone else. I'm not going to tell anyone who's going to run and tell the press. You're not going to tell the press..."

"You don't understand, Terry." Natalie moved to kiss her gently on the lips. "I love you. I want to live with you, and how can I live with you and not have everybody know?"

"How do you feel about cramped spaces and hour and a half commutes?"

"Sounds like heaven if it's with you."

Chapter 4

Natalie woke up and stretched. She couldn't remember the last time she had slept so well.

"It's so quiet out here," she whispered in her lover's ear.

Terry stirred and mumbled, "Till some woman's talking in your head."

"Come on Terry," she rubbed her body against Terry's back. Her reward was to have Terry roll over and throw her on her back. Terry laughed at the startled look on her face and then she started kissing her and Natalie found herself wondering just how long the 'actress' had actually been awake.

Natalie looked through the cabinets and the refrigerator again. There were eggs, apples, oranges, carrots, and celery in the refrigerator. There were three jars of peanut butter and hundreds of cans of sardines in the cabinets, coffee, green tea and honey on the counter, and that was it.

Terry walked into the small kitchen area dressed in tattered blue jeans and a tank top.

Natalie pointed at the cabinets. "Honey, there's nothing to eat in this house."

Terry grinned impishly. "Yes there is, the refrigerator and cabinets are full."

"Sardines and eggs," Natalie said making a face.

"Well I don't eat them together. Usually. It's a healthy diet," Terry defended.

"There's not a lot of variety."

"Sure there is. You can have sardines and a piece of fruit. Or eggs and a piece of fruit. Or you could just have fruit or you could have celery and peanut butter, or a couple of carrots. Choice of beverages, green tea or coffee. Though I usually have coffee first thing in the morning and then drink green tea the rest of the day."

Natalie made a face. "My parents would be so proud that I'm keeping kosher."

"You're the one who wanted to live together," Terry reminded.

"I'm going to get some groceries before I come back," Natalie said. "Just till I get used to your sardine, egg, fruit, vegetable and peanut butter diet of course." She sighed.

Terry filled the coffee maker with grounds and water and turned it on. A year and a half ago she'd been alone – well mostly – boiling coffee and water in a pan and straining it through an old T-shirt that she'd put on later when it dried. Her life had definitely changed for the better she thought, looking over her shoulder at Natalie who was still trying to decide what she wanted.

"Might I suggest the scrambled eggs and a piece of fruit?"

"I'm assuming you can cook, because I can't." Natalie changed to her best valley girl voice. "It's so primitive. At home I just call and a man brings food to my door, we call it order in."

"I can cook," Terry bragged. "Scrambled eggs, boiled eggs, not fried and not with cheese. I can open a can of sardines and I'm really good with the smearing of peanut butter, not just onto celery but also pieces of bread, which we don't happen to have because of the whole weight issue."

"Eggs sound good. So... do you suppose that if we're eventually going to live together, here in the middle of the nowhere, that one of us should maybe learn to cook?"

"I have a perfectly good diet without the cooking," Terry said. "Learn to desire less, grasshopper."

"I can make sandwiches," Natalie announced.

"Are you trying to make me fat?" Terry said in mock disgust and started making the eggs.

After breakfast Terry threw a few logs in the heater.

"So, I've got the day off, it's our first day *almost* cohabitating. What are we going to do?" Natalie asked.

"Well, you want to hike around the place? I can show you where I've been putting the fence up... You know, Nat, you're probably going to be bored to tears out here. We could maybe drive up the coast..."

"I don't bore easily." Natalie smiled broadly. "I actually like the woods and hiking a lot. So show me your place."

It turned out that Natalie wasn't just saying it, she really did love to hike. Apparently her family's idea of a dream vacation was to go camping and hiking in the country's national parks. She'd been to all of them, and she told Terry all about it as they walked around the property hand and hand, just looking at everything and enjoying being alone together.

"My parents will just love this place. I can't wait for them to meet you. Mom and dad are so happy that I'm settled."

"It must be so nice to have parents who are actually supportive. My own dear departed mother had an absolute and complete meltdown when she caught me at sixteen screwing a twenty year old photographer in between shoots," Terry said and stopped there.

Her mother had never really seen her as anything more than a meal ticket. She'd been a homely woman with a beautiful child that she hated. Making money off the brat seemed to be the only reason to keep her around. If she didn't do well on the set or acted up, her mother would beat her with a belt, always where it wouldn't show.

Terry's childhood was not the sort of thing you walked through the woods telling your lover about. She realized only now why it had been so easy for her to slide into a useless life of self-destruction after the show ended. It was just too easy to remember all the awful things her mother used to say to her, how she was really only good to look at. That she was stupid and dim witted and slow and lazy. It was easy to believe that when all the fame and praise ended. Being famous had given her a sense of self that her mother had purposely beaten out of her, and losing her career had taken it away again.

The day her mother had caught her with Judy, she'd come after Terry with a broom handle and worked her over so well that they'd had to cancel the rest of the shoot. Mother Dearest had Judy carted off to jail but had to drop the charges when Terry threatened to have her mother arrested for child abuse if she didn't.

That was the sort of lovely relationship she'd had with her mother. Her father, from whom she'd gotten all her looks, had died on a construction job when she was two, leaving her mother with champagne taste, too damn lazy to work, and unable to get along on Social Security. Someone had said Terry was pretty enough to model, and her mother had her new meal ticket.

Plenty of people had known what Karen North was doing to her daughter, but no one ever turned her mother in. No one intervened. Her mother told her it was because no one but her gave a damn about her and that she should learn to appreciate how much her mother cared.

The day Karen had beaten her with the broom handle and had Judy arrested was the day Terry's fear of her mother had turned to just plain hate. It had been the first time she had ever stood up to her. As soon as she'd turned eighteen she'd turned her back on her mother and struck out on her own, even though it meant leaving all the money she'd made till then behind. She could have sued, but that would have meant contact with her mother, and she was just better rid of her. Besides money wasn't really an issue. By that time she was getting more work than she could do. The cash was rolling in, and that was in the days before she'd learned how to blow it. So she'd been doing fine and when her mother had died her first thought was that she was finally going to get back the money she'd worked so hard for.

Making that money had cost Terry her childhood. She'd lived on movie sets, TV sets, on runways. She had tutors and rarely got to play with children her own age. No school days to reminisce about, no senior year, no prom, just work. She'd gotten more warmth from directors and fellow actors than she'd gotten from her mother.

She didn't know how she'd kept from going down the drug path like so many young stars did. Maybe she'd always known that if she went down that road there wouldn't be any going back. Besides, Terry didn't really have an addictive nature. Even when she'd been drinking all the time she hadn't been an alcoholic, she'd just been a drunk. She'd gotten drunk because she wanted to have an excuse to go numb, an excuse to screw up. Quitting hadn't been a problem, which more or less proved that she wasn't addicted.

"What's wrong?" Natalie asked.

"Nothing." Terry forced a smile and held Natalie's hand tight. "I... well, except for playing *Dark Avenger* nothing good has ever happened to me. I was sure that nothing good ever would, and then... Now I have a new life. It's not really what I would have chosen for myself, but it's all right, and I have you, and you're perfect. I just keep thinking that someone somewhere's going to realize they made a mistake and then you're going to be gone."

Natalie squeezed her hand back. "That isn't ever going to happen. You're never going to get rid of me."

"Good, because I don't want to."

Natalie was at work and was expecting several late nights so she probably wouldn't be back for three or four days. Terry sighed and continued digging the hole, slamming the posthole digger into the bottom of the hole and pulling the dirt back up.

Natalie had only got to stay two nights and two days, but she had gotten used to having her around. Very quickly. In fact, maybe the whole thing was going too quickly. Natalie wanted to take Terry to meet her parents the next time she was off, and wasn't it way too early in their relationship to be doing that?

She stopped digging for a minute and looked up the row of posts, and was suddenly sure that she was never going to finish this project and was not at all sure that she wanted to.

She was sick to death of all the construction noise coming from the twenty acres next to hers, and it had only been three days. Someone had bought it and was now busily building some – no doubt – ostentatious piece of shit. The noise started early in the morning and didn't end till late at night. Luckily they hadn't started till Monday, or Natalie wouldn't have found this a quiet and peaceful place at all. If she looked real hard she could just make out the dirt moving equipment through the trees, and that really pissed her off.

I should have bought that acreage when I had the money. You buy a place in the middle of nowhere to have a little peace and quiet, some privacy, and then some asshole starts building on your fucking line... All right, it's not on the line, but it's close enough that I can see it from my property line... Almost.

Her arm itched and she scratched at it. The stitches were out. It was almost healed, and now it was really starting to itch. She smiled remembering her moment of triumph over the forces of evil.

What a charge. Wish I could just do that at least once a day, no doubts, no self-worth issues. You do something like that and you know instantly that you've made a difference and... I could walk over there and kick those construction workers asses. Except they're just doing their jobs and besides they're all in good shape and I'd no doubt get my ass kicked... There is always some slack-jawed jerk throwing his weight around in some bar who needs a serious ass kicking.

She knew it was crazy, but she threw down her posthole

digger and started for the house. She'd just pop down to town and get a beer. She was thirsty. And if anyone started some shit, well that would be all right, too.

It wasn't an actual biker bar, but it was damn close. Terry walked up to the bar and ordered a lite beer. The bartender looked at her and grunted.

"Ain't got no lite beer."

"Then I'll just have whatever's on tap."

The bar was dark, so she wound up taking off her sunglasses because she just flat couldn't see, even though she thought she looked much cooler and far more intimidating with them on.

The guy handed her the beer.

"Thanks," she said.

He smiled at her then showing that he only had about half of his teeth. Apparently he had just noticed that she was a beautiful woman. She didn't consider herself egotistical, but she knew when she was in good shape – like she was now – that she was considered one of the planet's most beautiful women.

Men were drawn to her like bees to flowers, always had been, and most of them just didn't believe that she wasn't interested in them.

"So, where have you been all my life?" he asked, and she fought the urge to laugh out loud.

"Hanging out in lesbian bars," she answered with a smile.

"Maybe you ought to think about coming over on our side of the fence."

"What makes you think that being on your side of the fence isn't how I wound up over here in the first place?" she asked with a smile.

He obviously wasn't exactly sure what she meant, but it didn't stop him continuing his clumsy attempt to try to talk his way into her pants. But he stayed on his side of the bar and didn't cross the line.

Unlike the scrawny drunk that decided to walk out of his corner and plop himself on the bar stool beside her to announce, "So, you must be tired because you been running through my head all night."

This time Terry couldn't prevent her laughter.

"She ain't interested in you Benny, she's a lesbian," the

bartender said.

"I didn't see that stopping you from trying to open her legs."

"Well ain't you a charmer?" Terry asked, thinking she'd found herself the ass that needed kicking.

"All you split lickers... all you really need is a real man to lay you out and..."

"If your main objective is to make me puke, I think I should warn you that I have a pretty strong stomach."

"All you need is a little persuasion." He took hold of her arm hard.

"That's enough, Benny," The bartender warned.

Of course no one would ever know whether ole Benny would have unhanded her or not, because he'd actually touched her, and that was all the incentive she needed to kick his ass.

She smacked him in the nose hard with the heel of her palm, breaking his nose and sending blood flying. Then she slung the barstool out of her way and brought her knee up into his gut. When he bent over she brought a palm down into the back of his head driving him face first into the floor. She stepped on the back of his head and held him there.

"Be still or I'll break your fucking neck." Terry reached over to the bar and picked up her beer. She finished it, then set it down and took her foot off the back of Benny's neck. "It's been fun," she said to the bartender, who was still stunned.

"You... you're fucking *Dark Avenger*," he said.

Terry just nodded and headed for the door as the drunk started to roll onto his back screaming that she'd broken his nose, and the bartender broke out laughing.

She got in her car and headed for the house. Now she could get back to the fence.

Chang got up off the mat and bowed to her. Straightening with an effort, he said, "The student now teachers the master."

Terry smiled with pride. "Thank you, sensai."

When she got out of the shower a familiar voice asked, "What happened to your ribs?" And she almost jumped out of her skin.

"Christ, Nat, you scared the hell out of me." She hugged her anyway, they kissed, and then she finished drying off.

"You didn't answer me."

"Chang must have got a good kick in." It was a lie. She'd been going from bar to bar for the last three weeks teaching assholes a little manners. It was a rush. Even this last time when the guy she'd tried to teach a lesson to had kicked her ass good. Fortunately jujitsu had also taught her how to take a hit, so that she'd taken minimal damage. He had laughed at her when she ran out of the bar away from him, but she had known her ribs were cracked and had no desire to get them broken. She'd get stronger, become a better fighter, and some day she'd go back and make him wish he'd never laughed at her.

Terry knew Natalie wouldn't understand her strange compulsion and saw no reason to tell her.

"I wasn't expecting you to come home till tomorrow," Terry said.

"Should I go back to the city then?" Natalie asked with a mock pout.

Terry laughed and took Natalie's hand. "Not unless you want to drag me back with you. Come on let's go home."

They left the school.

"Hey let's go to the coffee shop... for old times sake."

"All right, but when I get all jacked up on coffee..."

"I'll help you burn the energy off." They walked into the coffee shop. Natalie started steering them towards their usual table where a middle-aged couple was seated, and Terry knew she'd been set up. She was about to meet the parents.

"This really sucks, Nat," Terry whispered in her ear.

Natalie just smiled. "You would never give me a good time, Terry. You just kept making up really lame excuses. They want to meet you, I want you to meet them, now come on."

Terry sighed and walked behind Natalie to the table.

"Mom, Dad this is Terry,"

"Nathan," the Dad said, holding out his hand. Terry shook his hand, noticing that her palm was sweaty. She, who had grown up in the public eye and who had never actually been nervous about meeting any one, was suddenly petrified.

"Paula," the Mom said, taking Terry's sweaty palm and shaking it.

Terry fought the nausea. She'd never experienced any form of stage fright, but she was experiencing it now. Why? Because it mattered to Natalie whether her parents liked Terry or not, and Terry was just sure that they weren't going to like her. And because Natalie was so close to her parents she was going to leave Terry and then what would Terry have?

Twenty acres in the middle of nowhere with hobbies that included building fence and going to bars and kicking jerks' butts.

What was she wearing? She looked down because she couldn't remember. Tight tattered blue jeans, a wife beater T-shirt and black leather jacket which had seen it's last good day five years ago. She looked like a hood.

Oh my dear God! I'm meeting my girlfriend's parents for the first time and I look like a reject from a James Dean movie. They're going to want to know how old I am, what work I've done lately, what my hobbies are, what religion I am, and none of those questions have answers parents want to hear. I'm an actress. I need to act like someone else. But who? What's my motivation? Besides liking to have sex with their daugh-ter? Damn! I never should have thought that. Think about some-thing else. What! I don't fucking know! I have no idea how to play this part. I'm so completely screwed!

"Honey, why don't you sit down?" Natalie asked patting the seat beside her.

Am I still standing? I didn't realize I was still standing they're going to think I'm trying to act all superior, or worse still that I'm a freaking moron. Terry flopped down in the chair quickly. *You're an actress, Terry; try acting like anything be-sides a total dumb ass. Deep breath let it out, focus on not being an asshole, act intelligent and ambitious and... They're only going to keep staring like that until you tell them the truth. Nat doesn't want you lying to her parents, or does she? God why didn't she tell me what I was supposed to say to them? Why can't there be a fucking script for moments like this?*

"Terry, Mom asked you a question," Natalie said with a smile.

"I'm thirty-three, I haven't done anything but game and talk shows in years, and I basically live off royalties from the reruns of *Dark Avenger*. I like to work on my place and I don't really like any religion; I lean towards Buddhism."

Natalie and her parents started laughing – which Terry was pretty sure wasn't a good response.

"Honey, calm down," Natalie said. "My parents aren't here to judge you."

"Natalie loves you, and you obviously care about her or you wouldn't be so nervous. All I asked was if you wanted cream in your coffee."

Terry looked down at the cup in front of her and where Ms. Stein was holding the cream. *When did they bring the coffee? Did I order? I don't remember ordering.*

"No thanks," Terry said. She looked the longhaired middle-aged man and his thin, gray-haired wife over, noticed the way they were dressed, and immediately calmed down. Of course they were going to be cool with their daughter's choices. They were old hippies. Everything was going to be all right.

"Natalie tells us you teach Jujitsu," her father started, "isn't that considered the most violent of the martial arts?"

Or not.

"Dammit, Nat, stop it," Terry said in a harsh whisper.

Natalie laughed. "Why? Come on, Terry, it's been like five days."

"Keep your voice down," Terry whispered. "I told you. I can't do *it* with your parents in the house."

"Terry... that's just ridiculous. We're in the bedroom, and they're all the way in the living room on the hide-a-bed."

"I just can't."

Natalie laughed again. "Honey, they know that we do *it*, you know." Natalie started feeling her up again, and Terry grabbed her hands.

"Dammit Nat, I said quit."

"I can't believe you're so uptight that you're wearing pajamas when you never do. Why don't you just relax and be yourself? Which means you would have already had your way with me an hour ago."

"I just don't feel right."

Natalie got out of bed went to the bedroom door and opened it. "Mom, Dad, do you care if Terry and I have sex?" Natalie screamed.

"Not at all, dear, we are," her mother yelled back.

Natalie closed the door and crawled back into bed with Terry who had now covered her face with the blankets. "See, Terry? I told you it would be all right. Now come on and give me what I need."

As Natalie's hands ran over her body her own need beat the shit out of her sense of propriety, and she and Natalie made love till she forgot about everything else.

Except that her ribs hurt.

Natalie's parents were intensely impressed with everything Terry had done on the place and the place in general. They just hung out hiking around the place and talking till late in the afternoon.

"Why don't you follow us to the hills and we can have dinner at The Yorkshire, our treat?" her dad asked.

"Nat doesn't want..." Nat cut her off with a sharp elbow in her sore ribs. It was all she could do to keep from screaming, and it was an effort to catch her breath.

"We'd really love to, Dad, but I have an early call in the morning and..."

"So you could stay in your apartment, be that much closer to work," He looked at Terry. "Didn't you say you had to go test for something at the studio tomorrow?"

"Yeah, but Nat and I..." another sharp rap in her sore ribs. Tears came to her eyes, and she decided it was probably safer to just say nothing.

"Terry and I are both on diets, you know how it is..."

"Well I don't get it," Nathan Stein said. "Come on, Nat. it's your favorite restaurant. You can diet again tomorrow."

Natalie looked at Terry, and Terry couldn't figure out whether she expected her to say something to get them out of it, or if she was daring her to say anything at all. Since she didn't want to get hit again she was silent.

Natalie hadn't been able to talk her parents out of dinner. On the drive down Natalie was way too quiet. "Why did you keep hitting me?"

"I don't want my parents to find out that I don't want to be seen in public with you."

Terry laughed. "Let me get this straight. It's all right for your parents to know that you're having sex with a much older woman..."

"You're only eleven years older than I am."

"I'm a has-been, and that's all right. I'm basically everything but an atheist, and that's all right..."

"But they'd have an absolute fit if they knew I was trying to hide the fact that I'm a lesbian and in a relationship with you from the press. Yes. They'd have a complete meltdown. They have always taught me to be proud of everything I am, Asian, Jewish, gay. They would feel as if they had failed in some way, and since I already feel guilty about it, I don't want the lecture. They don't really approve of my acting except that they know it's all I've ever wanted to do so they've been very supportive, but if they found out I was hiding what I am and who I'm with. You understand it, but they won't."

Terry nodded.

When they got to the restaurant Natalie asked for the darkest corner table available and then tried to sit with her father, but he slid her chair over next to Terry's.

When it looked like no one had noticed her, and after she'd had a couple of glasses of wine, Natalie started to relax. In fact, she relaxed a little too much. She leaned over and kissed Terry on the cheek, and a camera flashed. Natalie looked up in a panic and the camera flashed again.

The paparazzi took off running.

"Excuse me." Terry jumped up and took off after him.

"Terry, don't..." Terry lost whatever Natalie said after that as she chased him out of the restaurant and across the parking lot. She jumped up on the hood of a car and then pounced on the guy, driving him to the ground. She twisted his arm behind his back and shoved his face into the pavement.

"You paparazzi fucks really piss me off," she hissed.

"Jesus Christ, you're breaking my arm. Christ, I'm hurt, let me up."

Terry got off of him as the maitre d' and half of the staff ran out of the restaurant. She picked the guy's camera up from where he had dropped it and smashed it into the parking lot, breaking the camera into five different pieces. She reached down and grabbed the film. Whispering in his ear. "If you go near Natalie again, I'll break both your arms and your legs. I am the darkness."

The maitre d' walked up to her as she was walking back to the restaurant. "Ms. North," he said, "I am so sorry. Do you want me to call police, file charges?"

Terry smiled and held up the film. "That won't be necessary."

"I am very sorry. We cater to a lot of celebrities here. I want you to know we don't appreciate scum like that in our restaurant. I don't know how it happened, but it won't happen again. You and your lady friend can come here any time;

we will not allow you to be molested by the press."

Terry felt a momentary surge of pure ego. He knew who she was, but had no idea who her date was. It was that strange generation gap thing – he'd been a lot younger when *Dark Avenger* had been on the air, so he'd been their target audience, now he was older so Natalie's show which had the same target audience as hers had didn't appeal to him.

"Thank you very much." Terry threw the film in an ashtray standing just outside the front door as she walked in and went back to their table.

"Well?" Natalie asked anxiously.

"I explained the circumstances to him, he gave me the film, and I destroyed it. No harm, no foul," Terry answered in a whisper. But from the look on Natalie and her parents' faces, it was obvious that the lecture Natalie had hoped to avoid had already started.

"If you live your life in honesty, then no one can hold the truth over your head. That's all I'm going to say about it," Paula Stein said.

Terry greatly doubted that would be the case.

"Doing what you do," Nathan actually clicked his tongue. "How long do you really think you can stay in the closet, Nat? It isn't fair to Terry, it isn't fair to you."

"It doesn't bother me," Terry said with a quick shrug.

"Well it ought to," Paula said.

"The business can be pretty unforgiving. If she came out she might not get any more work than I do. No, that's not fair, it certainly isn't right, but it is absolutely the truth."

Paula nodded. "Maybe if more people came out..."

"Nothing will change as long as the Republicans are in office," Nathan said. Paula nodded. "Natalie's made her decision. Terry seems to accept that, so we have to support them in what they're doing even though we might not approve."

Natalie's apartment was large, sparsely furnished and obviously mostly unlived in.

"Maybe they're right. I mean how long can I go on living a lie? Sooner or later someone's going to find out. It would be nice to be able to just go places with you and not worry about it. Take you to cast parties and go out to eat and..."

"Honey, you're letting your parents whip a big guilt trip on you."

"What do you think I should do? You have never really said what you *want*. What do you want me to do?"

Wait a minute... she didn't just ask me to make a life decision did she? She did, have we been dating long enough for that? I mean when was that convention? She started scratching at her new scar. *Three weeks, four tops. We've only even known each other like what maybe six months. We're practically living together; I've met her parents and now this.* She knew what her answer had to be. She plopped down in a very comfortable looking recliner – which besides a couch was the only thing in the living room – and patted her leg. Natalie willingly climbed into her lap, wrapping her arms around her neck and resting her head on Terry's chest.

"I can't make a decision like that for you. I won't," Terry said gently. She wrapped her arms around Natalie's waist. "You certainly don't have to decide today. You shouldn't let either your parent's or my desires influence your decision."

"I'd rather just be with you all the time, Terry. You know, like real people. I miss you when I'm here and you're up there."

"It's a nice apartment," Terry said.

"I guess I haven't even taken the time to furnish it. I don't see the purpose. I just feel like it's part of my front. I feel like it's a really big, very elaborate closet that I hide in."

"Boy, your people really do have the whole guilt thing down, don't they? You aren't doing anything wrong, Nat. Being with me isn't wrong, and wanting to stay in the game isn't wrong, and no one knows for sure whether you could do both."

Natalie nodded and Terry could actually feel the tension leaving Natalie's body. "So, you want to tell me how you really got that film? And don't give me that bullshit story you fed my parents. I'm not as willingly naive as they are, and I know there is no way in hell that a paparazzi gets a prize picture like me kissing you and just turns it over because he appreciates my situation."

"I chased him down, threw him to the ground, took his camera, smashed it, and destroyed the film," Terry said proudly.

"Dammit, Terry... I love it that you keep saving me, but I hate it that you just keep throwing yourself in harm's way. I'd much rather be exposed than have something – *anything* – happen to you. I swear, sometimes I worry you have some kind of death wish."

"I don't have a death wish. I just like playing the hero, especially for you." She wanted to change the subject because she suddenly felt guilty about lying to Natalie about where she'd gotten her bruise and for hiding her hobby from her. "So... you ever have any other chicks up in here?"

"No." Natalie slapped at her playfully. "Unlike some people, I'm not the sort of girl who just goes around picking up women for sex."

"Ouch," Terry said. "And for the record I didn't pick them up, I let them pick me up, which is different. Mostly it takes a lot less effort."

"You... Terry... I'm the only one now, right? I mean we've never really said it but we're exclusive, right?"

"Nat... I thought that was obvious. I didn't know we had to say it. We both know what we want. I love you. Admittedly, I have been a grade-A, number one dog in the past. But how stupid would I have to be to cheat on you? You're the best thing that's ever happened to me. I still wake up every day and wonder what you see in me... I mean besides the fact that I'm stunning and give really great head. I'm not looking to take my act on the road. You make me happy, and it's been a very long time since I was actually happy. And for the record, I don't like to share my toys. If you fucked around on me, you'd have a dead girlfriend, and I don't mean me. "

Natalie laughed. "Once a girl has slept with *Dark Avenger*, no one else will do." Then getting serious she said, "I don't have any desire left over for anyone else, Terry, I love you with all my heart and soul."

I just wish it was enough, Terry thought. *I wish I didn't still feel like something was missing. Wish I didn't feel like I had to do the crazy shit I do. Things you'd probably leave me for if you knew I was doing them. At the very least you'd make me go to a shrink. You were right when you said I was nuts, but at least I ain't a cheat.*

Chapter 5

"Damn!" Terry yelled as the hammer missed the fence staple and damn near hit her thumb.

"That wouldah hurt."

Terry swung on him and stopped the hammer just short of his head. "God dammit, Paul, don't fucking sneak up on me." Then she laughed. "I have the reaction time of a freaking jungle cat."

"I'll remember that," he smiled. "You do have hellishly good reflexes."

"Yeah." Terry's heart rate was returning to normal. "Lucky for you, or you'd have hammer claws through your skull." She threw the hammer down, walked over and hugged him. He hugged her back.

"Heard you got a movie role," he said.

She nodded, smiling. "A little one. They shot all my scenes in a little more than two weeks. It was a good role, though. I'm this kick-assed mechanic in some future world, and I have a really dramatic death scene. Dan says he's sure once people see me I'll get some more work. If I could get enough roles to live a little more comfortably that would make me happy. Isn't that the way it always is? As long as you're busting your ass for something it never happens, but the minute you just don't care anymore, there it is." She gave him a curious look. "How did you find me?" He'd called her a couple of times since the convention, so she didn't doubt that she'd told him where she lived at some point, but she was all the way up on the farthest corner of her property.

"I followed the sound of the hammer."

"So what brings you to the middle of nowhere?" Terry asked, taking the leather fencing gloves off and throwing them in the can with her staples.

"I've got a proposition for you..."

"Yes – if you've written something and you want me to even have a bit part – yes. I'd do it in a heartbeat."

"It's not exactly that. Follow me down to the house?"

She nodded, her curiosity aroused, and started through

the woods towards the house cutting in front of him to lead the way.

"What if I told you that you could be *Dark Avenger*, not play her but *be* her?"

Terry laughed. "I'd say you'd gone round the bend, bud."

"It would be as crazy as say, oh I don't know, a thirty-four year old actress going to dives and picking fights with drunks."

Terry stopped abruptly and turned to face Paul. He stopped to keep from walking into her and held her gaze. "Are you fucking having me followed?"

"Yes, and I have been for months. You see, I had to make sure that you were the one."

"Paul, I don't like being followed..."

"No one likes being followed, Terry, but face it, I already knew about the girl, and that's not what I was interested in. I had to see if you still had it."

"Had what?" Terry was really mad. "You better come up with a good answer quick, Paul, because I'm about to forget all about our past friendship and just get right to the ass kicking."

"What it takes to be a superhero." He walked around her and started towards the house again so that she was now following him again. "It's all going to make sense when you see *it*."

At the house he walked over to a jeep she assumed was his car and opened the door. "Get in and I'll show you."

Terry didn't know what possessed her to get in the car. Paul had admitted to having her followed and he was acting like some sort of perverted stalker. Maybe it was that in spite of the strange way he was acting she trusted Paul, or maybe it was just that she was sure she could take him in a fight. Whatever the reason she got in the car. Paul drove down her driveway, turned right, and then turned into the first driveway on the right and drove right up to the huge new house that had just been built there.

"This is my new house."

"You're the asshole who bought the place next door? The one who brought six months of noise to my little slice of peace and quiet? What are you, some weirdo stalker, Paul? I mean, you move next door to me, you have me followed... were you lying about being queer?"

"We're going to need to be this close if we're going to work together. Just chill, Terry, I'm not any kind of weirdo that you need to worry about. I'm about to make your dream come true, so just try to relax." As he neared it, the garage door opened seemingly of it's own accord, which wouldn't have been such a big deal except that she hadn't seen him use any sort of garage door opener. He drove right in and then down and down and down into the ground. There had to be at least two stories of cement ramp. Finally the vehicle came to rest in a room as large as a gymnasium filled with high tech looking equipment and computers.

"Christ on a crutch," Terry breathed. She watched in the side view mirror as the door closed behind them. *Well, now if he wants to kill me or gut me and turn me into a cyborg, I'm just screwed.*

"The garage will only open for two vehicles – my jeep and your motorcycle."

"I don't have a motorcycle. I had to sell it years ago to pay a bar tab... I think... Well, you're a freaking nut job, Paul, and I want you to take me home right now, preferably without yanking my guts out and replacing them with transistors."

"Calm down, Terry, all this is about to make sense." He got out of the Jeep. "Coming?" he asked.

Terry nodded and got out, seeing no alternative. "You see, Terry, what the country, what the world needs is a hero. Not some stupid system that serves the rich and the powerful. That frees criminals in the millions to commit their crimes over again. Some people don't deserve a second chance."

Terry just nodded as she walked around looking in awe at all the equipment.

"I had a dream, Terry. A dream to bring real justice to the people who need it most. I wanted to make a suit. A suit that – when it was worn by the right candidate – would make them the perfect crime fighter. They could blend in so they were almost invisible, the suit would shield them from most blows and bullets. It would be able to read their vitals and tell when they needed what vitamins, nutrients, medications. Smart fibers, bio fibers, fiber optics all melded into one perfect suit that would be able to both heat and cool the wearer so that they would be constantly comfortable, so that they could always perform at their best.

"They kept tying my hands. My research costs were too high. The suits would cost too much. I tried to explain that my idea was just to make a few. I tried to explain that if such a person, such a suit existed, that they wouldn't need that many. They didn't understand the psychological aspects of the suit. They wanted me to make something cost effective that you could put on every soldier... Well, you try to explain to those bureaucratic idiots that you don't dare put a suit like that on just anyone because it would just give them too much power."

"Dude, could you maybe calm down just a wee bit? You are freaking me the hell out as it is," Terry said.

Paul nodded and went on more calmly. "You don't make a suit like this and give it to just anyone. You certainly don't give it to a war mongering, idiotic, administration like the one that's in power now. You know, the same administration that allowed terrorist attacks on American soil to boost their political agenda and pushed gay rights back twenty years. I said as much to my employers, and that's when they fired me. Well, when I ran out of money I sold my stock and..."

"More money than God," Terry finished for him.

"Exactly, so I started working on the project myself. And I did it. I built the suit, but then I was stuck. I mean who did I put in the suit? It has to be someone with my same sense of justice. Who understands the responsibility that goes with the power. Someone who wants to do it. When you stopped that whacko at the convention, I knew I had found the person to wear the suit."

He walked towards a closet-looking thing, motioning for her to follow, which she did. He opened the door and there was the suit, but it was hanging in a fairly large room, not the small closet she had imagined.

Terry made a face. "It's sort of plain, I mean couldn't it have a little color a cape or something?"

Paul laughed. "Sorry, you can't accessorize it. Just put it on and when you see what it does you'll know why."

"Will it fit me?"

"I made it for you. No one else can wear it. I suppose they could put it on, but they couldn't operate it."

Terry thought about it for a minute. This was crazy. She knew that this was crazy. But... she looked around her. He'd either spent a hell of a lot of money just to try and make her believe his bullshit story, or he was telling the truth, and she wanted to believe the latter.

"You'll have to take all your clothes off, even your underwear," he informed.

She nodded as he pointed her towards the room the suit hung in. When she walked through the opening, the door shut behind her. She put the suit on. It wasn't easy; the fabric was tight and didn't give easily. To make matters worse, gloves and feet had been made into it as well as a hood that went over her head so that only her face was sticking out. She zipped the front closed and felt like a grade A number one moron dressed all in gray. She was burning alive by the time she got it on. There were holes where her ears were, but she still felt like she couldn't hear a damn thing. When she moved towards the door looking for a way to open it, it just opened and she realized it was motion activated.

"All right I look like shit and so far I don't see how this is going to make me super human. So is this like one of those 'play a practical joke on a celebrity' shows? You know the kind where they always make a has-been the brunt of a joke because they'd get the shit sued out of them if they did it to one of the big shot A-list people?

Paul reached into the cubical and pulled out a gray helmet. He handed it to her. "Here put this on."

She did. "All right, Paul, still not feeling the power. This thing is really uncomfortable, and now I can hardly see or hear."

"That's because the suit hasn't been activated."

"Well how would I go about activating it?" Suddenly she felt a strange humming sensation from the suit and she wasn't hot any more. She watched in amazement as the zipper disappeared and the suit began to change color, becoming almost a reflective surface.

Paul literally laughed with glee. "Fiber optics match their surroundings, making the wearer almost invisible. The suit is activated when you put the helmet on and say the word 'activate'."

"I can hear you breathing," Terry said in amazement.

"There's an audio amplifier in your helmet. It can get louder, or you can turn it down just by saying 'audio up' or 'audio down'. The same is true of the visor screen. It's lexan impregnated with smart fibers. It's your most vulnerable area – remember that. It will stop a bullet, but after it's hit it probably won't stop a second one. To bring your visual to normal 20-20 just say 'visual normal'. If you're trying to see something far away, take a guess on the distance and say 'visual seventy-five feet magnify', etc. You need it lighter say 'make lighter'. Something's too bright say 'make darker'. You can see in pitch black or look at the sun.

"Look up to the left hand side of your visor, do you see the grid there?"

"Yes."

"Say, 'computer display room temperature'."

"Computer display room temperature. Seventy! Christ, Paul."

"Ask it the distance between you and the jeep."

"What is the distance between me and the jeep? Twelve feet six inches. Paul, this is amazing!"

"It can tell you how much the jeep weighs. It can identify unknown objects. It can detect explosives, chemicals, and poisons in the surrounding area and tell you what they are. It will tell you when someone is lying, and that's just for starters." Paul picked up a bat and moved to hit her with it. Instinct kicked in and she caught the bat with her palm, shoving it away from her body. The bat shattered but her hand... didn't hurt at all.

"Your suit is made of smart fiber impregnated rubber coated with a layer of bio steel. It's made from the same enzymes found in spider silk. It will stop a bullet, but I'm guessing you'll still take some damage. Look up at the right hand side of your visor. What does it say?"

"No damage," Terry answered.

"That means you're not hurt and neither is the suit. If either you or the suit were damaged it would tell you. If you were hurt badly enough it would sound an alarm. You're hooked up to all this hardware here, to these computers. So we'll be with you the whole time, we'll see what you see, be able to read all the data the suit's collecting.

"Most blows won't hurt you at all. If you're knocked down you'll almost bounce, but remember that your helmet has to remain on at all times. The rest of the suit works because of the helmet. You take it off and you'll still have the bio steel and the protective rubber layer, but you won't be hooked up to the computer any more. The suit will lose its environmental control, and depending on the circumstances, you'll either be too hot or too cold, and of course you'll lose you camouflaging capabilities.

"The camo mode only works really well in indirect light. Get it in bright light and you're going to look like a lump of camouflage in the room. It will be obvious that there is something there.

"The suit will know if you're hurt or if you need more energy. It will inject you with necessary chemicals and vitamins...

"Wow... hold the phone. I don't want to get shot full of all sorts of crap! I don't want to grow a beard or a penis or some shit."

"You'll get a shot of adrenalin if you need the extra energy. A shock if your heart stops. Vitamin K if you're bleeding. Nothing is a hundred percent safe, Terry. You have to use your head. The suit will only stop just so much damage even when it's fully operational. You aren't *Dark Avenger*. You're Terry North in a really neat suit. You won't regenerate in minutes. You can't jump off buildings, and if you get shot with a big enough bullet it's going to kill you. If you get hit by a bus, it's probably going to kill you. You can't run any faster or jump any higher than you normally can. But lets face it, chick, you've got game. Take your abilities, and mix them with this suit, and you're going to kick ass."

"All right, boy genius, here's a question for you. Why aren't you wearing the suit?"

"Asthma, remember? And unfortunately I appear to be allergic to everything in the suit. Remember it's by and large made from organic fibers. I'm in crappy shape. I'd have to work out for a year to even begin getting in shape, and you've already done that. I have no martial arts training. Besides, look at me, I'm the behind the scenes guy, always have been. You're the out-front person. You're the superhero and I'm the sidekick. You're *Dark Avenger* and I'm Marilyn."

"With a dick."

"It's hardly large enough to warrant consideration," he said with a smile. "The helmet has to be recharged weekly, and the chemicals and vitamins and such have to be replaced as they're used. It can't give you a shot of say adrenalin or steroids..."

"Steroids! I told you, Paul, I don't want anything that's going to make me grow body hair."

"Steroids occur naturally in the body. They help repair

damage, and fast. This one has been specifically modified for your body chemistry."

"How do you know what my body chemistry is?" Terry asked suspiciously.

"Your DNA. I took it off the bottle you drank your water from at the bar at the convention. You left to go have your tryst, I took the bottle, got your fingerprints and your DNA all in one fell swoop. The helmet modifies your voice automatically so that it's unrecognizable. You ask the computer a question it is answered on the left side of your visor. Your vitals, any damage you or the suit takes, any drugs the suit might be administering will be on the right hand side."

"You said something about a bike?"

"Ah, yes. Since you can't fly, and you don't have super speed, you've got to have wheels. Owen!"

A medium sized guy with his long brown hair pulled back in a ponytail wearing grease-coated coveralls came walking down a flight of stairs eating a sandwich.

"My better half, Owen," Paul announced.

"For the record I ain't wearing the suit because I think you're both fucking crazy." He smiled at her. "Only you could make even that ugly-assed thing look good." He wrestled his sandwich into his left hand and shook Terry's hand. "Pleasure to meet you."

Terry noticed that the left side of her visor was feeding her information about Owen. He was six foot tall, Anglo-Saxon, his temperature was slightly below normal, he was telling the truth, and his blood alcohol was point zero seven.

"Well, now that you know all about me," Owen started, "come right this way." She followed him to another cabinet. The door opened to reveal a sleek black motorbike.

"It's a X-eleven side winder, completely elevated back cam plate motivated." Or at least that's what Terry heard. Mechanic crap didn't make much more sense to her than the scientific crap that spewed forth from Paul's mouth.

"Keep it simple," Terry said. "I've got no idea what magnum covered ramitsframs even do. Just tell me what I need to know."

"Son of a bitch will do zero to sixty in three seconds flat, and will run one-eighty without any wobble. It's been coated in bio steel. It will only start for you, or me or Paul. Put your hand here," he showed her where, "on the gas tank."

She did and the bike started.

"Put your hand back on it and it will stop." She did and it did. "Or you can give it a voice command. It runs just like a normal motorbike with one small exception. It can drive itself if it has to. If we lose contact with you for some reason we can call the bike back to us. If you need the bike to come get you, you can call it and it will come. If you're injured, the seat and sissy bar, which have been impregnated with smart fibers, will grab you like Velcro when you sit on it. You tell the bike to go home and it will bring you here."

"Or to a hospital if the need arises, where I will have a surgeon and staff waiting. There are people who we know who want to help us and who are happy to know as little as is possible to do the job we might have to occasionally ask them to do," Paul informed. "We have to keep our identities and what we're doing totally secret because what we're planning to do is highly illegal. Law enforcement can't do the job you're going to be doing, but they won't appreciate being outclassed by some vigilante in a smart suit. So we can only trust each other. When you're out in the suit, one of us will always be on call here watching the monitors. We'll see what you're seeing so we'll be able to help you if you need it."

Terry nodded her understanding. They spent the next few hours just telling her how the suit worked, letting her test it out a little. After she had worn it for a while it was completely comfortable. In fact she could move as if she weren't wearing anything at all.

"So... it's dark now. You want to take this puppy for a test run?"

"Yeah, and I know just the place."

Terry raced down the road like a maniac because she wasn't afraid of spilling the bike. If she did the suit would protect her.

She pulled up outside the bar and walked in.

Sure as hell, the big greasy screw that had kicked her ass was at a corner table intimidating all hell out of a much smaller man and his date.

Every eye turned to look at the door that had opened of its own accord. Terry kept to the shadows in the darkened interior of the bar. If the patrons of the bar saw her at all they weren't letting on.

She walked right up to the asshole in question's back.

"Hey, monkey fucker. Why don't you leave these people alone?"

He turned around quickly throwing a punch, which she dodged easily. She hit him hard in the face and he went flying. She started laughing. The suit added significant strength to her blows.

The guy jumped up shaking his head trying to clear it. Trying to get a true bead on her. "What the fuck?" he asked the air in front of him.

"You're a maggot. A festering pile of dog shit on the face of the planet. You think because you're bigger than most that you can pester women and pick fights with those smaller than you. It's time you got a taste of your own medicine." She slung a good strong kick into the guy's ribs knowing she was breaking them. When he fell to the floor screaming in rage and pain she stepped on his broken ribs and just held her foot there. "Now I could just step right on down and force your ribs into your lung, but I'm not going to do that. I'm going to give you a chance to repent from your sins."

As the whole bar started clapping she took her foot off him and ran for the door. The patrons watched as once again the door seemed to open and then close by itself.

Terry realized that she could see the bike just fine through her visor even when it was on camouflage mode. She jumped on the bike, started it and took off.

This is it. This is what I was meant to do. I am Dark Avenger. No... I'm not Dark Avenger. I'm Terry North in a neat suit. Still, I need a name. A superhero has to have a bitchin' name.

She had taken the suit off and put her own clothes back on. Paul was busy checking the suit out as Owen checked out the bike.

"I should have a name, don't you think I should have a name?" Terry asked excitedly.

"I told you, didn't I tell you?" Paul said to Owen with a laugh. "I told you Terry would be in."

"Like Flint. Now about my name, I think I should have one."

"What about the bar room brawler?" Owen said lightly. "After all you seem to have this compulsion to kick the shit out of barflies."

"People ought to be able to go a bar and get a beer without being hassled by some bully. It's a simple freedom I'm fighting for."

"I didn't create the suit to make bars safer for drunks," Paul grunted. "There are real criminals out there tonight walking the streets, and because their victims aren't rich or important enough the police aren't even trying to catch them. That's what we're going to do. We're going to try to stop crimes before they happen. We're going to bring down those criminals who keep slipping through the cracks."

"But I really need a name, and I can't use *Dark Avenger* because everyone will know."

"Why do you need a name?" Paul asked.

"Because... well, what am I going to tell these creeps when I take them down and they ask, "Who the hell are you?""

"What about Midnight? It's sort of sexy," Owen supplied.

"Too sexy, sounds like a stripper's name," Terry said, making a face.

"What about Butch?" Paul suggested with a laugh.

"Come on, I'm serious. I have to have a name..."

"Terry... this isn't some character you're playing. This is real. If you fart around playing like this is some part, you're going to get yourself killed."

"I know all that, but I still have to play a part, don't I? Like you said it's the psychology of the superhero that works. Don't give me any shit; part of the reason you chose me for this project is because you know I can give the performance. That I can play the character. Make it all you need it to be in order to be successful. So quit giving me shit and help me pick out a name. If nothing else when we're communicating I'll need a code name. You can't be shouting my name out."

"She's got a point there," Owen said. Paul nodded thoughtfully.

"Night Blossom," Owen suggested.

"Drag name," Terry protested.

"It does sound familiar," Paul said. "What about Night Stalker?"

"Been done," Terry said.

"Dark Angel," Owen said.

"Another TV show," Terry said with disgust.

"Oh yeah," Owen smiled and shrugged.

"What about PMS Woman?" Paul laughed, looking at Owen.

"Ha ha. Hey, what are we going to do about my period? I mean the suit won't even let me wear underwear, and if it detects blood it's going to think I'm injured."

"I thought a tampon would take care of that," Paul said.

"Most of the time, but sometimes when I get active there is overflow."

"Now see? That's way too much information," Owen said making a face.

"We may have to design a special tampon," Paul said thoughtfully.

"Two gay men designing a tampon. I don't think that's such a good idea."

"Don't you stereotype me. One of my best friends happens to be a gynecologist, and he's every bit as queer as we all are."

Terry suddenly started laughing.

"What?" Paul and Owen asked.

"Well... who would have thought it? The first real super crime fighters and it turns out to be a bunch of queers. Wouldn't the current administration and the moral majority just love that?"

"So, I'm back to Butch for a name," Paul said.

"What about a smart fibers tampon? Something that automatically moves to stop leaks," Owen suggested.

"That could work," Paul said thoughtfully. "I'll get with my gynecologist friend and see what we can work out."

"Taking a piss would be a real bitch, too," Terry told them. "I'd have to get completely undressed."

"Maybe we should just stick her in a depends. This would have been a hell of a lot easier if we just put a guy in the suit. No bleeding, and just unzip to piss," Owen said.

"I'll just piss before I put it on and try not to drink anything while I'm wearing it... What about Thug Killer?"

"Too WWF raw," Paul said making a face.

"What about Vigilance?" Terry asked, nodding her head in approval of her own suggestion.

"Vigilance," Paul said letting it roll off his tongue. "I like that."

Terry started pacing around the room. "I am Vigilance, guardian of the night. I am Vigilance, and I'm kicking your sorry ass. I am Vigilance, and I'm your worst nightmare."

"I'm thinking she's Vigilance," Owen said.

"So what are you going to tell Natalie?" Paul asked.

"Fucking Christ!" Terry said she looked at her watch. "She's coming home tonight. She's been there for an hour. My car's there, so she's going to think I'm dead or something."

"Come on I'll take you home," Paul offered. In the car Paul asked again. "What are you going to tell her, Terry?"

"That I'm working on some special project with you, and that I lost track of the time."

"I mean about the whole Vigilance project. You'll have to be gone some nights. There is going to be a lot of weirdness. She's going to ask questions, and what are you going to say?"

Terry shrugged. "I don't know. I can't tell her. She'd never understand. She wouldn't want me to do it. I'll have to work on some sort of cover story. She's not home all the time. We could work around her schedule when possible. What are we going to do any way Paul?"

"We can talk about that tomorrow."

"Natalie's going to be home tomorrow. I just got a personal life and I'm not going to give it up, Paul."

"All right, then, I'll see you the day after. We'll talk then." He parked the car.

"You have to come in with me or she's never going to believe I wasn't out getting drunk and screwing some dyke."

"What are we going to tell her?"

Terry thought quickly. "That I was out working got tired of all the noise coming from your place and decided to go read you the riot act and got the surprise of my life when I realized that the noisy neighbor I've been bitching about for months was none other than my good friend, Paul. We got to talking and decided to work on a project together and I just flat lost all concept of time. You'll say goodbye and go home, then the ass kissing can begin. I'll screw her silly and she won't even think about questioning my story."

"Oh, you're good," Paul said and followed her in the house to meet Natalie.

Natalie was sitting on the couch looking worried when they walked in, and she actually got up and ran to embrace Terry. Terry hugged her back and Natalie started to cry.

"I thought you were dead. I've been all over the property with a flashlight. Where the hell *were* you?"

She and Paul told their well-fabricated story and things more or less went as planned.

Chapter 6

Paul pointed to the picture on the screen. "He's actually been convicted of sexual assault not once but twice, and he's only served a total of twenty-two months." A map filled the screen. "Now here's his old stomping grounds, and these," three X's appeared on the map, "are where the 'serial' rapist's victims lived. The rapist is wearing a stocking over his head, and carrying a 357. It matches Jordan's MO. The police have questioned him three times, but his girlfriend keeps alibiing him."

"What about DNA?"

"He's gotten smart, learned things from his other incarcerations. He's making the victims bathe afterwards and taking the sheets. He's wearing a rubber, and he's apparently shaved all his pubes off. There is no DNA. He's wearing rubber gloves so there aren't any finger prints either."

"So what do I do?" Terry asked.

"The attacks are happening one week apart; the computer has calculated this," a circle appeared on the map, "is the next place he'll target. Further we've made a list of his possible targets." Their residences appeared on the screen.

"Why haven't the police done this?"

"They don't have the technology, and quite frankly they just don't have the man power. They'd much rather solve a crime after it happens than prevent it happening in the first place. An attempted crime is hard to prove and even harder to convict."

"So I try to watch all five of these houses that are roughly six blocks apart and I try to stop him."

"He'll be trying to get into a back window someplace not visible from the street. You'll need this." He handed her a weapon in a holster.

"Ah, superheroes don't carry guns, Paul," Terry protested.

"You do. It's a laser pistol, completely silent and very deadly up to two hundred feet. Don't aim it at anything unless you want it to be dead. Aim, pull the trigger, and release. A continuous beam will burn through a human body and through a two-foot thick brick wall in a little under two minutes, so don't hang onto the trigger unless you're trying to go through a wall. You might have to kill someone. If he aims that gun at you, I want you to fire on him without hesitation. Can you do that?"

Terry thought about that for a minute. Could she kill some-one? He was scum, if he aimed his weapon at her. If it was him or her...

"Yeah, I can kill him if I have to."

"Good girl."

Terry strapped the weapon on and smiled.

"What?" Paul asked.

She held out her arms and spun around. "Finally I'm accessorized."

Paul laughed. "Only you can fire the weapon. If you lose it or someone takes it from you, it won't fire. It's camouflaged the same as you and the bike. Remember you and the bike can't really be seen at night, so don't expect people to drive like they can see you. Also the camo only works completely when you're in the dark or perfectly still, as long as you're moving and in the light you can be seen. The bike has been programmed for your destination. So... are you ready Vigilance?"

"I'm ready Control."

"Be careful."

"Yeah, right." Terry smiled, got on the bike and took off. The bike told her when to turn. At an average speed of one twenty-five, Terry got to the neighborhood in question in a little under forty minutes. She found a secluded place in an alley close to victim number one's house and parked the bike.

She got off the bike and started walking around the house. She'd left the bike running. The bike was very quiet, but it could certainly be heard. Terry wondered how badly it would freak someone out if they heard the motorbike but didn't see it, and decided that was cool all by itself. There was no one lurking around house number one, so she walked through the alleyway to the next one thinking it was a lot more fun to just walk into a bar, pick an obnoxious drunk, and kick his ass. She might walk around all night and never see anything. Hell, she might walk around for several weeks and not catch this guy. Then she heard something that didn't sound right.

"Audio louder, louder. All right there." She heard something that sounded like wood breaking. She turned towards the sound. "Visual one hundred twenty feet."

She saw him then, behind the house hiding behind a bush with a crow bar. She smiled; it was definitely their man. She ran as fast as she could and just smacked right into him because she thought it would be fun. She grabbed his foot as he lay dazed on the ground. Being smacked at full speed by her bio-armored body was the equivalent of being smacked with a hundred forty pounds of bricks.

She dragged him to a dark spot in the alley where she knew her camo would work best. While he was still dazed she searched him, found his weapon, and took all the bullets out of it slinging them towards the garbage cans across the way.

"You're a big man aren't ya, Jordan?" she said when his eyes opened. "A big strong man with a gun who likes to force women to do unthinkable things."

"Who... who's there?"

Terry laughed. "I am Vigilance, protector of the night, and you are scum." She threw the gun into his chest. "I'm wondering what justice needs, and I'm thinking you need to be dead." She jumped up and landed in his chest.

He looked up at the being he could hardly see with terror in his eyes. She put a foot against his nose. "So easy, so easy to kill you, but maybe too easy." He punched out at her and she jumped off him now placing a foot against his nuts. "Maybe castration." She started to apply some real pressure.

"Oh, God! Please, no."

"You know I bet all your victims beg for mercy. I bet you get off on that don't you, you malignant tumor." She kicked him hard in the groin and backed off a bit as he writhed on the ground in pain.

"What the hell are you?" he screamed.

"I told you, I'm Vigilance."

"Vigilance, get out of there. The police are on their way. Apparently someone heard the struggle," Paul's voice said in her ear.

"I read, Control," she said. Then to the criminal screaming in pain on the ground, "The police are coming this way. Now you tell them what kind of scum you are and what you've done. You confess to it all and spend some time in jail learning what rape's all about, or I'm going to track you down like a dog and kill you in ways you can't even imagine, and... more than once."

She heard the sirens then and took off, jumped on her bike, and was gone before the cops had even begun their search of the neighborhood.

"Vigilance, I'm sending his exact location as an anonymous tip. Except for your shitty adlibbed lines you did good, damn good. Come back in now."

"Since I was in town I thought I'd scoot on by and see my squeeze."

"In the suit on the bike?" Paul said in disbelief.

"I brought a change of clothes."

"What about the bike?"

"It *can* look like a normal bike. I'll just be in and out. I'll be back in dock way before it gets light."

"Are you fucking crazy?"

"No, what I am is fucking horny. Don't worry. I'll get the toys home way before curfew, Dad."

Natalie didn't even seem to be mad that she'd woken her up. She believed her story that she was trying out her new motorbike, though she wasn't happy about the whole motorbike thing. When Terry just wanted to make love and leave, Nat believed her story that she had an appointment with Paul early in the morning to work on their project.

Terry felt bad lying to Natalie, but at least she wasn't doing drugs or cheating.

She decided to drive through the worst neighborhood possible on the way home.

"Dammit, Vigilance, please come home. I would like to go to sleep some time tonight," Owen said in a sleepy voice.

"Taking a short cut is all," Terry answered.

"By the way, the cops picked Jordan up and he confessed on every count. Seems he was scared shitless by some invisible neighborhood vigilante calling themselves Vigilance."

"Bitchin'." To her left she saw some gang-bangers chasing a boy down the street. "Hot damn we got some action!"

"Dammit!" Owen yelled.

She slung the bike up on the sidewalk and between the hunters and their prey. They damn near ran into her before they realized there was something there.

"What the fuck!" one of them yelled.

"You little piss ant punks." She got off the bike and stood

up. "Five of you all against one guy, how about we even the odds a bit?"

"What the fuck do you think you are?" one boy screamed.

"I am Vigilance."

One of the boys pulled a gun, but she easily kicked it from his hand then smacked him in the head with her foot.

One of them stabbed her, and their cheep-assed dollar store blade disintegrated on her body – the visor read no damage. She punched him full in the face and drove him to his knees. She punched and kicked till no one was left standing, then she walked over and grabbed the gun, unloaded it, and slung gun and bullets into a rain gutter.

"Let me impart a little wisdom to you gutter rats. Go home, do your homework, go to bed, then get up in the morning and go to school. In short, keep your little hoodlum wannabe asses off my streets, cause I'm going to kick your asses every time I see you."

She got on her bike and took off.

As stories of the nighttime apparition Vigilance filled the TV and the newspapers, Terry realized she had to streamline her life, so she gave Chang two weeks notice and gave up teaching classes. Despite Owen and Paul's protests she was actually seeing more of Natalie because she'd swing by after a night of being Vigilance and then leave and come home before daylight. Since Natalie had to go to work at 5:00 most mornings, most of the time she even slept over.

Paul picked a crime he wanted to stop, did all the homework, and then she went out. Some nights she would go home or to Nat's with no more information than she'd had when she'd left. Then she'd just drive around till she found some minor hood that needed a good ass kicking.

As Paul had predicted, the police absolutely hated Vigilance. Of course, so far they didn't even know what sex she was much less how they'd go about catching her. It was hard to set a trap for an invisible superhero who was collaring crooks they either didn't know existed or hadn't been able to catch. They had no way of knowing who she was after let alone where she was going to strike next or when, since she purposely went out very randomly. So far the suit was doing its job protecting Terry and making her an enemy of criminals. It had gotten her the unwanted attention of the police, but it was hiding her from them, too, so the suit was doing its job.

She'd go out anywhere from one to three times a week, depending on whether she accomplished their objective or not, but she never came home without doing something for the reporters to buzz about. Paul screamed and carried on, but Terry could see no reason at all to be out and accomplish nothing, so even if she didn't do anything more heroic than spray-painting a tagger's nuts, she did it.

She'd finished her fence, including a gate, and had started on a shop building – someplace she could keep the motorbike she had bought when Natalie asked to see her new cycle.

There were two bikes in case one needed repairs. She also now had two suits and helmets, so that one was always on charge and the other she carried in a box that she didn't go anywhere without. After all, you never knew where and when evil might strike. It was a big box, large enough to hold both the suit and the helmet. It was made of biosteel and covered in the same fiber optic camouflage, as was all other Vigilance wear. Only she and Paul could open it. Of course normally it just looked like a large ugly gray box with a handle.

So it was only natural that Natalie would start to ask questions about it eventually. After all, it would have been more than stupid to have a large invisible box lying around where Natalie could trip over or run into it. Not to mention that if the light was bright enough it would look like a shimmering form, and when she went to check it out... Anyway, it was only a matter of time till Natalie would start to question the ever-present box.

Like the very first day Terry had it.

"What are you carting around in here anyway?" Natalie said working at the latch trying to open the case. Terry walked out of the bathroom at Natalie's apartment and when she saw what Natalie was doing she must have looked every bit as horrified as she was. "What's in here?"

"Ah... secret stuff Paul and I are working on for our project."

"Just what is this project? You guys have been working on it for three months and you still won't tell me what it is."

"It's just a project, you know a movie thing. Nothing really."

"Yet it consumes a great deal of your time and now you're hiding stuff in some sort of coded case. How do you open this thing anyway?"

"It... ah only Paul can open it," Terry said.

"Yet you're taking it every where you go. What the hell is going on Terry, and how come you never take me to Paul and Owen's house? How come you only work there when I'm gone?"

"Because I want to work when you're not here and spend time with you when you're home. I didn't realize that made me suspect. It's not like I'm dressing up in some weird suit and playing vigilante late at night when you aren't home."

Natalie gave her a strange look. "Tell me what's in the case."

"I can't," Terry said helplessly.

"Why not?"

"Because it's a secret, Nat," Terry said.

"I don't have any secrets from you, Terry. You've been acting really weird. What the hell's going on?"

Have I been acting odd? I don't think I've been acting weird. It's just a big case. Lots of people carry purses and shit. I don't ask her what she's carrying around in her purse, God only knows what she's got in there. Why does she have to know what's in my case? Isn't that sort of an invasion? What about my personal space? Doesn't it show that she doesn't trust me? Of course, why should she trust me? I lie to her damn near every time I open my mouth.

"Nothing's going on. Why do you think anything's going on?"

"Let me see what's in the case," Natalie demanded.

"I told you, only Paul can open it."

"Then why are you carrying it around? Why isn't Paul carrying it around? And why does it have to be carried around at all?"

"Don't you trust me?"

"How can I when you won't answer simple questions? When you're acting so weird."

"I'm not acting weird, Nat. I have a right to have a life of my own, you know. We don't always have to be in each other's pockets." She was mad. Mad because Natalie was asking her to tell her things that she couldn't, and because she already felt bad enough about the lies. "Since my case bothers you so much, I just won't keep it around you."

"What the fuck is in it?" Natalie demanded in a scream. Boy, she was really getting pissed. Her face was all red and her eyes were bulging and she wasn't at all pretty when she was mad.

"It's clothes all right! It's a costume for the project that Paul and I are working on. It's another damn superhero show, all right? Paul's making me carry it around everywhere because he's that paranoid that the idea is going to get stolen. I'm not the one who's weird, he is. He told me to cart it around so I am. I really want to do this project, so I don't want to piss him off. I can't help it if Paul's a warped little monkey, that isn't my fault."

Natalie bought it and walked across the room to hug her. Terry hugged her back. She didn't want to fight with Natalie.

I am getting way too good at this lying thing. I wish I could tell her, but she'd just have a cow. If she thinks I'm taking too many chances when I chase one of the paparazzi down, beat him up, and take his camera, how would she deal with what I'm doing now? With the whole Vigilance thing. I don't think she could handle it. I think she'd leave me. They always say shit like they're going to love you forever and that you're their sun and moon and bullshit like that, but when it comes right down to it they just can't handle it when you're a superhero.

A week later they were sleeping at her house in the woods when her beeper went off.

She walked in the living room and called Paul, glad that Natalie seemed to still be fast asleep.

"What is it?" she asked in a sleepy annoyed tone of voice.

"It's Dixon, he's on the move. I've got him on GPS right now. He's heading into West Hollywood and you know what that means."

"If he's the guy."

"He is, come on, Terry, get a move on."

Terry automatically lowered her voice even more. "Dammit, Paul, Natalie's here. What excuse am I going to make for leaving in the middle of the fucking night?"

"That's your problem, Terry, not mine. Listen... we've been tracking this guy for weeks and losing him. He's a fucking contract killer. Someone's going to die tonight if you don't stop him. Now what's going to weigh heavier on your mind, telling your girlfriend another lie, or somebody's dead body?"

"Give me a second..."

"Dammit, Terry!"

"All right, I'm coming. Christ on a crutch." She hung up.

"Where are you going?" Natalie asked hotly as she stepped out of the hallway into the kitchen.

"Dammit, Nat! Are you spying on me now? Fuck!" She shook her head. "Quit asking so many fucking questions. I've got to go, that's all. I've got to go."

"Just tell me where. Just tell me why. That shouldn't be too much to ask."

"I'm not cheating on you, I'm not doing drugs, why should anything else matter?" Terry grabbed the keys to her bike and headed for the door.

"Dammit, Terry, if you leave I'm not going to be here when you get back."

"I have to go. You do whatever you have to do."

Terry jumped on her bike and took off for Paul's.

She ran into the basement and right to the cabinet to dress. As soon as the suit was activated she jumped on the bike and took off.

"You may have just cost me my God damned relationship," she cursed Paul.

"Maybe you should just tell her."

"Yeah, that's a good idea. Last weekend when we went to her parents' house for dinner I got to listen for a full hour about how anarchy is evil, and this Vigilance character needed to be stopped before it killed someone. So I'm sure she'd just pony right up to the idea that I'm Vigilance. Besides, make up your mind. A week ago you told me I couldn't tell her."

"Don't let your personal life effect your work," Paul said helpfully.

"You know what, Control? A job is something you go do and you get paid for, not something that people guilt you into doing even when it might cost you everything you care about. Right now I'm thinking that I shouldn't allow *this* to interfere with my personal life."

"Just be careful. Don't let yourself get rattled. This guy will literally kill someone for five hundred bucks. He won't think twice about shooting you."

"See... not the sort of thing you hear an employer say." She gunned the bike and rounded the corner. "I ought to at least be getting paid. Why am I not being paid?"

"Super heroes don't get paid," Paul said in disgust. "They do it for truth, justice, and the American way..."

"Yeah, well Superman ain't real," Terry said, then muttered. "I ought to get time and a half for getting woke up in the middle of the night to do some shit like this."

"Vigilance, please just concentrate on the job."

How am I supposed to concentrate on anything but the fact that Natalie might not be there when I get back home? He's in a relationship. I wonder if he'd be so complacent if Owen was the one threatening to leave because of all this shit. Maybe I could tell her. Maybe she was just saying all that shit about my alter ego because her parents were. It wasn't that bad, was it? I mean she did say that she understood what I was trying to do, just that I was going about it the wrong way, and... What the fuck is that supposed to mean? How is a superhero supposed to go about their work? I get bad guys off the street. That's what I do. Maybe the big difference is that I don't think there is any wrong way to do it.

She ran down the road at breakneck speeds with Paul constantly updating Dixon's position. Paul felt it was necessary to tell her that he had gotten into his car, though that was obvious from how fast he was suddenly moving.

She turned onto the docks just in time to see him raise his high-powered rifle and point it at a dockworker. She didn't take time to think. If she had, there was a good chance she wouldn't have done it. She gunned the bike and ran between the hired assassin and his mark. The rifle jerked in his arms, and then something plowed into her. Terry went flying towards the intended victim, and the bike kept going straight before it stopped in an upright position, the kickstand catching it automatically. An alarm was sounding and her visor was registering both damage to the suit and to her body. Then she got a rush of energy and the pain was gone. She jumped to her feet pulling the laser sidearm for the first time. She looked at the hit man, his rifle pointed right at her face – her most vulnerable spot – and she didn't hesitate, she fired. She'd never know whether he had actually seen her or if she was just between him and his target. The laser hit the guy in the chest and his gun fired harmlessly into the air as he went down. She ran towards the bike, her vision blurring as the pain returned. Another shot of energy, the pain was gone, and she was on the bike and out of there. She slipped right past the police who were no doubt responding to a call about the shots fired.

The pain came back with a vengeance, and now there was no energy and no release. The visor was telling her that this was because it couldn't deliver any more adrenalin or pain killer. It was also saying other things like suspected internal bleeding, elevated heart rate, and lowered blood pressure.

"Dammit, Vigilance, can you hear me?" Paul was screaming. Had he been screaming all that time? If he had she hadn't heard him.

"I read," she said.

"Oh, thank God. Listen, you're hurt..."

"No shit, Sherlock!"

"Put the bike on auto pilot, Terry. It will take you to a hospital. I've got a doctor and staff enroute. They'll be ready when you get there."

"You're supposed to call me my code name."

"Fuck that. Bike on auto pilot now, Terry, or I'll do it from here."

"I'm doing it. Bike on auto pilot," she ordered, and leaned back into the sissy bar. It immediately grabbed her, and she was glad. The visor was now saying a lung had been punctured. She could feel blood running out of her nose and knew that wasn't good.

I'm going to die, and the last thing I did was fight with Natalie. Christ! What a fucking mess. I killed someone, I'm sure I did. Fuck!

"Control?"

"Yes."

"I'm bleeding out my nose. My visor says my right lung has collapsed; I have two broken ribs, and unidentified internal bleeding. Am I going to die?"

"No."

"Then could you please call my house and see if she left me? And if she didn't, would you please tell her not to leave me that I'm sorry and I love her?"

"I really don't think..."

"I don't care what you think right now! If I'm going to die I want her to know how I feel, and if I'm not going to die I don't want to lose her. Are you my fucking friend or am I just a warm body for you to put in this fucking suit?"

"You're my friend. I'll call your house. Now calm down. You need to calm down and conserve your strength."

The monitors said she had lost consciousness.

"So what now?" Owen asked.

"We do a lot of praying. Call Terry's house. Tell Nat Terry's been in a car accident and to meet us at the hospital."

"If she's not there?"

"Then try her fucking cell phone, just get her."

"This is all your fault, Paul. You just had to push. This was too dangerous, all of this. She may be dying."

"You aren't helping, Owen," Paul hissed. He was making his own calls. "Just find Natalie and get her to the fucking hospital if you have to track her down on foot and drag her there."

Terry woke up in a hospital bed. There were tubes and lines running out of every orifice in her body, and there was not one single spot on her entire body that didn't hurt.

"Terry, can you hear me, are you awake?" Natalie's voice. She looked around till she saw her and smiled.

"You didn't leave," Terry said in a voice that didn't sound like her own even to her.

"No – I didn't leave. I was just mad. I could never leave you, baby, you ought to know that. How do you feel?"

"Like hammered dog shit," Terry said.

"All right, I guess that was a stupid question." Natalie smiled. "I mean you got hit by a car, how do I expect you to feel?"

"A car," Terry frowned. She looked around. She was in the hospital, a real hospital. "How did I get here?"

"In an ambulance. You were lucky. A doctor and an ambulance both happened to see the accident and they responded."

"Hit by a car?" Terry asked. Had it all been a dream then? The suit, the bike, Vigilance. "When, where?"

"They said you'd be disoriented. Remember Paul called and you had to leave in the middle of the night, you left..."

"Then it's all real," Terry mumbled out.

"I never want to fight with you again, Terry. I'm so sorry..."

"No... don't apologize," Terry took a deep breath and it hurt like hell. "I have to tell you..."

"That she's very, very sorry and she'll never play in the road again," Paul said, stepping into the room with a big bouquet of roses and followed by Owen who was remarkably clean and not eating – something she'd never seen before.

Terry smiled, "I had the strangest dream, and you were there and you and I was a superhero and..."

"I get the joke," Paul said laughing nervously.

"I have to tell her," Terry said.

"Yes, all about our film."

"No, Paul I have to tell her about the suit."

"Have you been up long enough to know what's going on?" Paul asked, fixing her with a stare. "You know how the police and the FBI are now all hot to find this Vigilance character. Seems they've finally gone and killed someone."

Natalie fixed him with a *what does that have to do with anything* stare, and then said, "We all knew it was only a matter of time."

"They're wanted for murder one. The authorities are paying a twenty-thousand dollar reward for information leading to the capture of this person," Paul said. "If you ask me, someone kills a penny-ante hit man like that, they're doing the world a favor."

"Oh come on, Paul," Natalie said, shaking her head. "We can't have that kind of stone age justice. Where one person runs around playing judge jury and executioner."

OK, so... I'm not telling her, at least not today, but I'd give everything I've got to know how the hell I wound up here.

"How bad was I hurt?" Terry asked. "How long have I been out?"

"About twelve hours," Paul started, talking like the computer. "You have two broken ribs, there was some minor internal bleeding around your spleen, but they say it didn't do any permanent damage. Your lung was punctured, but they repaired it and blew it back up, and they say that will be fine in time, too. God damned hit and run driver."

"What was I doing in town in the middle of the night?" Terry asked, because she mostly just wanted to see Paul crawl the way he always made her crawl.

"I sent you down there to pick up some fresh bread I needed for the project. You know me. I'm such a perfectionist. I'm so sorry."

Natalie was glaring at him and Terry got the impression that they'd had words while she was out. She closed her eyes.

"I wish the suit would give me another shot of adrenalin,"

she said, half asleep already.

Paul's nervous laughter let her know that what she had said was all wrong.

"Damn, give me the drugs they're giving her," Owen said nervously, making Terry smile. These two were not actors, and if they were ever questioned they were all going to jail. Yet another reason for her to be in the suit.

A nurse walked in. "I'm sorry, but this is intensive care. No flowers and no more than one visitor in the room."

Paul looked at Terry with meaning. "Watch what you say and who you say it to."

Terry nodded and watched as Owen, Paul and the roses left.

The nurse checked the IV and her monitor and then she left, giving Natalie an odd look. Terry looked at Natalie and realized she was looking nervous and why.

"I'm going to be fine. Why don't you get on out of here before the press gets here? You ought to be at work any way. It'll be OK."

"I can't go Terry. I can't." She started to cry. "I thought... I thought you were going to die and that the last thing I ever would have said to you was that I was leaving you. I don't know what the hell you're up to, and I don't believe any of the utter crap that comes out of you or your friends' mouths. I just know that I never want to lose you. That I never want to live without you, and..."

"Come closer."

Natalie moved her head closer. "If you can wait till we get home, I'll tell you the truth. Everything. Now why don't you go on to work before you get caught here with me?"

Natalie cried harder. "I don't care. I don't care if I get caught here with you, I just..."

"I'm going to be fine, baby. Really."

"I have to be here, Terry."

"No you don't. There is a whole hospital full of staff here to take care of me, and you know as well as I do that being even the minor celebrity that I am the press will be here at any minute in full force. Now go on."

"Hey, kid, how you doing?" Janey asked, taking a seat by her bed.

"I've been better," Terry said.

"I ... you know you forget to make time for your friends in this fucking business. It wasn't until I heard about your accident that I realized it had been months since I'd seen you, or even called."

"I've been busy, too."

Janey smiled. "So I saw. Natalie Stein was leaving just as I was walking in."

"That doesn't mean we're screwing," Terry said quickly, moving to try and get comfortable. It didn't work.

"If you say so. I ran into Paul and his beau. He said you and he are working on a project. That you'd gotten a part in a movie."

"Yeah, a small part but a damn good one. Of course the movie won't be out for another six months. You know how that is." Janey nodded.

"See, you didn't need to be *Dark Avenger* after all. Speaking of your preoccupation with super heroes, what do you make of this Vigilance character?"

"Anyone who's kicking crook's asses and giving the little guys a piece of justice is all right by me." Though right that minute she didn't care if she ever saw that damned suit again.

"Have you read what this guy says? Sounds like copy straight out of a *Dark Avenger* script. I'm thinking he's some sort of uber-fan."

Damn I never thought of that, better change my routine a bit.

"When you going home?" Janey asked.

"They said two more days at least. I'm ready to go home, though. I am already so fucking tired of all this hospital shit, and you're the first person whose visited me who hasn't found it necessary to tell me all about their hospital stay."

Janey laughed. "But I was just getting ready to."

"God why do people do that?" Terry asked, once again trying to get comfortable without much success.

"I guess so that you'll understand that we know how you feel." Janey shrugged. "I bet if you think about it you have done the same damn thing."

Terry thought about it for a minute, then nodded. "Yeah, I guess I have. I guess when you're looking down at someone laying in a hospital, and they're the wrong color, look like shit, have tubes hanging out and going into places that tubes shouldn't be, it's hard to just make polite conversation."

Janey nodded.

"So... Natalie's producer saw me at a party and asked me to do a guest spot on their show for sweeps. I wasn't going to do it, but if Natalie's your girlfriend... Well, I'd do the spot just as a favor to you."

Terry laughed then stopped because it hurt a lot. "You ought to do the show."

"That's what I thought. You old dog she's like what, twenty years younger than you are?"

"Eleven years, but until this shit I was in really good shape."

By the time she got out of the hospital she had heard about the accidents, injuries, and hospital stays of everyone she'd ever known who'd paraded through her room making sure that she was cheered up plenty and subsequently making sure she couldn't get any real rest. She also started to wonder what she had ever missed about being a celebrity. The press was there every few minutes, and people she hardly knew sent flowers till there was no more room for them and she asked the hospital staff to just pass them around to the other patients.

Dan came by three times with different offers to do talk shows and walk-ons on several TV shows. She said yes to them all, but that she didn't know when she could do them.

She was way ready to go home.

Except that being home again meant two things, first that she was going to have to do without the high-powered pain killers, and second that she was going to have to tell Natalie the real reason she'd landed in the hospital.

"Don't tell her, Terry," Paul begged as he drove her home.

"Oh, I'm telling her," Terry said emphatically.

"She's never going to understand, Terry," Paul said.

"Well, duh. I don't expect my sane girlfriend to understand the crazy shit that I do. I'm not really sure I understand myself. But she deserves to know, and you won't believe some of the conclusions she's jumping to."

"We'll all go to jail."

"You are such a fucking drama queen. She might bitch at me, or even leave me, but she isn't going to turn me in. Even if she did no one would believe her and there is no proof. All that aside, how would you and Owen go to jail? You didn't kill anyone."

"True, but I can think of about a billion laws we've broken, conspiracy to name one." He parked out front and sighed when he saw Natalie's car. "It's your funeral, kid. Here." He handed her a small bottle of pills. "I made these for you. They should help you heal. By the way, just for the record, that bullet he popped you with? This guy liked to make sure. Forty-five caliber, Teflon coated, and it still didn't breach the suit. It damaged it, but there was no hole."

Terry smiled. "So the suit didn't fail, he just had some really good shit."

"You said it." He took a deep breath. "Listen, in case you're going to be fighting with your woman or you wind up single, and for almost getting you killed. I really am incredibly sorry."

"Don't sweat it, except for the last few days I wouldn't trade it for anything, except maybe Natalie. Help me get to the house?"

He nodded, but before he could get out of the car and open her door Natalie was there. "I've got her," she growled at Paul. Paul looked at Terry and shrugged.

Paul got Terry's bag and brought it to the house, holding the door open for Terry and Natalie. Natalie scowled at him again and took the bag while she was still supporting Terry.

"I can get that."

"All righty, then. I'll just be going." He looked at Terry. "I'll see you later."

Paul left.

"Nat, you think you can cut Paul some slack? He did us a favor bringing me home. The press was everywhere. If you had come to get me..."

"It's his fault you got hurt in the first place." She helped Terry sit down in a new recliner she'd obviously bought for the purpose of recuperation. It was very thoughtful and so-lidified Terry's conviction to tell Natalie exactly what she'd been up to.

Natalie sat on the couch so that she was eye level with Terry. "I also can't stand it that he has some secret with you. That he knows things about you, what you've been doing, and I don't."

"Could you please bring me a glass of water?" Terry asked. Natalie nodded and went to the kitchen as Terry read the directions on the side of the bottle. Take one every six hours. She took one out of the bottle and looked at the clock as

Natalie handed her a glass of water. She took the pill. "I need another one of these at six."

Natalie nodded and then wrote it down. Terry smiled. Natalie wanted to take care of her. That was sweet. She wondered if she'd feel the same way after she told her.

All right I change my mind. I don't want to tell her. Maybe she forgot. Maybe she's decided she doesn't want to know. But when Natalie sat back down and just stared at her, waiting, she knew she hadn't forgotten. That she still wanted answers.

Terry took a deep breath – which hurt like hell – and then let it out. "You know, I tried to think of a really good believable lie to tell you, because let's face it I'm a really good liar."

"So I've noticed," Natalie said in a voice that crystallized in the air. She was trying to remain calm, but she just wasn't quite making it.

"Go get the case," Terry said, resolved.

Natalie stood up went to get it out of the bedroom. When she carried it into the room and set it in front of Terry it was obvious that she had tried to get into it – probably with a crow bar. There were scuffmarks and dings all over it. Terry smiled.

"You tried to open it."

"Well, duh." Natalie bit off as she sat down. "All right, Terry, who is the bitch?"

"Huh?"

"Who is she? Is it Janey Williams? She's married, too, so you're fucking around...'

"Christ, Nat! I told you I'm not cheating on you, and I'm not taking drugs."

"You also said you're a good liar. It's obvious that your friend Paul is covering for you. A call in the middle of the night – it's obviously a booty call." She was screaming by now, and she jumped to her feet. "This stupid case!" She kicked it. "What's it got some of her personal effects in it, so that you don't have to be separated from her? Does her husband know? Does she know about me? Does she even care, and..."

"Christ, Nat, you are so far off the mark. Sit down." Natalie just glared at her. "Please." Natalie sat down and Terry reached down with an effort, lined her fingers up just right on the pad so that it could read her DNA, and the latch opened. She opened the chest. She pulled out the suit and the helmet. "I'm Vigilance." She threw the suit in Natalie's lap.

Natalie looked at the ugly gray suit and helmet, then she threw them down and got to her feet. "This... this is the best you can do, you've had days, and this is what you bring to the table. This weak assed lie."

"It's true, that's how I got hurt."

Natalie started to cry. "I don't know what you want from me. Dammit, Terry, do you actually expect me to believe such utter crap?"

"You called me two weeks ago here at the house and said you wanted to see me. Forty-five minutes later I was knocking at your door. How do you think I did that?"

"It's a fucking cell phone, Terry. I figure you were at *her* house and you left there to come be with me."

Terry hadn't thought of that explanation. When she thought about it she had to admit that except for the long shot on why she was carrying the case around, that it did look like she was having an affair.

"You know what, Terry? If you would just admit what you're doing we could work through it. But I'm beginning to feel like you are playing me for an idiot, using me for an in-between snack, and I can't stand that you think I'm so fucking stupid. Call your friend Paul or your lover Janey to come take care of you. I'm leaving." She stomped into the trailer part of the house and Terry could hear her in the bedroom packing her things.

"Dammit, Nat, would you just listen..." No she wasn't going to listen, and Terry couldn't really blame her. It did sound absurd. Terry looked at the suit on the floor, stood up and got undressed. Putting the suit on over her broken ribs almost killed her, but she did it and slammed the helmet on her head just as Natalie walked in carrying her bags.

"What the fuck are you doing now?" Natalie yelled at her.

"Activate," Terry ordered the suit, and it did. The zipper closed over and the fiber optic camouflage kicked in.

Natalie dropped her bags and flopped back on the couch, looking like a discarded marionette with her arms and legs laying around hap hazard and her mouth hanging open.
"You're Vigilance," she said quietly, as if letting it sink in. Then she screamed, "You're fucking Vigilance! Are you out of your tiny little mind? Are you telling me that you're Vigilance? That you didn't get hit by a car, that you almost died because you were shot?"

Terry took the helmet off and the suit deactivated. "But I'm not having an affair," Terry said defensively.

Natalie got up and walked around Terry. "Make it work again."

Terry put the helmet back on. "Activate."

Natalie touched the shimmering suit as if to make sure that Terry was still there. "It's fiber optics, smart fibers. It copies its surroundings. It works best in indirect light."

"Terry... you nearly got yourself killed."

"But the suit saved me."

"Terry... you killed someone."

"Well," Terry took the helmet off again, "It's not like he was a nice guy. He was a hit man, and not the kind that hits mob bosses. The kind that kills a wife's husband so that she can collect his life insurance. He had a bead on his mark, and I drove between them. The bullet hit me and slung me off my bike..."

"Have you got any idea how fucking crazy that sounds?" Natalie screamed right in her ear. "How fucking crazy it is!"

"Someone was going to get killed."

"Someone *did* get killed, you killed him, and you almost got yourself killed playing at being a superhero." She flopped down on the couch again and looked up at Terry. "God... why couldn't you just have been having an affair like a normal person?"

"Listen... could you help me get this suit off? It damn near killed me putting it on, and..." Natalie got up and helped her without a whole lot of compassion for Terry's broken ribs. She looked at Terry's naked, battered body and hugged her, again without too much concern for the ribs and started crying even louder.

"Oh, God, Terry, I love you. I love you, and you're completely insane. Couldn't you have just gone on being perfect? I love you, why isn't that enough to make you happy?"

"Why isn't it enough to make *you* happy? I lied to you, I'm sorry. I lied to you to keep doing what I wanted to do, what I *needed* to do to feel like a whole person. And you're lying to the public about yourself and me to keep doing what you need to do to feel whole." Terry was crying, too, now, because she was in a hell of a lot of pain and because she couldn't stand it that she was making Natalie cry. "Honey, you're killing me, and I need to put my clothes back on because I don't want to be having this conversation naked."

Natalie nodded and helped her get dressed and back into the chair.

Terry couldn't look at her as she asked. "Are you going to leave me, Nat?"

"Are you going to quit doing this crazy shit, dishing out this Neanderthal type justice?"

"It's actually very high-tech justice. Paul uses the computer to profile and track the criminals, I catch them – before they can commit another crime – and I take them down..."

"And how did I know that Paul was going to be behind all this? Honey, you have to realize, at least now, that you can't do this. If there were no other considerations you're going to get yourself killed."

Terry was silent.

"You have no intention of quitting, do you?"

Actually the whole time she'd been in the hospital and right up till Natalie had asked the question she'd been sure that she had the whole Vigilance thing out of her system, but now... the thought that she'd just quit, she knew she couldn't do it. "I... I'll think about it," Terry said.

"Think about it. Terry that's crazy talk. You almost got killed. You killed a man."

"He shot me, and he was about to shoot me again. The suit had been damaged, I couldn't have taken another hit. I didn't have any choice."

"Yes you did, you didn't have to be there."

"And if I hadn't, a man with two kids would be dead, a hit man would be getting ready to look for more work, and a murderer would be raising two kids and counting her blood money. Someone has to protect the little guy. Someone has to bring a little justice and a little hope to those who can't get it for themselves."

"Well it doesn't have to be you, Terry. You aren't *Dark Avenger.*"

"No, I'm better. I'm Vigilance, and I'm real. Listen for a minute. The bullet that guy was using, it was huge and Teflon coated. Over-kill in the truest sense of the word. The suit stopped it. I got hurt... all right, I almost died, but I didn't. I'm good at this, Nat, it's all I've ever wanted to do, and I'm damn good at it."

"I'll tell you what. I'll go to the press this minute. I'll come out, tell them all about us, if you'll just quit this crazy shit."

"Oh, that's a fucking beautiful idea!" Terry bellowed back, and then lowered her voice because it hurt to scream. "Then neither of us will be doing what we want to be doing, and it will be the other one's fault. Everyone knows that resentment and frustration are a perfect foundation for a strong relationship."

"It might not kill my career, but what you're doing... it will get you killed. If you keep doing it long enough, someone's going to hit you with something big and bad enough to kill you." Natalie sat down again and buried her face in her hands. "I love you, I don't want to live without you, Terry. I don't understand why you have to do this crazy shit to feel 'whole.' You're getting acting jobs again..."

"And that's great; it pays the bills. But Vigilance is actually making a difference. You read the papers, watch the news, a lot of namby-pamby doves are complaining about Vigilance, but the truth is that inner city crime in the LA area is down by twenty percent, and most of that isn't because I stopped the criminals. It's all because I *exist*, because when the criminals think something unnatural might peel out of the darkness and kick their ass they think twice about committing crimes. Finally there's something out there that makes *them* afraid to go out at night. The bureaucrats are complaining about Vigilance, but the people on the street, the ones I care about, are all in love with the character. It gives them hope, makes them feel safer. What could be evil or wrong with that?"

Natalie pulled her hands away from face and looked at Terry, her makeup smeared with her tears. "And what about me, Terry? Am I supposed to just sit back and wait for the call that you're hurt again, maybe dead? Am I going to have to worry that you're dead in a ditch somewhere every time you're out of my sight for ten minutes?"

"It takes me longer than that to get the suit on."

"I'm really not in the mood for your smart-assed shit right now, Terry," Natalie snapped.

"You know what, Nat? You knew I was like this when you got with me. For Christ's sake, we met in a jujitsu class. In fact, the day we were first together I stopped a sword blow from cleaving your head in two. What would have happened if I hadn't? If I hadn't put myself between you and him, you'd be dead, your parents would be childless, the world would have been robbed of a great artist, and I would still be alone. Without you my life would be bankrupt. I don't want to stop standing between people and death, Nat, but if it's the difference between having you and losing you, I'll give it up. I'll give it up and go back to putzing on the place and doing cameos and walk-ins. But think about it, please, because part of me is now tied up in the suit, and Vigilance doesn't just belong to Paul and me. Vigilance belongs to everyone. You can't give the people a hero and then take it away. It's just not right."

In the next three weeks the papers reported that Vigilance had apparently been killed in the gunfight with the hit man. They had come to this conclusion since all sightings of Vigilance had stopped. Crime jumped by thirty percent – everyone trying to catch up for lost time. It didn't escape either Terry or Natalie's attention.

They'd had a break in shooting, and that had allowed Natalie to stay home for the first week and take care of Terry. Since she'd gone back to work she'd been going back to Terry's house every night. The three hours of commuting and all the stress of their situation were about to kill her. To make matters worse, people on the set were noticing. The makeup girl had told her she looked like crap, and everyone from the director to her costars kept asking her if something was wrong. Since she couldn't talk about even one of the numerous things that were bothering her, it did nothing but stress her out even more.

She couldn't keep up with everything, and so it was that day that she had noticed that Terry was healing fast, too fast. When she questioned Terry about it and found out that the "medicine" Terry was taking four times a day had been prescribed by Paul, something inside her snapped. She waited till Terry was sleeping and then grabbed the bottle and headed for Paul's house.

It was time for a showdown.

She knocked on Paul's door and Owen answered it wearing greasy coveralls and chewing on an apple.

"Honey, the rain for your parade is here," Owen said. He motioned for Natalie to come in as Paul walked into the room. Paul visibly shrank when he saw who it was and what she had.

"What the fuck is this shit?" Natalie asked shaking the

bottle in the air.

"Just some supplements to help Terry heal."

"At what cost? God, do you ever stop to think! She's not some guinea pig you know. She's a person."

"I didn't make her do any of this, she wanted to."

"Oh I have no doubt, and isn't that what makes her the perfect guinea pig? The fact that you offered her a chance to be just what she's always dreamed of being, a fucking super-hero, and now that she's done that she'll never be happy to just be normal again."

"You're right. I did give her exactly what she wanted. Now, the question is, are you going to take it away from her and everyone else? I know you know what's happening in the city, and I know you know what that means. Vigilance does make a difference."

"Then you do it, put your own ass on the line, better yet, let your lover risk his neck doing it. Why do you have to put Terry's life in danger? Why does it have to be Terry in the fucking suit?" Natalie screamed feeling a rage she had never felt before in her life.

"Because I can't do it, I'm allergic to every part of the suit, to the point of anaphylactic shock," Paul said, remaining calm in the wake of her rage.

"And I don't want to," Owen said, and took his apple and left the room.

"You have to have the physical strength, but more than that whoever wears the suit has to have the desire, and the right ethics. Their sense of justice has to be beyond reproach. Like it or not, the only person I trust to wear the suit is Terry. Those pills aren't going to hurt her; they'll just help her heal faster. They've been formulated specifically for her body chemistry."

"So that she can get right back out there, protecting the masses. Well, I wish you all could get this through your thick skulls. I don't give a damn about the masses. I only care about Terry."

"Then let her do what she wants to do, Natalie," Paul said gently. "Let her be who she is. Vigilance is a part of her. Take it away and I'm not sure what you'll be left with, but it won't be Terry. Do you know what she was doing before she got the suit?"

"Having a normal life."

"Only if you think going to bars and picking fights with the first bully that pisses her off is normal. I've got news for you, she wasn't getting bruised up in Jujitsu classes, she was getting bruised up in barroom brawls. She *needs* to do this, it's a release for her."

Natalie nodded, feeling defeated, took the pills and went out to her car without another word.

Her girlfriend was Vigilance. It wasn't a problem that was going to go away. She started the car and headed for home.

Terry is Vigilance. The only woman I have ever loved is a fucking lunatic who puts on a magic suit and goes out and kicks people's asses in the name of justice, and that's just one of the problems we have. There's the whole me in the closet thing. Trying to have a relationship with someone who's in many ways a bigger celebrity than I am, who's completely out while I try to stay in. She killed someone, and she almost got caught. But do I really disapprove of Vigilance, or am I just mimicking what my parents think?. I didn't hate it when she stopped me from getting my head cut off, and if I admit it I didn't hate it when she beat up that paparazzi, either. Why do I assume that my need is any more important than anyone else's?

I don't want Terry to get hurt, but we all take risks every day, and I think Paul's right. I don't think she'd start living a safe life if you took away the suit. At least with the suit she's got some protection.

Natalie parked the car. She sat there for a minute, then she got out and walked in the house. She put the bottle of pills down on the counter and headed for the bedroom, taking her clothes off as she went, so that by the time she got into bed with Terry she was completely naked. She slid up to Terry's back, wrapped her arms around her and started kissing her neck.

"If you're trying to wake me up, you've succeeded," Terry rolled over to face Natalie.

"How do you feel?" Natalie asked.

"Like we're way overdue for the make-up sex. We are making up, aren't we? You aren't going to leave me, are you, Nat?"

"No, I wish I could, because that would mean that at least one of us was sane. But I can't, my heart is too tied up in you. I understand about Vigilance. I don't like it, it scares the living hell out of me, and it *is* completely crazy, but I understand. My girlfriend is Vigilance. I can deal."

Chapter 7

So, you still look tired but you look a lot happier," Marie said as she applied Natalie's makeup.

"So... did you get a little?" Roxanne Beats, the star of the show asked as she walked in.

"Ah... na... no," Natalie stammered out.

Roxanne laughed knowingly. "You're such a little liar. So I'm guessing some fight with the boyfriend and then you made up."

"Something like that," Natalie said, and she could almost hear her mother and father lecturing her about living a lie. Of course she was just living in the closet. She wasn't acting by day and killing criminals by night, and... They'd only say two wrongs don't make a right.

"Big news, big news," the show's creator and producer said walking into the make up room. "Janey William's has said she'd do a show with us, and she had a really great idea. She suggested we try to get Terry North. We could do this sort of spoof thing like where Terry winds up working with Natalie and Roxanne winds up working with Janey. You know the old superhero with the new sidekick and the old sidekick with the new superhero. I'm going to call Terry's agent, but she did save your life, Nat, so she at least likes you that much. Do you think you could maybe talk to her, feel her out, find out what she's going to need to do it, if she'll do it at all?"

"I could try," Natalie said, feeling like a total moron.

"Good girl." He seemed to sense Natalie's discomfort then. "What's wrong?"

"Well... You know she's still convalescing, she just got hit by a car three weeks ago."

"Everyone knows. It's one of the reasons she's hot again," he said, and practically skipped from the makeup room as he said. "I'm such a huge *Dark Avenger* fan, this is going to be so great."

"Fucking beautiful business we're in," Roxanne said, shaking her head and pissing the makeup artist off. "So... what's she like?"

"I... I don't know her that well," Natalie lied. "She's nice."

"She's fucking gorgeous. I'm glad you're going to be sharing more frames with her than I will. Sounds like a stupid fucking idea to me."

"Yeah."

"He told me to ask you, and I did," Natalie said throwing up her hands.

"Why are you so upset?" Terry asked with a laugh.

"Because I'm worried and scared. If you're on the same set as I am, then everyone's going to know, and I'm so stressed out. Dammit I'm just exhausted. The drive is killing me, and..."

"I can take care of myself now, Nat."

"I know but... I don't like to sleep alone, Terry."

"You don't like to sleep alone, or you've figured out that Vigilance only comes out when you're not with me?"

"Both."

"All right, listen. I'm not going to put the suit on for another two weeks, Paul's orders. Let's go stay at your place. Believe me I know how to sneak in and out of places. I know how to be discrete. You can get some sleep. We can be together."

Natalie nodded with a sigh. "That would be great."

"If you don't want me to take the guest shot on *Monster Killer* I won't."

"You better take it. Fred was all excited. I have a feeling I'll lose mega points if I can't produce you. I might even get shit canned."

"No way, you've become the foil for the main character. You're way too insecure for someone who's as important to the show as you are. You and Roxanne have chemistry; you can't buy that shit. I think it will be fun to work together, and, no, I don't think people are going to look at us and know we're a couple. After all, we're both talented actresses."

There it was, the lying thing again. Natalie felt like a total fraud.

Terry knocked on the door to Janey's dressing room. "Hey, Janey, are you decent?"

"Yeah," she hollered back. So Terry walked in. "So... when did you grow a semblance of manners?" Terry shrugged and Janey laughed. "Since your girlfriend's on the set?"

"She once accused me of having a secret affair with you."

"Oh, you've got to be kidding."

"I wish I were. Janey, do me a favor…"

"Don't worry, Terry. I'm not going to out your girlfriend."

"Thanks."

"This has been a lot of fun so far," Janey said.

"Yeah, now if only they could find a way to let me wear tights, a mask and a cape," Terry said with a smile.

"No seriously, Terry, I have to tell you I forgot how much fun it could be to do TV. How nice it is to be able to go home every day," Janey said. "Don't get me wrong, I love my career, it's just…"

"It sometimes doesn't leave any time for anything else."

"You said it. You sure look a hell of a lot better than you did when I saw you in the hospital. How are you feeling?" Janey asked with the real concern of a true friend.

Terry smiled. "I feel great actually. Not much worse than I did before the accident."

"They ever find the pud that hit you?"

"No, I'm afraid not."

"Well maybe now Vigilance has returned he'll get him." Janey laughed.

"Maybe so."

Terry got back to the apartment before Natalie because of course Natalie had more scenes. Natalie walked in and immediately walked over and collapsed in Terry's lap.

"I was a nervous wreck all day," she announced.

"Well it didn't show," Terry said.

"Your friend…"

"Janey," Terry said as if she thought Natalie couldn't remember her name.

"She knows about us doesn't she?"

"Yes. Honey, Janey's one of my oldest and dearest friends. She's not going to tell anyone."

"But she is going to keep giving me that "I know what you're doing and with who" look, just to watch me squirm."

Terry laughed. "Yes, she probably will."

"I have no one, no one but you. You can tell Owen and Paul everything, you can tell Janey about us. But I have no one I can tell things to."

"Your parents know about us."

"Yes, and they so approve of me wanting to stay in the closet that their advice is always so helpful."

"You can talk to me." Terry held her close. "You can tell me anything."

"I can't bitch to you about you," Natalie said with a sly smile.

Terry laughed. "So... you have nothing to eat in this house. No sardines, no vegetables, no fruit, no peanut butter."

"Ah, but I do have a Chinese restaurant with delivery on the speed dial."

"Make food woman, my hungry," Terry grunted out.

Natalie got up and went after the phone. Terry watched her with a smile, she looked good enough to eat, and she was.

She'd had fun on the set. It was a good set, cast and crew. It was great to work with Janey again, and it was fun to work with Natalie, although it was off-putting to hear Natalie talking with a Chinese accent since her normal speaking voice sounded just like every other California beach-raised girl.

The script was funny. She and Janey were playing two actresses who used to work on a superhero TV show, which wasn't much of a stretch. Being has-beens and wanting to get back in the limelight, they had come to the town of Harvest View, which is heralded with being the center of all sorts of paranormal activity. They go there basically in character to try to rid the town of monsters. They have brought a couple of their actor friends to be monsters so that they can "overcome" them. Of course the monsters that attack them aren't their friends, but real fiends. Then Roxanne and Natalie have to save them. Then they get paired up with the girls and wackiness ensues as the actresses try to use their "skills" to track the monsters and of course mostly get in the way.

It was a blast, and it had been a long time since she'd had a fun script in her hands.

"I couldn't believe you let them douse you in mud," Natalie said, hanging up the phone after making the order.

"Because I'm normally so prim and proper," Terry said, making a face.

"Because you're so beautiful." Natalie walked over and sat back down in Terry's lap. Her whole manner changed. "Are you going out tonight?"

"No, not tonight."

"Good," Natalie rested her head against Terry's chest.

"Honey... you have to sleep when I'm out."

"I try, Terry, I just can't. I'd like to see you sleep if I was the one running all over the city trying to get killed while you were home safe in bed."

"I'm sorry."

"I'll adjust. Sometimes I just pretend like I still don't know. That I'm just here and you're in the woods and that's why we aren't together. And when we're home, and you're not there I pretend that you're off shooting some movie."

"Paul strengthened the suit, and I'm more careful than I was," Terry said reassuringly.

"And see both of those things might make me feel better if I didn't know what a really good actress and subsequently good liar you are." Natalie snuggled closer. "Let's not talk about it."

"OK. So... do you like Janey?"

"I think I would if she wasn't having so much fun teasing me about you, why?"

"She and Tom want us to come for dinner one night. That might be nice for both of us. To do something together – besides sex – that's almost like normal couples do."

"I think I'd like that, yeah," Natalie said.

Natalie was sleeping soundly, but Terry was wide-awake. Her eyes fell on the case, but she'd told Natalie that she wasn't going out, so if she did there was going to be shit. They also had an early casting call tomorrow. She didn't have her bike, and she just didn't feel as Vigilance-y when she was driving around in a car. It was too easy to see, too easy to track. Besides, there couldn't be anything much more disconcerting to the casual motorist than to look over and realize that the car driving up next to you has no driver.

She had just been out two nights ago. Compromise. It was all about compromise. She had to juggle Vigilance with some semblance of a normal life or she'd wind up with no life whatsoever. Vigilance would consume her, and all she'd be was the suit.

Natalie rolled in her sleep and wrapped herself around Terry, and suddenly Terry didn't want to be anywhere else. She wrapped an arm around Natalie and soon she was asleep.

They woke up at five and got dressed. Terry was ready

first, and they wouldn't be going to work together, so she grabbed her case and headed for the door. "I'll see you at work, baby."

"All right, be careful," Natalie answered from the bedroom where she was still getting dressed.

"You, too." Terry opened the door and walked out. She heard... something. She looked around carefully, wishing that she was in the suit at that moment. There was nothing. For a second she almost went back in to put the suit on. Then a look at her watch said there wasn't time.

Still she felt uncomfortable enough that she didn't leave until she saw Natalie get safely into her car and take off.

Series TV was always so cool because you shot a whole story in one week. The producer must have thanked Terry and Janey about a thousand times. He even asked if they'd be interested in playing the characters again sometime, and they both said yes.

In spite of Natalie's fears, if anyone had guessed they were lovers they were better actors than Terry gave them credit for.

Terry came home to her place early one morning after a hard night of crime fighting to find Natalie on the couch in tears.

"Baby," Terry said gently. She sat down beside her. "What's wrong? I thought you were staying in your apartment to-night."

"It's two o'clock in the morning, Terry," Natalie said accusingly.

"I'm sorry, I was working," Terry defended.

"I'm sorry. I know. I just... I needed you. I needed you here."

"Honey, you could always call Paul and get in touch with me. What happened? Are your mom and dad all right?"

"This, this happened." Natalie handed a stack of pictures to Terry. They were mostly Terry and Natalie walking in and out of the apartment, and the last one was Terry kissing Natalie goodbye. "They came with this."

Natalie handed her a typed note that said, "The tabloids have offered me one hundred thousand dollars for these. What will you give me? Leave your answer and a better offer in an envelope on the corner of sixth and main at six o'clock PM tomorrow. If I don't hear from you, I'll take what I can get."

"I knew it. I knew I heard something. Boy did this stupid fucker pick the wrong dyke to mess with. I'm taking this fucker out," Terry said, starting to stand up.

"If I'd just come out this wouldn't have happened. People can't blackmail you if you're telling the truth. You know why I'm so upset, Terry? What if he had gotten a picture of you in the suit? What if some stupid fucker is trying to catch me with you so he can out me and he winds up getting a picture of Vigilance?"

"If I was in the suit I would have had his number. He sure as hell wouldn't have gotten any pictures."

"I have to come out, Terry. I have to stop this."

"Natalie... this isn't your fault. You don't deserve, and you certainly didn't ask for this kind of invasion, this kind of abuse. You come out if and when you want. Till then no one's going to do this sort of shit to my girl. I'm fucking Vigilance. Tomorrow you go make the drop and go home. I'll take care of the rest."

"Terry, I don't want you to hurt anyone, even this scum, for me. I don't want you to take any risks for me."

"Now that's just stupid shit, Nat. I come home and you're crying, he hurt you, and he deserves a good ass kicking. He's spying on me, too, and as you pointed out, I can't have that, not being who I am."

"I knew it, I knew you were going to do this." Natalie got up and started pacing back and forth. "I knew I shouldn't tell you, that you'd blow it all out of proportion."

"What part of this guy's watching you, watching us, and then blackmailing you do you not understand? Do you think if you come out he's going to have learned his lesson and he'll never do this sort of thing again? No, he'll just find a new target. That's why there are soooo many shit heads in the world, because most people just give in, let them do as they damn well please. They cause other people pain, but they never experience it. When they have the pain, when they have the fear, then everything changes."

"My God, Terry, do you ever listen to yourself? You might as well be reading from a *Dark Avenger* script."

"Did it ever occur to you, to anyone, that I played that part so well because, except for being straight, that's who I was? Who I *am*? This guy's a blemish on the face of humanity, and I'm gonna pop him like a zit, with or without your help. With or without your permission. Because that's who I am. Even if I wasn't Vigilance, I wouldn't let anyone push you around. You've got to know that, Nat. Since I am Vigilance, it just makes it a little easier to deal with this fucker."

Natalie nodded, too tired and too upset to fight. "I have to get some sleep. I have to be to work at six o'clock in the morning."

"Come on." Terry took her hand and started leading her towards the bedroom.

They stripped and got in bed. Terry curled up around Natalie, holding her close. "Don't worry about anything, I'm going to take care of it. You go to sleep, I'll get up with you and take you to work in the morning. That way you can sleep in the car on the way in."

"Someone might see you bring me to work," Natalie said, yawning.

"No, because you'll be asleep all covered up in the back seat. You know they'll let me on the lot, no questions asked. I'll park somewhere out of sight. You'll get out and I'll take off. I'll give you an envelope in the morning to put in the phone booth. I'll be watching, so you'll be perfectly safe. I'll take care of this, and then you won't have to worry about it any more."

Natalie nodded and fell almost instantly asleep.

Two and a half hours later the alarm went off and she could hardly drag herself out of bed. She was barely aware of Terry helping her dress and practically carrying her to the car. She climbed in the back seat and was out like a light. The next thing she knew Terry was shaking her, her hand on her butt and whispering, "Nat, we're here,"

"Huh?"

"Baby, we're at the studio," Terry said.

Natalie uncovered her head, rubbed her eyes, and sucked the drool off her lip, still not sure where she was or how she'd gotten there. Then Terry was pressing an envelope into her hand. "Put this in the phone booth."

When Natalie felt the envelope in her hand, reality came flooding in and she remembered everything they had talked about the night before. She just wanted to go back to sleep so she could forget everything, but she got up reluctantly, the envelope in her hand.

"Be careful, Terry," she said as she got out of the car.

"Aren't I always?" Terry said with a smile.

"Actually, I don't think you know how. I love you, Terry."

"I love you, too. Now get going before someone sees you."

Natalie nodded and got out of the car. She watched Terry drive away and suddenly wondered how she was supposed to "make the drop" or even get home since Terry had just driven away in her car.

Her cell phone rang and she pulled it from her jacket pocket. It was Terry. "Hey, baby."

"Well, at least you finally sound awake. I'm going to park your car in the lot with everyone else's. I'll get a cab and go to the apartment. Paul's bringing the bike to the warehouse."

Because of course she never traveled anywhere without the suit, and she really had thought of everything. Natalie looked at the envelope in her hands. "Thanks, Terry."

"Don't open the envelope."

"Why not?"

"Just don't. After you went to sleep last night I called Paul and that was waiting on our kitchen table this morning. Paul didn't go into any details, but I imagine it's got a little surprise in it for our blackmailer," Terry explained.

"Great, probably some fucking explosive charge," Natalie mumbled, then said, "I love you, Terry."

"I know, love you, too. Now stop worrying and get to work."

Stop worrying, like it's ever that easy. What the hell's in this envelope that I can't open it? No doubt some super concoction Paul whipped up just for my blackmailer, and the simple fact is that I couldn't have a blackmailer if I wasn't living the big lie. Of course not every girl happens to have Vigilance in her back pocket or wrapped around her pretty little finger as the case may be. Damn, how did I get here?

She walked through the back door and started for her dressing room.

Everything was going my way and it was supposed to be so easy. Do my part, get some recognition, get movie roles, win an Oscar, and I'm set for life. If I'd never met Terry everything would have been so easy. Of course, if I hadn't gotten the role for which I needed the martial arts training I never would have met Terry in the first place. So it's all this part's fault, but of course if I hadn't gotten the part I'd never have a chance to get movie roles and someday win an Oscar, and if I'd never met Terry I never would have known what love is, not to mention all the intense sexual satisfaction. I'm twenty-three years old making more money than I know what to do with, and I'm living in an almost unfurnished apartment in the middle of one of the biggest cities in the world and a travel trailer with an addition on it in the middle of the woods. I'm on at least the Hollywood B list, and I can't go anywhere or do anything because all my spare time is spent running back and forth over the highway to be with my girlfriend who thinks she's a fucking superhero. My life is like I'm playing two completely different roles just like my crazy girlfriend, and now I'm being blackmailed but... Don't worry!

Her thoughts were so all-consuming that she literally ran into Roxanne in the hall on the way to the room where they did their read through. She'd only practiced the script with Terry once, but since she knew for a fact that some of her costars didn't even bother to look at their scripts till the day of the read through she wasn't really worried. She just thanked God that they weren't shooting today.

"Hey, girl, you all right?" Roxanne asked with real concern.

"Yeah... I'm sorry. I wasn't paying attention. I'm so sorry."

"My God, Natalie, you look like you slept in your clothes." She picked up Natalie's chin and looked in her eyes. "If you slept at all. You know you passed the reading room, right?"

Natalie turned and looked in the direction Roxanne was pointing and took a deep breath.

"You aren't doing crank are you, Nat?" Roxanne asked with concern.

"Would I be this fucking tired first thing in the morning if I was?" Natalie all but screamed at her. "I'm sorry, I'm just... I'm completely stressed out, and I got like three hours sleep last night."

"Do you need to talk about it, Nat?" Roxanne asked gently.

"I can't," Natalie said, close to tears. "I can't talk to anyone about anything, that's part of the problem."

"You could you know. I'm a pretty good listener, and I know how to keep a secret."

Natalie held up the envelope. "I'm being blackmailed." She quickly deposited the envelope in her jacket pocket.

"Blackmailed. First a stalker and now this. What, are you

just trying to make the rest of us feel unloved?" Natalie gave her a look that let her know she didn't think it was funny at all. "Natalie, what is he blackmailing you over, some old porn movie, some baby you gave up?"

"I'm queer, all right? I'm queer," Natalie said in an angry whisper.

"Chill out, I don't care. Do people really worry about that anymore?"

"Name me one actress who stayed in the game and got hugely famous after she came out."

"Anne Heche."

"Last I heard she was mostly a has-been, and besides she jumped back over the fence when the going got rough."

"True, and the Republicans are in office. What's the blackmailer have?"

"Pictures of Terry going in and out of my apartment and of us kissing."

"Terry North?" Roxanne asked with shocked surprise.

"Yes."

"Yeah, since she's openly gay that would be pretty damning." Roxanne smiled, "I have to tell you, you guys played it pretty cool on the set. I never would have guessed."

"Really? I was sure everyone would know."

"Well, not me."

"Well... we are actresses after all," Natalie said feeling a strange sort of pride.

"So... what are you going to do?"

Natalie shrugged. "Terry says she's going to handle it."

Byron, one of their costars, walked up to them then all smiles. "So," he looked at Natalie with meaning. "I just ran into Terry North in the parking lot. Funniest thing, Nat, she was getting out of your car."

"This day just keeps getting better and fucking better!" Natalie snarled, turned and headed back for the reading room.

"Get off her back, Byron," she heard Roxanne hiss.

Byron ran to catch up with her. "I was just ribbing you. I didn't mean anything by it, Nat."

Natalie nodded, walked into the reading room and took her seat.

Fred walked up to her shoulder and asked in a voice filled with concern. "You all right, Nat?"

Natalie took a deep breath and let it out. "I'm just tired."

"I want to talk to you in my office," Fred said.

Better and fucking better.

When he shut the office door and took his seat behind his desk she felt like a kid who'd been sent to the principal's office. She sat down, half expecting to be fired, just because that was the sort of day she was having.

"I'm fine, Fred, just having trouble sleeping."

"Yeah, well I'd have trouble sleeping, too, if I was in bed with Terry North."

"What?" Damn, Terry brought her to work one day and now everyone knew.

Fred took an envelope from the drawer, pulled some photos from it and handed them to her. "Our executive producer found these in his mail box this morning."

They were the same pictures she'd been sent.

"I can explain," though she really didn't know how.

"There's no need for you to explain, Nat. I wish you felt like you could have told me, but I understand why you didn't, what with the Republicans being in office and all. He wants money from us to keep it quiet."

"Me, too," Natalie said sadly. "I got the same package yesterday."

"Nat, Bill and I talked. We're not going to pay this clown, and I don't think you should, either. Only a tabloid rag is going to pay him for these pictures, no one really believes those anyway. You don't believe me ask your girlfriend. They must have printed hundreds of pictures of her with different women..."

"You aren't helping, Fred," Natalie said.

Fred laughed. "The point is no one thought the rumors were true till she came out... and then there was the video..."

"Oh yes the video."

Fred laughed again. "Whatever you decide to do, we want you to know that the cast and the crew... We'll stand behind you a hundred percent. Your job with us is secure."

Natalie sighed with relief. "Thanks, Fred, I can't tell you how much that means to me."

"So... I'm guessing as cool as you played it when she was working with us that you've been together for awhile or it didn't start till we'd finished shooting?"

"We've been together for almost a year."

"Which would explain why you were such a mess when

she had her accident. You could have told me, Nat. We would have worked around it. You're very important to the show, and I have to tell you, you're quite a trooper. None of the rest of these clowns are as dedicated as you are. You've been dealing with a pile load of crap, and you've never let it show in the quality of your work."

"Thanks, Fred." She sniffled. She would have liked to have told him that there was very little chance that the photos would ever see print, but she couldn't, and one day there would be more.

She could keep this job and come out, he'd told her that and she trusted him, but shows got canceled or died a natural death. There was no guarantee that she'd ever work again. Of course there were never any guarantees about anything.

Except that for the time being, at least, her secret was safe. She'd have a little more time to think about it. She started to relax.

Chapter Seven

Ken Keylor watched as the actress – dressed in a scarf and sunglasses – got quickly out of her car, went to the phone booth, set the envelope down inside and left. It was nearly dark and in this light it wasn't likely that anyone but him would have even recognized her. He waited till she was out of sight, and then he went and grabbed the envelope, pocketed it, and headed for his own car. He thought he saw something move out of the corner of his eye but when he turned there was nothing there but some bum. Still if she'd gone to the cops didn't they sometimes dress up like bums in a sting operation?

He hurried to his car and reminded himself to drive off slow. No one was following him. *Of course not. Miss Priss doesn't want anyone to know she's a split licker. This will teach her big, stupid dyke girlfriend to beat the shit out of me and break my camera.*

Only when he was safely alone in his apartment did he take the envelope from his pocket and open it. At first it appeared there was nothing written on the paper, then the words "Watch your back" appeared. Then the page burst into flame. He dropped the paper, stomped the flame out, and then turned slowly around. There was something there, but what? Something hit him hard in the chest and he went flying across the room. He landed on his ass on the floor and then something was on his chest, a foot by the feel of it. He tried to grab at his attacker's leg, and when he did the other foot stepped down hard on his wrist.

"Now you... you're a fucking problem," the shimmering slightly human shaped image said in an obviously synthesized voice. "Because I don't know that your crime deserves a death sentence, and yet what else can I do? If I turn you over to the cops as I normally do and you confess your crime you'll expose someone who doesn't deserve to be exposed. What crime has she committed?"

The creature's voice – deep, sinister, and not at all human – gave Ken the distinct impression that the creature would like nothing better than to rip his head off and watch his headless figure flop around on the floor.

"Please, please I'll do anything," Ken begged the apparition.

"Anything?"

"Yes anything, just please don't kill me."

"I bet I could come up with a whole list of things you wouldn't do even to save your own neck, but since most of those wouldn't serve anything but my very morbid and perverted curiosity, I guess what I want you to do is run around this dump you call home and pick up every piece of film, every camera, every photo you have, and bring them to me."

The creature stepped off him and he got up. He made a run for the front door and found himself kicked across the room again for his effort. The air was knocked out of him and he felt like his belly was on fire.

"I don't think you understand what's going on here, Jack. See, I would like for you to give me a reason, any reason at all to kill you dead where you lay. I *want* to kill you. That being the case, if you really want to stay alive I suggest you start acting like a man who's three seconds from having his arm ripped off and being beaten to death with the bloody end of it," the creature said, then picked him up by his belt and half dragged, half kicked him from one room to the next. He watched as the creature dumped his kitchen trash in the middle of the room then systematically went from one room to the next rummaging through his things and taking everything that even resembled a tape, film, disk, or camera and throwing them into the trash can. Then it dragged him and the trash can back into the living room.

"Now here's the deal, scum bag. You so much as breathe a word about Natalie Stein to the press, if you go to the police, if I so much as hear that you're bothering anyone else, I'll slip out of the night and I'll pull your liver out your throat. This was your big chance. This was me being a nice guy. You're lucky I'm in such a good mood today."

The front door opened and in the haze his pain was causing it looked like his trash can walked out of his apartment of its own accord.

It had been everything she could do to keep from killing the bastard, because he had made it personal when he'd gone after Natalie.

"Don't fuck with Vigilance's squeeze," she mumbled. She threw the trashcan into a dumpster and used her laser to start it on fire. As the dumpster blazed she took off into the night.

"I'm coming in," Terry announced.

"I'm opening the warehouse now," Owen said.

"The warehouse" was in Terry's opinion Paul's best idea yet, because it made life a whole lot easier for her. The gate opened and closed behind her. Then the "warehouse" door opened and she drove in. The door closed behind her and she got off the bike and stripped out of her suit.

Paul had bought up an old storage rental center and converted one of the stalls to a mini-hideout. It was perfect, located in the heart of the city and completely hidden from view.

She slipped into her street clothes and helmet and jumped on her regular bike. The door opened again and she roared out of the building. She drove to the front gates and took off down the street as the gates closed behind her. Her other suit and helmet were secured in the case on the back of her bike. She tried to remember not to drive as fast on this bike, after all she wasn't protected now. It was hard, because you got used to a bike that could compensate for your mistakes and being practically impervious.

When she walked up to the door there was a lot of noise coming from inside the apartment and she remembered thinking there were an awful lot of cars in the parking garage. She made sure she was at the right apartment and then when she was sure that she was she walked a little ways down the hall and called Natalie.

"Hello, baby, how's it going?" Natalie sounded more than a little inebriated.

"I'm in the hall, what the hell's going on?"

There was no answer. Instead Natalie appeared in the hall staggering ever so slightly, walked up to her, kissed her full on the mouth, then took her hand and started dragging her into the apartment. It was crammed with people and food and drinks. She saw Natalie's parents across the room. Natalie pulled her in the room and closed the door behind her.

"Hey listen up!" Natalie screamed and the din in the room mellowed though it didn't go away. "For anyone who hasn't met my girlfriend already, this is her. Her name's Terry and she's amazing in bed." She staggered back against Terry, and Terry caught her to keep her from falling as everyone in the room applauded.

"What the hell are you doing?" Terry whispered in her ear, working at keeping a smile on her face. Natalie turned to face her and wrapped her arms around Terry's neck.

"It's my coming out party, it was Roxanne's idea. Cool, huh?"

"Honey, are you sure you know what you're doing?"

"I wasn't drunk when we started this. Halfway through the day I just realized that it's too hard to hide everything all the time. I'm not ashamed of my relationship with you, and I'm tired of hiding." She lowered her voice even more. "I don't want you to ever have to save me again, not over something like this. Fred told me they'll stand behind me, and if I never work again when the series ends, say lovey, I'll still have you."

"You'll always have me." Terry kissed her gently on the lips. "I just hope you aren't going to regret this when you sober up."

"I hope so, too, because it's a little too late to go back now. I invited a photographer from one of the entertainment magazines. Please don't kick his ass," she laughed, then whispered in Terry's ear. "Speaking of which did you kick his ass good for me?"

Terry smiled broadly. "Oh yeah."

"That's my girl. Now come on I want to show you off to some of my friends you haven't met."

Like she could ever remember so many names. She found herself wishing that they had nametags like at the conventions. It had been a long time since she'd been to a Hollywood party, and she found that she recognized a lot of the people but had never actually met them. Of course she was familiar with most of the cast and crew of *Monster Killer* since she had worked with them, but she found herself suddenly feeling very out of place and very old. Most of these people were Natalie's age or younger, and she was never so happy to see two people in her life as she was when Janey and Tom arrived.

"Janey!" She waded through the crowd half loaded from all the drinks Nathan had been feeding her. She hugged first

Janey and then Tom, and noticed the room had gotten very quiet and knew why. Janey was amazingly famous even in this crowd, and they were impressed.

Terry would have liked to know how Natalie had pulled this off so quickly.

Natalie came over and hugged Tom and Janey then grabbed Terry's arm.

"Dance with me," she ordered.

There was a loud rank rock song playing, and Terry was happy to oblige. "I'll talk to you guys later," she said as she allowed herself to be led to a spot in the room where other people were dancing.

Roxanne approached Janey and Tom. "So... I suppose you knew all along."

"Yep, mostly," Janey said. "Terry and I have been through a lot together, there isn't much she can hide from me."

"I don't really know, Terry, but well... do they seem well matched to you?"

Janey smiled and shrugged. "They look good together."

"Give me a break. They're two of the most disgustingly attractive people I've ever known. Of course they *look* good together. It's just... well, Nat's always joking and cutting up, when she isn't having a meltdown, and well, Terry seems... I don't know, a little stiff."

"Well I don't really know Natalie, so I can't say how well matched they are, but I can tell you this. There isn't anything stiff about Terry North," Janey said with a laugh.

"If you say so," Roxanne said, sounding less than convinced.

"Hey, Terry, how are you healing?" Janey yelled across the room.

"Wanna see?" Terry asked, not stopping dancing.

"Yeah sure why the hell not?" Janey looked at Roxanne. "Did you bring your boyfriend?" Roxanne nodded. "Then be glad the bitch is queer."

"Why?" Roxanne asked.

Terry's shirt hit Janey in the face. Janey took the shirt and slung it onto the floor. Tom laughed and looked at Roxanne. "Because you give the girl a couple of drinks and her clothes come off."

Terry danced over. She stopped in front of Janey and Tom

in her sports bra and pointed to the tiny scar on her rib cage.

"They put a straw in there and blew my lung up," Terry said as if they didn't know.

"It's nice," Janey said with a smile. "Did you ever show Roxanne your tattoo?"

Roxanne watched in amazement as Terry undid her jeans, pulled down her pants and turned to show Roxanne the yellow smiley face on her ass.

"Honey," Natalie stumbled over and pulled Terry's pants up. She looked around on the floor till she found Terry's shirt. "Put your clothes on." She handed the shirt to Terry, and Terry threw it back in the floor.

"Too hot, let's dance," Terry said.

"Show Roxanne your piercing," Janey prompted.

"No don't," Natalie said, pulling on the bottom of Terry's bra to stop her. She took Terry's hand. "Leave your clothes on and come dance with me."

As they were walking back across the room Nathan pushed another drink in Terry's hand, and a few seconds later he was obviously fighting with his wife.

"Still think she's a little stiff? Well then let's move her to a party where her in-laws aren't and it's all *her* friends," Janey said.

"Point taken," Roxanne said with a laugh. "You know I think they're perfect for each other."

Morning sucked. Her head was pounding and she thanked God and Fred that she didn't have to go into work. Terry was laying all over the California King – leaving barely enough room for Natalie – buck naked, the smiley face on her ass seeming to laugh at Natalie's hangover.

She didn't even want to walk into the rest of the apartment and see the devastation left in the wake of last night's party, but she figured it had to happen sooner or later and she desperately needed some coffee. She stumbled to the bathroom where she pissed for way longer than she thought was normal. She slung on her robe, tried to brush the dirty sock taste out of her mouth, and then stumbled out and towards the kitchen. She tripped over something in the middle of the floor, and when it yelped realized it was Roxanne and Byron tangled together on the floor, not wearing much more clothing than Terry was – which was probably why Roxanne's boyfriend had left the party so early.

She hoped the reporter was going to use a little discretion. Half way through the party she was pretty sure that no one remembered he was even there.

She saw the case that contained Vigilance's suit sitting next to the couch, being used as a coffee table, covered with half-empty drinks. She cringed and marked this as yet another reason to get more furniture.

"I hope you're heading to the kitchen to make coffee," Roxanne moaned.

"Yep."

"Thank you, God." Roxanne got up dragging the items of clothing she was almost wearing back into place, as she searched for other items that she found thrown around the room.

Roxanne appeared in the kitchen just as Natalie was pouring the water into the coffee maker, sat down at the bar and let her head drop onto the countertop. "I feel like death warmed up, and I came with Ryan and woke up with Byron." She picked her head up and looked at Natalie with a broad smile. "Great party."

Natalie laughed and then wished she hadn't. It hurt, but then so did sunlight and the sound the water running through the coffee and into the pot made. "Thanks for helping me put it all together at the last minute." She grabbed a bar stool and sat across the counter from Roxanne. "You realize that you're wearing Terry's shirt don't you?"

"That's all right. I think Byron's wearing her pants," Roxanne said with a smile.

"I made a total ass of myself," Natalie said.

"Did you have a good time?"

"I think so," Natalie said. "I hope so, otherwise this mess and this hangover are for nothing."

"At least you have the same partner this morning as you had last night."

"I'm sorry about Ryan."

"Don't be. I was ready to be rid of him; he's too clingy. Of course screwing one of my costars on your living room floor probably wasn't the smartest thing I've ever done."

"At least everyone else was gone, and I didn't hear you."

"How could you, with all the screaming and moaning you two were making, and might I add jealously, for a lot longer than we were."

"Hey I was drunk," Byron defended as he walked into the room. He sat down next to Roxanne. "I must have put on five pounds last night. My pants feel like they're three sizes to small."

Natalie and Roxanne just looked at each other and laughed.

The phone rang, sending a wave of pain through her brain that was only intensified when she answered the phone and it was her mother, who was nearly hysterical.

"Mom... calm down, of course he looked... because she's a very beautiful woman. It's perfectly normal, mother... Hell everyone was looking at her... Mother... it isn't even close to the same as looking at me... Mom you're blowing this whole thing out of proportion... Of course he isn't going to apologize. He didn't do anything wrong... if I had a dick I would have gotten a boner, too."

"I know I did," Byron said from where he had moved to stand hopefully by the coffee pot, waiting for the dripping to stop, signaling a relief from pain.

"See mother, Byron got a stiffy, too," Natalie explained to her mother. "No, I don't think Daddy no longer finds you attractive... He didn't say he wanted to have sex with her, Mother... No that's not what that means."

"The little head has a will all its own," Byron said helpfully.

"See, Mom? Byron said the little head has a will all it's own... well, maybe you should go to counseling then... Mom I have to go. Byron has just poured the coffee and I could really use it. Maybe next time you go to a party you should make him be the designated driver... It's supposed to mean that maybe you wouldn't be so judgmental and Daddy wouldn't have had such a good time if you'd been the one drinking...Well sometimes it seems like you don't want Daddy to have a good time... If I'm not upset I don't see why you should be, I mean it's my girlfriend he was apparently lusting after... You know as well as I do that Dad's not going to go after Terry or any other woman for that matter. For God's sake you don't leave him with any sexual energy left... It was just a stiffy, Mom, it's not the end of the world. Listen, I have to go someone else is trying to call." She hung up. "No one else is on the line. I'm just tired of hearing what a perv my dad is."

They all laughed. Terry walked in wearing boxers and a tank top, and she was obviously not in the least hung over, though she did take the coffee Natalie handed her when she sat down beside her.

"You aren't hung over at all are you?" Natalie asked scowling at her.

"No, not at all," Terry said smiling. "I got a few years of partying over you youngsters." She squinted at Roxanne and Byron, a confused look on her face.

"No, we didn't come together," Roxanne said, "but considering that you have put Nat's parent's in divorce court and now don't even have the good taste to be hung over I don't think you should rush to any judgments."

"Your mom and dad are fighting?" Terry asked.

"Apparently my dad got a boner when you were doing one of your many strip routines, and what's up with that anyway? Janey asks you to take off clothes and you do it?" Natalie said, more than a little angry.

"Yeah, what is up with that?" Roxanne asked.

Terry just looked from her to Byron and they both looked down at the countertop.

"Don't tell me you're going to start that shit about me and Janey again," Terry said to Natalie. "I was drunk. Anyone could have suggested I take my clothes off and I would have done it."

"That *is* what Janey told me," Roxanne said.

"Well that's very comforting to know," Natalie said. She got up and started to walk away and Terry grabbed her and pulled her into her lap.

"Unlike some people, who shall remain nameless, I didn't forget who I came with." Terry kissed the side of Natalie's neck and she melted against her.

"Oh, ouch," Roxanne said in mock pain.

"Isn't that my shirt?" Terry asked.

"That's all right those are Byron's boxer shorts you're wearing," Roxanne said with a laugh.

"I thought they looked familiar," Byron said.

"Damn, and I thought I lost weight," Terry said with disappointment.

"If you'd lost weight *and* you weren't hung over we'd have to kill you," Roxanne said.

Natalie leaned against Terry. Normal, it all felt so normal. All right, maybe not normal by most people's standards, but normal by hers. Just a bunch of friends sitting around talking and joking over the events of the night before.

Then her eyes fell on the case. Only a few feet away from where they sat was a secret so profound that no one would believe it unless they saw it. That Terry North, a well-known actress and Natalie's partner was also Vigilance, street vigilante with a magical suit.

Suddenly she felt a peace come over her. She had made a decision, a decision that would remove her from the status of target. It was her decision, and she was completely happy with it. Somehow she knew she'd made the right choice.

And it was all hers because Terry had removed the problem. She had done it and probably hadn't even worked up a sweat. Of course she hadn't, the suit didn't allow her to sweat. *She puts it on and she's Vigilance, but when she takes it off she's still just Terry, it hasn't really changed her except in positive ways. She's more self-confident, less depressed, less anxious than she was when I first met her.*

Suddenly Terry's alter ego didn't seem like such a big, terrible problem, a thing to be worried and lose sleep over.

It just was.

Chapter 8

When the movie came out, Terry's short but memorable role was getting more praise than the rest of the movie. She got asked to do a bunch of talk shows on both coasts, and the studio all but begged her to do them. She did a bunch of them in LA.

Natalie was shooting a film in *Monster Killers'* hiatus, and it just happened to work out that they would be shooting for three weeks in New York. So Terry let Dan book her onto the New York talk shows and went with Natalie.

So did Vigilance.

"Is Paul still pissed off about the party?" Natalie asked as she sat in her seat in first class.

"He thinks you hate him," Terry said, putting her case in the overhead compartment. She sat down next to Natalie and buckled up. "Put your seat belt on."

"We haven't even started to taxi. Besides, I don't think a seat belt will save you if the plane crashes."

"Just put your seatbelt on, Nat," Terry ordered.

Natalie did it, smiling at Terry. "You're afraid of flying."

"Well, it isn't exactly my favorite thing," Terry whispered back.

"Imagine, the big bad Super Hero afraid of flying," Natalie teased in a whisper.

"Just stop, all right?"

Seeing that Terry was actually sweating and almost white, Natalie did stop, and changed the subject. "I didn't not invite he and Owen to the party on purpose, and I don't actually hate him... not anymore."

"Janey and Tom and everyone else were there, and he just felt like you purposely left them off the list," Terry said.

"It wasn't like I spent weeks planning it, for Christ's sake. Roxanne and I put the whole thing together in an afternoon before and after I made the drop."

"I told him that, and then he said the fact that you didn't think to invite them showed that you hated them. He was acting very much like a stereotypical gay man, which really kind of threw me. I wish everyone could just get along."

"We should have them over when we get home."

"If we get home," Terry mumbled.

"You all right, Ms. North?" the stewardess asked.

"I'm fine," Terry said, quickly forcing a smile.

"Here," Natalie said, helpfully pushing an airsickness bag into Terry's sweaty palms.

Terry saw the smile on Natalie's face and growled. "It's not funny you know, Nat."

"Yes, it really is, Terry," Natalie laughed.

Terry wondered if Natalie would think it was so funny if she knew that Terry didn't have a fear of flying at all. If she knew the real reason why she was so freaked out about them being on the plane.

A couple of weeks ago she had seen a man she thought she recognized. The computer had popped the guy back as one of the suspected terrorists the government was looking for. She'd followed him and he'd taken her back to a nearly condemned warehouse where he and five others were obviously hard at work making some sort of plan. The problem was that there were government agents everywhere, obviously doing the same thing she was trying to do.

She didn't understand why they weren't just taking them in. Paul suggested they were watching them to see if they might lead them to bigger fish. Terry thought maybe they were watching them to find out what they were going to target and then make sure no one important was around when they did it. People were bitching about the war. If there was another terrorist attack they'd shut right up.

Paul pointed out that Terry didn't trust anyone, and that her conspiracy theories tended to grow all out of proportion.

Either way she'd never been able to get close enough to gather enough information to find out what they were planning or when they were planning if for because the damn government had been everywhere, and Paul warned her that they had equipment that might be able to detect her – maybe even see her.

Then one day they were all gone, both the government agents and the terrorists, leaving no evidence that was worth anything. She would have liked to believe that the government had picked them up, but she somehow doubted it. If they had they would have been crowing about it.

She scoured the area and Paul had used every computer trick he knew, but they hadn't found the terrorists again. Paul was profiling different targets, but there were just too many and no way of narrowing it down.

Paul had said that statistically they should be perfectly safe to fly. But Terry had never trusted statistics, not even Paul's, and getting on a plane when you knew there were terrorists on the loose in your city was not, in her opinion, her brightest moment.

She had sweated all the way through boarding that they were going to pick her luggage to search even though she knew all they'd find when she opened the case was an ugly gray suit, which she could explain away with a simple lie. She just didn't like cutting it that close.

She was as jumpy as everyone else was with all the orange alerts and warnings every day on the news. The difference being that she knew that the bastards were actually planning something in LA. The fact that the government apparently knew and wasn't doing anything only made her more nervous. In fact, one of her crazier conspiracy theories centered around the notion that the government agents weren't there to watch the Middle Eastern thugs at all. That they were there because they figured Vigilance would show up and the government would love nothing better than to get their hands on that suit.

She knew that was crazy, and somewhere in the back of her head she wasn't expecting any sort of a disaster on this flight, but she'd still feel better when they touched down.

She was starting to calm down when a man of Middle Eastern descent sat down across the aisle from her. He was wearing an expensive suit and new shoes. She looked him over closely for any bulges in his clothing.

He'd better hope he doesn't have to so much as piss during this flight. If he so much as moves I'm going to jump up and beat him to the ground.

She had purposely gotten them a flight with a stop over in Dallas, knowing that the cross-country flights with more fuel would be more alluring to a terrorist.

Natalie leaned over, got right in her ear, and whispered in an angry tone, "You know something don't you?"

"No, I'm just paranoid," Terry whispered back, never taking her eyes off the man.

"Great, " Natalie flopped back in her seat and fell silent. "I wish I could tell when you were lying," she mumbled.

The plane started to move. She watched the guy; did he look nervous? She couldn't tell. She was worthless without the suit, no way of detecting an elevated heart rate, no way of asking him a question then seeing if he had lied. She wondered if they had searched this guy, and then knew they hadn't. They were so afraid of being politically incorrect that they rarely screened the people they needed to be screening. They had screened a middle-aged woman traveling with her husband and her adult daughter, and a WASP college girl with designer luggage who'd obviously just had a nose job. They'd searched an obese black man wearing a Hawaiian shirt and traveling with his wife, but they hadn't checked this guy.

She wasn't the profiler, that was Paul's job, but even she knew that people who loved themselves didn't fly planes into buildings. That people traveling with family members weren't likely to use the plane for a missile, unless of course they just hated that family member. She smiled then. *I would do it if my mother was on board. If she were still alive and I were a terrorist.*

"What are you grinning about?" Natalie asked with a smile, apparently forgetting that she was mad at her.

"How much I hated my mother," Terry said.

The plane started to lift off. She took Natalie's hand, still keeping a half an eye on the "Arab."

"You hated your mother, why?"

"I'd rather not talk about it," Terry said. The pilot was talking, and she was trying to listen to him and still watch the "Arab."

"I think he's all right, Terry," Natalie said. "Look what he's reading."

"Some Arab crap," Terry said nodding her head.

"That's a Hebrew newspaper. He's an Israeli Jew, honey."

"Well he looks like an Arab, maybe he's trying to pass. Maybe it's just a clever disguise."

Natalie leaned over Terry and spit out something Terry assumed was Hebrew because she couldn't understand a word she said. The guy looked as shocked as Terry was, then laughed and rattled something back.

Natalie laughed.

"*Monster Killer,*" he said, snapping his fingers, and it was obvious that he had been raised in America. "I watch your show all the time." He pointed at Terry. "And you, I loved you when I was a kid. I had all the *Dark Avenger* stuff."

Terry smiled, and feeling too completely idiotic and old to actually speak, just nodded.

Natalie talked to him for a few minutes. It turned out the guy was a rabbinical student who had just gotten back from Israel.

The plane had reached its cruising altitude and the stewardess came by to collect drink orders. Terry asked for a scotch neat, she felt like she needed it.

"So what did you say and what did he say to you?"

"I said my girlfriend thinks you may be an Arab terrorist, and he sa..."

"You told him?"

"Yes, and then he said, you don't look Jewish, either."

"Ha, ha every one has a good laugh, and I look like a big, stupid jerk."

Natalie took her hand and leaned over to whisper in her ear. "Hey, *Dark Avenger*, why don't you quit fighting crime for awhile and just try to enjoy our trip?"

Terry nodded her head, and squeezed Natalie's hand. "I'll try."

A limo met them at the airport, and so did a huge press core. They asked them questions that they half answered as they tried to get in the limo. Security sent by the studio kept the press back. The driver tried to take Terry's case, but she shook her head no and brought it into the car with her. Two of the security guards got in the limo with them.

There was more press and a crowd of fans at the hotel. They waded through, signing a couple of autographs, and answering some more questions.

The first night she left the suit in the case, just enjoying being with Natalie and preparing for the next morning when she was supposed to appear on the Ronald and Donna show.

When she woke up and turned the TV on, some Republican senator was saying how much he appreciated Vigilance and what Vigilance stood for, and she almost puked. She was directly opposed to everything this fucker stood for, mixing religion with politics, nixing gay rights, and giving tax cuts to the rich, so it really rankled that he was all for her vigilante-style justice.

She wondered how he'd feel if he knew his hero would love to plant a laser bolt in *his* chest, was a lowly woman and a queer woman to boot.

This was probably the reason why when Donna asked her, "So, you used to play a superhero on TV, what do you think of Vigilance?" she told her just what she thought.

"We're living in a time when no one knows what's next. When the rich have taken over our government and passed laws to make themselves richer while they make everyone else poorer. The economy is in ruins. Tax cut after tax cut to make the rich richer has cost jobs and caused essential programs to suffer. The religious right is running rampant over our basic rights to exist, to read, and to watch what we find fit. We're in a war and no one knows whether we actually need to be there or not. Faceless Corporations are eating everything. There aren't enough police to stop crimes, and most of the police we have seem more concerned with writing traffic tickets than actually protecting and serving.

"People have lost hope, hope in our government, hope in our future, hope for the world. Vigilance gives a little slice of that hope back. Vigilance actually stops criminals from committing crimes, actually saves lives, what a terrible thing. This horrid vigilante has taken one life, but did it while saving another, and how many people are alive today because of Vigilance? The fact that the same police force that says they don't have the time or manpower to actually cruise the poorer neighborhoods is wasting time and money to try to track down Vigilance is obscene. I think that tells us just how much we can count on the government for anything remotely resembling justice."

The rest of the interview went more or less normally.

When her cell phone rang on the way back to the hotel, she knew who it was.

"God dammit, Terry, do you just hate to work?" Dan screamed. "Tell me you didn't just get on national television, dis the current administration, question the war effort, and endorse Vigilance."

"I didn't get on national television and…"

"Dammit, you smart ass! I'm in the middle of negotiations for a good supporting role for you in a major motion picture and you pull this shit."

"Don't have an aneurysm, Dan," Terry said. "Very few people like the current administration, even more are confused about the war, and the last poll taken gave Vigilance a higher popularity rating than the president. Besides, do you really think that anyone who loves this administration would tolerate my openly gay, agnostic ass anyway?"

"An actor shouldn't have an opinion, it's the best way to make sure you get work."

"Plenty of very famous actors have voiced opinions a whole lot stronger than mine."

"Yes, and plenty have been blacklisted for doing so. You accused the police force of being incompetent, the government of being corrupt..."

"Is and is."

"That's not the point, Terry. I swear, if I didn't know better I'd think you were afraid of success."

"My dear friend, and the guy who gets twenty percent of every dime I make, I've finally reached a point in my life where fame and fortune no longer determine my success as a human being. Since this is the case, I assure you that I will be getting parts for the rest of my life."

Not too far behind Dan's call – in fact she was still in the limo on the way back to the hotel – came the call from Paul.

"Tell me you didn't just get on national television and endorse Vigilance."

"I didn't just get on nationa..."

"God dammit, Terry!"

"Wow, déjà vu," Terry mumbled.

"You *are* Vigilance, you dumb ass. The last thing we want is for some idiot government official to put two and two together and figure that out. You'd better just cancel any going out in New York. People might figure out that Vigilance is anywhere that Terry North is."

"You worry more than my grandma."

"That's not hard since your grandmother has been dead for twenty years," Paul said. "I didn't like this anyway, Terry. You're there without the bike, without any support team..."

"I'll be fine and I'll be careful."

"What made you say that anyway?" Paul screeched as if getting mad all over again.

"This morning on the news that idiot Rhoyd Thornsen was endorsing Vigilance. Since I'd love to kill the worthless preacher, butt-sucking creep it just got on my last nerve."

Paul laughed then. "Gee, Terry don't hold back, tell me how you really feel."

"I'll try to behave during the rest of my interviews, boss."

"Do, let's not give the government any clues."

She was just wondering whether it was dark enough to go out yet when Natalie walked in looking exhausted and plopped in the nearest chair.

"They tried to talk me into coming back, getting you and going to Studio 51." She sighed. "I was ashamed to tell them that I was just flat too tired," Natalie said.

"Well, we did lose two hours, not to mention the number of amphetamines your fellow cast members are eating," Terry said.

"Ah, come on, Terry, you don't really think so?"

"Bet on it. You can't party all night and work all day the way those fuckheads do unless you're popping pills to wake you up and more to make you sleep. We're a rare minority in tinsel town."

Natalie smiled. "How do you know I'm not popping uppers and downers?"

"Not funny, Nat, but if you were popping pills you wouldn't be so tired all the time. Besides, the suit would have detected it."

"Well, you *do* pop pills, dear, and God only knows what they do to you," Natalie said, looking over at the bedside table where the pill bottle sat. Her whole manner had changed. No more joking now.

"They're just supplements, Nat. We've gone over this about a billion times."

"A simple supplement wouldn't allow you to thrive on five hours of sleep instead of eight. It wouldn't keep you from being hung over after a night of binge drinking," Natalie said.

"Paul says it's perfectly safe, there haven't been any side effects."

The phone rang and Natalie answered it. "Hello... Mom so good to hear from you... What? No, I didn't see Terry's interview." Natalie turned and gave Terry a quizzical look and Terry cringed. "She has a right to her own opinion... Well, see you agreed with everything else she said... Don't ask because you don't want to know, Mom... All right, then I do agree with

Terry… No, I didn't like it at first, but now, well the crime rate in the entire area took a huge downward thrust, didn't it?… One hit man was killed, which isn't any great loss, is it, Mom?… How many people do you think it has saved, Mom?.. No I haven't become a member of the violent majority Mom, I just don't think Vigilance is such a bad thing… Mom I just got back to the hotel and I'm bushed. If you don't have something more pleasant to talk about, then I'm going to hang up… No, I'm not mad, just tired." Natalie sighed and glared at Terry, who just shrugged helplessly and mouthed the words, "I'm sorry."

When she finally got off the phone with her mother she flopped back in her chair. "Let's go out and get something to eat."

"I thought you were tired."

"I am, but if I stay here my mother's just going to call back." She took her cell phone out of her pocket and left it on the bed. "Come on, I love New York pizza." The phone rang. "See? Now come on."

They left the hotel followed by security, and Terry wondered how she was going to get out of the room without them noticing. Of course they weren't here for her, they were here for Nat. Still, they were bound to notice the door opening and a shimmering form walking out and then the door closing on its own.

"Quit working," Natalie demanded, seeing the look on her face. "Besides, they only stay around till I tell them I'm definitely in for the night."

They walked to a pizza place and got a couple of slices of pizza and a couple of beers, then sat down.

"You know, Terry…"

"I know, I know I shouldn't have gotten all political on TV. Someone with such seemingly opposing views is just bound to piss off just about everyone, and besides I shouldn't mention Vigilance, and…"

"That's not what I was going to say. Terry, we've talked about everything, but we've never talked about your family. Yesterday you said you hated your mother, and I just can't get that out of my head."

"You know how you said you weren't like most adopted kids, that your parents had let you meet your mother and you just didn't care to have anything to do with her? That you were glad she had given you away because no one should keep a child they don't want. Well, I wish my mother had given me away, 'cause she sure didn't want me. Let's just leave it at that."

"No, let's not. Terry we're a couple, if you can't share with me who can you share with?"

Terry took a drink of beer to try to stop the burning on the roof of her mouth. It was one of the downfalls of pizza. Cheese napalm peeling off the roof of your mouth. Of course that didn't stop her from eating it before it was cool enough. After she'd swallowed her beer she glared at Natalie across the table. "Dammit, Nat, you're ruining my big New York pizza reunion here. I hated my mother, all right. I'm glad she's dead. I know that sounds awful, but it's true, and no I don't have any unresolved issues over it. My father died when I was so young I don't remember him. I wish I'd had the chance to get to know him, because maybe he wasn't a shithead like my mother. I got my father's good looks and my mother hated me because of it. See she hated him, she wanted to leave him, but she also hated to work and she hated for anyone to think that she looked less than proper, so she couldn't leave him and not take me, and she sure as hell didn't want to have to take care of me on her own.

"When he died I'm thinking she resented me even more because she could have gotten her life back completely if it hadn't been for me." Terry put her folded pizza down and took another drink of beer before she went on. "She probably would have eventually killed me if I hadn't started bringing in money. And no, that isn't an exaggeration. She was a cold, evil bitch with not a single redeeming quality. She beat me all the time, made me work till I was about to drop and never said anything kind to me. She was a passive aggressive and violent woman who stole all my money so that when I left home at eighteen I was broke. And yes, I'm well aware that this upbringing is doubtlessly why I identified so strongly with the *Dark Avenger* character that I eventually became Vigilance. I know what it's like to be the little guy with no rights, taking the hits with no one to step in for you. That enough information for you?" Terry snapped.

Natalie nodded silently, a tear falling from her eye as she did so. "I'm so sorry, Terry."

Terry calmed down with a sigh. "That's why I didn't tell

you about my childhood, Nat. Not because it's some big secret or I wanted to keep you out, but because there isn't anything good to tell, and I'm not looking for your sympathy or using it for an excuse for any of the things I do that drive you nuts. I don't like to talk about it because it's depressing as hell. You have wonderful stories about the things you did with your parents, and that they did with you and I have, well… that."

It was easy to sneak out of the hotel and easy to sneak around the streets. She badly needed to beat someone's head in, so she knew she had to watch it or she'd wind up crippling a guy for yelling at someone else.

"There's been a string of subway robberies in the Bronx. Seems like it's the same bunch of thugs. Why don't you check that out?" Paul said in her ear.

She nodded and headed for the nearest subway entrance. She jumped over the gate and got in the car. It was only about half full, so she found an empty seat and sat down. A dirty guy who looked like he was probably homeless, and who the suit told her was drunk, kept looking at her. Terry thought it was funny. No one else seemed to have even noticed that there was a strange presence on the subway, but this guy did. He walked right over, swaying and almost falling as he did so, and he sat down next to her.

"I got to tell you, Pete, am I ever glad to see you."

Terry smiled and said in a whisper, "Yeah it's been too long."

"Sure has, so… I could use another wish."

"Well, you flat wasted the last one," Terry said.

"Ah, Pete, ain't it the truth, but come on you got the power, help a fella out."

"Tell ya what, it's real simple. Quit drinking, sober up and get a job."

This seemed to agitate the drunk and he jumped to his feet looked down at her and yelled. "You're fucking out of your mind, Pete!"

"Hey, you crazy fuck shut up!" a big guy who looked like he might be a steel worker screamed from the other end of the car.

"Don't tell me to shut up, you tell him, Pete. Tell him, he can't tell me to shut up," the drunk yelled back.

"You filthy pile of puke I'm warning you right now. I've had a shitty day." The big guy started to get up.

Terry jumped up, grabbed the drunk and sat him back in his seat.

"Listen, you dumb fuck," she hissed in a whisper. "Right now I'm starting to wonder who I should save. Do I save you from him, or do I save him from you? You're a worthless drunken bum, harmless but definitely annoying. That guy's just said he had a shitty day. He works for a living, he just wants to ride home in peace without any of your crazy shit."

"You're right, Pete." The drunk looked up at the big guy who was now standing up. "I'm sorry; I'll be quiet."

The big guy snarled, mumbled something, and sat back down. Terry knew how he felt. He'd had a bad day and he really just wanted to thrash someone, it didn't really matter who.

She almost felt bad she didn't just let the drunk keep it up till the guy felt he had just cause to kick the bum's ass. Maybe helping someone feel less frustrated was all he was good for.

"You know, Pete, you're not as much fun as you used to be," the drunk said in a whisper.

"Yeah... well I found God."

"You did?" the drunk whispered in awe.

"Yeah, damndest thing, everyone's always looking for this guy and there he was just sitting on a park bench feeding the pigeons."

"Did he talk to you?"

"Well of course he did it, wouldn't have been polite not to."

"What did he say?"

"He said hi, and then I said hi back, and then I asked him the big question, you know. What's it all about? He looks me right in the eye and says... are you ready for this?"

The drunk nodded.

"It's all about not being a dickhead. That's it. The whole thing. Just don't be a prick."

"That's fucking amazing."

"Yeah. That's what I thought, but then the dude was God and all, and what do you expect?" Terry was growing tired of this game. Like the construction worker, she was ready to kick some ass that needed kicking, so she got up. "Well, I'll see you later, dude. Good bye."

"Good bye, Pete."

Terry walked up to the door between the cars, opened it

and walked out. When she heard the gasp behind her she knew what she had done. She turned around to look at the car full of stunned faces, and then just closed the door. That ought to give them all something to talk about for a while. When the subway stopped at the next station she went on through the other door into the car figuring she wouldn't be noticed, and she wasn't.

The time on her visor said it was now twelve thirty-five. Lots more people got out of the car than got in and the entire atmosphere seemed to change. She stood up deciding to just hang onto one of the ceiling handles, to be more ready for action. The subway started moving. None of these people looked dangerous, just tired and maybe a little scared. But then they were quickly approaching the part of the burrow in which most of the muggings had taken place.

Look at them, they aren't stupid, they know this is danger-ous. They just don't have any choice. They work horrible shifts, and this is what time they get off. No choices. I know what that's like. It's an awful feeling, like being naked in a room with no walls. And where are the cops? Why aren't their cops in these trains? Because our wonderful president gave a huge tax cut to the rich, which caused huge gaps in funding for things like police protection. States are having trouble with-out federal funding. What police there are have all been sent to watch the rich neighborhoods because burglary is on the rise, that's what always happens when the economy's in the toilet and there are no jobs.

They didn't know it, but at least for tonight they were going to get home safely.

Suddenly she heard a noise. "Amplify sound," she ordered in a whisper.

Shooting from two cars down. She rushed to the door and kept moving. "Vision 75 feet."

She could see them then. There were at least five of them. She slung the door open and said to the stunned people in the car. "There's no need to fear, Vigilance is here."

To her surprise, they all started to cheer. She opened the door to the next car and ran through it to the next one. She slung the door open. One of the nylon stocking wearing punks was carrying a small gun. He turned and fired, but she had already hit the floor, rolled, and come up behind one of his buddies. She smacked her hand down hard on a pressure point at the base of his neck and he went down. She kicked out at the guy holding the gun, her foot exploding into his chest with such force that he hit the side of the subway car and slid down. She shot the barrel of his weapon with the laser, destroying it. One of the other guys had figured out where she was, and he stabbed her in the back, his cheap blade snapping on the bio armor and causing just enough pain to piss her off, so she rounded on him, slamming her fist into his face making blood splatter against the nylon stocking he wore over his head. One of the others had apparently had a gun she hadn't seen till now. He was aiming in the direction of an elderly man in a pizzeria outfit who was screaming.

She jumped at the gunman, catching the bullet he fired in her stomach. She still landed on him, knocking him to the ground, and this time she hit him so hard in the face that she knew instantly that she'd killed him.

"Damn, broke another one," she said.

"Dammit, Vigilance!" Paul was saying in her ear; no time to listen to him. The visor said no detectable damage to the suit. No damage to her. The adrenalin shot the suit gave her made her able to literally jump up off the man she'd just killed, spin in the air and land a kick to the side of the last punk's head, laying him out on the subway car floor.

"Vigilance will not be denied!" she yelled, and the passengers of the subway car started to applaud. She aimed her laser at the last weapon and melted its barrel. She walked around pulling the stockings off the heads of all the punks except the one she'd killed. That was the problem with jujitsu, everything ended with, *and then you finish them.* She was sure she should feel bad about it, but all she could think about was that Natalie was going to be pissed off that she'd killed someone else. The one who had first shot at her was coming to even as the subway car was stopping, and she turned to him and said, "Little boys shouldn't play with guns."

As the door opened she holstered her weapon and ran out into the station up the stairs and down the street.

She didn't stop till she was several blocks away and the adrenalin shot had worn off.

"Vigilance, are you all right?" Paul asked.

"I'm bruised a little, but damn," she leaned against the side of the building to catch her breath, "what a rush! Damn, Paul, the little bullets don't do shit to the suit, or to me in the suit."

"Call it a night," Paul ordered.

"That's a great idea, but I'm lost," she said looking around her. She was in a real bad part of the Bronx.

"Go to a street corner, find a sign, and I'll have the computer plot you a course back to the hotel."

"I could just go back to the subway station catch a train back uptown."

"No, by now the police will be everywhere. It's too risky."

"I ain't walking all the way back uptown, Paul."

"No, just to another station. In fact, why don't you take a bus?"

"All right." She walked a long time before she found a street sign that was still up, then the information and map were coming across her visor. There was another subway station five blocks to her right. She started walking. All around her she could hear people fighting, gun fire in the distance. There were a couple of streetwalkers standing on a corner; their combined age might have made them legal.

They were talking up a storm, and she stood just feet from them and listened.

"I'm telling you, Lucricia, Tyron is just using you the same way he uses us all. He don't care nothin' bout you."

"I know you're right, Dorella," she sighed. "All I ever wanted was to raise enough money to buy a Porsche and a boob job."

Dorella laughed. "With Tyron you'll be lucky to make enough money to buy a pinto and a water bra."

Both girls laughed. A car drove up and rolled down it's window, and the hookers went running over.

He of course wanted them to do obscene things for which he was willing to pay them the high price of fifty bucks. Terry figured that by the time ole Tyron got his cut it would be another five years before Lucrecia could get the water bra, much less the Pinto.

She walked over to the john's side of the car and smashed the window out with her fist. She reached in and ripped him out of the window of his car. She slammed him against the side of the car and took his wallet from his pocket. She looked at the guy's pictures, at his license. "So Robert, here's what I'm thinking. If you can't get your wife to do these filthy things for ya, then why do you think these girls should?"

"What the hell is going on?" the guy screamed in terror.

"Vigilance, dude. Justice, you're here cheating on your wife using these girls who aren't much older than your daughter, and you don't even want to pay them anything for their trouble." She extracted five hundred dollars from his wallet, put it back in his pocket and let him go.

He didn't stay to argue with her just got in his car and roared off.

The two girls watched with mouths gaped open as the money seemed to walk to them of its own accord. "Let's make a deal, girls. You can take what Vigilance is holding here in my hand, or you can go for what ole Tyron has behind curtain number two. Take the money get two bus tickets. Go somewhere far away from here where no one knows you. Get a job at McDonald's and start a new life. Or take the money, use it to buy more drugs, and end up dead before you're twenty. The world isn't all about having nice things. Nice things aren't worth a flying fuck if you can't look yourself in the face in the morning." She gave the girls the money and took off in the direction of the subway station again.

"Dammit I didn't create that suit so that you could go around terrorizing johns."

"You know what, Control? Fuck you! Vigilance isn't all about what you want. You heard what he wanted to do." She made a face. "Fucking sick ass pervert. I thank God everyday that I'm queer."

"Me, too, because it means I don't have to put up with any woman's shit. Except, no, wait a minute! I still have to put up with *your* shit. Do you think you can maybe just get back to the hotel without stopping to save any more hookers?" Paul all but yelled in her ear.

"I'll try," Terry said, and started skipping down the sidewalk.

"Vigilance could you maybe try not being so cheerful?" Paul asked, a disapproving quality to his voice.

"Why not?"

"Oh I don't know, because you just killed yet another person?"

"Oh that." She stopped skipping. "How's that?"

"Seriously, don't you feel anything?"

"Well I was feeling pretty happy till you started bringing me down."

She had a long time to think about it on the trip back to the hotel and realized there was a hole in her somewhere. She'd hated her mother so much she hadn't shed a single tear when she'd died, and she could kill a thug and feel no remorse whatsoever. That just couldn't be right; maybe she needed therapy.

At the hotel Terry quickly stripped the suit off and took a much needed piss. Natalie walked in before she had finished.

"Damn, have we already reached this stage in our relationship?" Terry said as she wiped herself and stood up. "What's next, farting in front of each other?"

"It's not funny, Terry," Natalie said. When she looked at her she could see that she'd been crying. "On the news... there was a news break and I knew I knew it had something to do with you. They said Vigilance was in New York. That she'd stopped a robbery on the subway. That one person was dead and that the witnesses believed that Vigilance had been shot."

"But I wasn't hurt. Look." Terry pointed at the small bruise on her stomach. "Hell, the one where I got stabbed actually hurts worse." She looked at her back in the mirror. "And it looks worse, too."

"My God, Terry, do you even hear what you're saying anymore? Does it even register how weird and wrong it is? You killed someone else..."

"Not on purpose," Terry defended quickly. "He shot at me as I was jumping on him. When I landed my training just kicked in and he was dead before I had a chance to think about it."

"So it's all right!" Natalie screeched.

"Honey, these little bastards have shot three people in the last six weeks. They've put six people in the hospital, and one person is dead. They killed one, I killed one..."

"So now what? Everything is even?"

"You know what, Nat? I'm naked, and I don't feel like it's fair for you to fight with me when I'm naked. I feel vulnerable when I'm standing around with no clothes on."

"You're about as vulnerable as a Desert Storm tank!" Natalie yelled and stomped out of the room.

Terry sighed. She really just wanted to get a shower maybe take a couple of aspirins and go to bed. She slung her robe on and walked out. "Honey, come on now..."

"Shhhhh," Natalie ordered, pointing at the TV.

Another newsbreak. Oh great, probably just something to get me into even more trouble. Maybe I should hone my acting skills looking like it really upsets me that I killed some worthless punk. Work up a tear or two for the dead guy who shot me.

"This just in, the robber killed tonight in Vigilance's upset of yet another subway train robbery has been identified as twenty-one year old Hector Rivera. Now if that name sounds familiar, it should. Hector was the boy who went to trial at age twelve for the brutal, supposedly wrestling-inspired killing of his twenty-two month old baby brother. He was given probation and ordered to undergo psychological counseling. He was released from both probation and counseling when the courts determined that he had been rehabilitated.

"Right now we don't know which gun actually fired the bullet that killed Anita Gonzales in the first of these robberies, but we talked to her husband who had this to say."

A Hispanic man's face filled the screen. "My children don't have a mother, I don't have a wife. I'm glad someone finally got the people who took her away from us. I don't care if one of them is dead. I wish they were all dead. Maybe if this man had been locked up where he needed to be, my wife would still be alive. He was sick and never should have been allowed to exist with the rest of us. I think it's a crime against justice that the police are looking for Vigilance. I thank you, Vigilance. If you're watching, I thank you."

Natalie turned to look at Terry, and Terry tried not to look smug and pleased with herself, which was almost too much for her acting ability to handle.

"OK... the guy was a brutal creep, but I'm still not sure that he deserves to be dead."

"It was an accident, Nat. I'm really, really sorry that it happened..."

"My shitting God, why don't you have an Oscar? I almost believe you."

"Well," Terry said, smiling in spite of herself. "I am sorry that you're pissed off at me."

Natalie sighed. "Well, in all honesty I'm doing a little acting myself, because I'm not as mad that you killed someone as I am that you didn't bother to pick up a phone and tell me that you weren't hurt."

"I thought we had decided that you wouldn't watch the TV while I was out. You should have been in bed asleep."

"Yes, well, I'm still having trouble with the whole sleeping while you're out trying to get yourself killed thing." She walked over and wrapped her arms around Terry. "I'm so glad you're all right, and so pissed off that you made me worry, and... Oh my God! I'm channeling my mother."

Terry laughed. "I need to get a shower, and we both need to get some sleep."

"I don't have to be to work till nine," Natalie said.

"Yeah, and it's two o'clock now. If you'd gone to sleep when I left, you would have been plenty rested. As it is we might as well have gone with your friends to the club."

"I'll get plenty of sleep. Of course if we'd gone to the club..."

"Don't go there, Nat. If we'd gone to the club instead, a subway full of people would never feel completely safe again, someone who didn't deserve it might even be dead, and some filthy pervert would have cheated on his wife and family with a couple of hookers who should be in junior high. It all comes down to weighing the evils. I killed a baby killer to stop a robbery and maybe worse. I think the balance is in my favor." Terry walked over and kissed Natalie on the forehead. "Now, I'm here so why don't you go to bed and try to get some sleep?"

Natalie nodded and Terry turned and walked back into the bathroom. She started the shower running and when it was warm climbed in and closed the doors. A few seconds later as she was soaping up the shower door opened and Natalie crawled in the shower with her. Terry smiled.

"Now what the hell are you doing?"

"I still couldn't sleep. Now... what's this about hookers?"

Chapter 9

Once she got back from New York she went to work every
night looking for the terrorist cell she had found and lost
before she left. Paul was working his computer magic – which
she was pretty sure included hacking into secret government
systems, and within two weeks they had located them again.
This time they were harder to get close to. They were holed
up in a run-down tenement building with civilians all around.

She could get a good vantage point of the room they were
staying in if she could get up on the fire escape that was
directly across from the apartment they were in.

She made a move for it when suddenly a red light started
flashing in the upper right hand corner of her visor, the same
one that flashed when she was shot or hurt or out of one of
chemicals or medication. The message underneath read. "Detected."

"What the fuck does that mean?" Terry asked.

"The feds must have rigged up something to detect movement, or more likely body heat, to try and find you," Paul said.
"Abort, get the hell out of there."

Easier said than done. The damn government boys seemed
to be peeling out of the darkness all around her, guns drawn,
and it was pretty obvious that they could see her.

"It's body heat. They're using an infrared scan," Paul said.

"Suit temperature fifty degrees," Terry ordered as she
moved slowly away towards the area which seemed to be the
least populated by what she now assumed from their move-
ments and their dress were some sort of special ops unit.
"Audio higher, higher." Nothing. Either they weren't talking
or they had the same cloaking device she had. That could be
both a plus and a minus. She could now clearly hear all the
movement around her, so that she knew exactly where each
and everyone of them were. If they were ordered to be silent
– if they didn't have the same system she had which allowed
her to talk to Paul without being heard outside the helmet –
that meant they couldn't communicate with each other. Ten
men – which was what she was now counting – working alone

were more likely to screw up than ten men working in coordinated groups. Of course, the down side was that she had no idea what their objective was. Were they supposed to catch her alive, or were they just not shooting at her because they couldn't afford to tip the Arabs off that they were here? And were they here for the terrorists and just didn't want her to get in their way, or were they using the terrorists as bait to catch her?

She was cold and they seemed to be looking around as if they'd lost her, so she assumed that her trick had worked.

She ran right between two of them, and when they didn't fire on or chase her she knew they could no longer see her. She ran down the alley to her bike, climbed on, started it and took off. Immediately a car started following her, so she assumed they had been watching the bike. They had definitely been waiting for her, then; the bike would have been hot when she came in, but it cooled quickly. They'd known the minute she had gotten there. Why had they waited?

They wanted to make sure they separated her from the bike.

They were still following her.

No problem.

She made the motor sing and took off through traffic at speeds no one with a brain would travel, and it didn't take her two minutes to lose them. She headed for the hills, suddenly finding a need to put some space between her and the city.

"These army boys are a real problem, Paul," Terry said, pacing back and forth in front of him.

"No shit," Paul said. He didn't look up at her, just kept downloading the data from the suit. "By the way, genius idea turning the temperature down on the suit."

"Thanks," Terry said, then, "Paul, these guys are right in my way, and I'm not at all sure now that my theory – you know the one you said was total paranoia – that these bastards don't give a damn about the terrorists they just want me, isn't exactly right."

Paul nodded, still not looking up. "That's what it's starting to look like to me, too."

"So what are we going to do?" Terry asked.

"Here's a far out idea for you two coconuts," Owen said from where he sat on a stool checking out the bike and chewing on a bagel, "why don't you quit all this stupid shit before Terry gets killed and we wind up in prison playing pin cushion? This ain't the local pigs after us anymore, it's the fucking federal government, and the military arm at that. They'll just keep on and on till they catch us. It's been a fun run, but it's time to call it a night."

"Earth to Owen," Terry practically screamed. "There are rag heads in LA…"

"Excuse me," Owen nearly screamed. "Can you get any more politically incorrect?"

"Bite my ass, Owen. What would you like me to say? That the poorly informed, misguided, Middle Eastern gentlemen are in LA looking for something to blow up!"

"And maybe the military can handle it. Maybe we're in *their* way," Owen suggested. "Maybe they're coming after you because you're going to screw up their operation."

"Expecting this government to actually do anything about terrorism is like expecting a can of sardines to get the taste of bad pussy out of your mouth," Terry explained.

Owen made a face. "Why am I thinking, here speaks the voice of experience? Christ, Terry! That has to go on my list of the ten nastiest similes ever."

"She's right," Paul said.

"About the pussy and sardines?" Owen looked – if possible – even more disgusted than before. "I don't want to know how you know that, but you gargle with bleach before you kiss me again."

"I don't know about the sardines, I'm talking about the government. Terry's right. If they wanted to stop the terrorists they would have rounded them up by now. Instead they seem more interested in Vigilance than they are the terrorists." Paul finally gave up on the computer, stood up and started pacing. As if the two of them pacing might actually solve all the problems of the world.

Owen watched as Terry and Paul paced against each other and out of sync, back and forth, back and forth, till it screwed with his head. So much he leaned into the bike pretending that he was fixing something.

"I can't get close enough to find out what the hell they're doing," Terry said.

"The terrorists are using so much slang and talking so gutturally that what I can decipher from what we've picked up doesn't tell us a God damned thing about what their target might be," Paul said. "Mostly just what they want to eat for dinner and what nasty American girls will do for a little cash. Hypocritical bastards. They're going to kill us because we're ungodly heathens, but before they suicide bomb whatever it is they're going to bomb they're going to do everything they say God hates us for."

"We have to get the military out of there so I can get close enough to figure out what their target is. You know... maybe I should just get a good laser bead on the terrorists and kill them..."

"That's going to tell the military boys just exactly where you are. And if you don't get every one of them, whoever's left is going to get in a car and try to kill as many people as possible. What if the military boys are legit? What if they're trying to trace these guys back to someone bigger, stop *something* bigger, like maybe the war?"

Terry stopped pacing and glared across the computer consol at where Paul suddenly stopped pacing to turn to face her. "You know, Paul... I keep coming up with ideas and you keep blowing holes in them."

"Well, one of us has to actually take a second to think, don't we?" Paul said with a smile. "This isn't like stopping some hood in an alley. This could have big, huge, long-range consequences. It would sure help a hell of a lot if we could actually trust our own government to be first competent and second looking out for the American public's best interests instead of their own political agenda."

Terry nodded. "That's what I'm thinking, Paul. I'm thinking I don't trust this administration not to purposely sit back and let whatever's going to happen just happen, because then people will get behind their unpopular war effort. The country has gone to hell in a hand basket ever since this joker got in office. What if they don't even want the suit? What if they're just there to make sure that I can't stop the terrorists from doing what they actually want them to do?"

"Here she goes again," Owen mumbled.

"Terry, I don't like this administration any better than you do, and I don't trust them, but your conspiracies within conspiracy theories boggle the boundaries of my strained imagination," Paul said. He rubbed at his eyes as if he had the beginning of a headache.

The phone rang and they all jumped. Paul answered the phone. "Hello..." he handed the phone to Terry, "it's for you."

"Hello... in a minute, baby... yes, I know what time it is... all right, I'll come right home." She handed the phone back to Paul who hung it up.

"You know, Terry, you can't just run out because your girlfriend calls. Lives hang in the balance, a terrorist cell is on the loose, and now the feds have seen you. Batman's girl-friend never calls him when he's in the bat cave."

Terry smiled as she headed for her car. "That's because he never has the same girlfriend from one movie to the next."

"And didn't he have a girlfriend who actually stumbled into the Bat Cave?" Owen asked.

Paul looked thoughtful. "No, I don't think so."

"Yes, I think it was the second one, the one where he's played by George Clooney."

"George Clooney wasn't Batman in the second one, that was Val Kilmer, and Robin was the one who found the Bat Cave not the girl, whichever one she was..."

"Speaking of Robin, what the hell does Batman need Robin for? Seems to me the little simp spends more time getting into trouble and being held hostage than anything else."

"Batman definitely doesn't need Robin," Paul said knowl-edgably. "The writers need him so that Batman can have some-one to save."

"I think they're a gay couple," Owen said.

"Boys!" Terry yelled, standing by the open door to her car. "Lives hang in the balance, a terrorist cell is loose, and the feds saw me tonight, do you really think it's time to worry about the love life of a comic book character?"

She got in, slammed the door and took off.

Paul and Owen looked at each other. "Are you sure Michael Keaton wasn't in the second one?" Owen asked.

"You're right," Paul said. "That's the one with Cat Woman."

"Thank God we cleared that up."

Terry crawled into bed and scooted over to Nat.

"You're still wet," Natalie protested.

"I was anxious to get in bed with you," Terry said. "Why are you so mad?"

"I'm not."

"You are." Terry rubbed at Natalie's shoulders. "You're so

tense you could bounce a quarter off your ass."

"Do you know what today... Well, yesterday was?"

"Friday. You're home for the weekend and tomorrow... well later this morning we're going to drive up the coast and go beach combing. I didn't forget."

"It was the anniversary of when we first met."

Terry started doing the math in her head. "Are you sure?"

"Yes, *I'm* sure. I *remembered*, Terry."

That sounds a whole lot like an accusation. In fact, it's the same tone of voice she uses when she's mad because I've killed someone. Is it that big a deal? Were we supposed to celebrate it or something? I thought our anniversary was like the first day that we did it. Do I know the date for that? No, so that won't work as an excuse. God dammit! I'm off saving the world, I can't be expected to remember every stupid date. The day I was told I had the Dark Avenger part, April 24th 1991. First day I wore the suit, March 15th... Oh my God! I'm a shitty girlfriend! Why didn't I remember? Why can't I remember the date for the first day we did it? I was at that convention... it was the first day of the convention. No, because it was after midnight, so it was the next day. I still don't know the date, I'll call Dan it will be on his little calendar, and...

"Terry, aren't you going to say anything?" Natalie asked again, with accusation implied.

"Ah... I love you," Terry said.

Natalie scooted away from her and jumped out of bed. She grabbed her robe and slung it on.

"Do I matter to you at all, Terry, or am I just a convenient fuck.?"

"You're hardly convenient, honey," Terry said, then realized it was all wrong, even before Natalie stormed out of the room. Terry got up sighing. She was tired. She just wanted to get a little and go to sleep. She didn't need all this drama; still she supposed it was her fault. "Baby, I didn't mean that the way it sounded." She found her own robe and then went off to find Natalie.

Natalie was standing in the kitchen getting a glass of water. There were two aspirins in her hand. No doubt the implication was that Terry had given her a headache. That was the problem with living with another actress, she wanted to be the only one using props and putting on a show.

"Come on, Nat, I'm sorry. I didn't forget on purpose. You

could have just told me, you know. How am I supposed to remember? Hell, I don't remember anything."

"I bet you remember the exact moment and time that you put on that fucking suit for the first time."

"No I don't, baby," Terry lied. "Is it really that big a deal?"

"I swear, Terry, sometimes you're so much like a man that I wonder why I'm bothering to be a lesbian."

Terry's face wrinkled up as she thought. *All right, is it just me or did that make no sense at all?* Suddenly she had the answer. "Baby... do you maybe have PMS?" Terry asked carefully.

"And so you prove my point!" Natalie screamed.

Terry cringed; maybe she'd just better not say anything.

"Because I'm not worshiping at the throne of your porcelain ass you naturally assume that I must be premenstrual."

Terry didn't say anything, at this point deciding that was definitely the direction she should go in.

"Aren't you going to say anything, Terry?" Natalie screamed.

"No, I don't think so. Every time I say something you just get madder, so I think I'm going to take my man-like, porcelain ass off to bed before I get myself into more trouble than I will ever be able to get out of. I'm sorry for forgetting our anniversary, and... Well, everything else."

Terry turned around and went back to bed. She heard Natalie mumbling and then heard her go into the bathroom where she could hear her mumbling and basically arguing with herself for almost ten minutes before she finally came back to bed. Terry snuggled up to her. "So you want to make up?"

"No, my period just started... And I swear to God, Terry, if you so much as snicker I'm going to kill you in your sleep."

Over the next few weeks attempts to get close enough to the terrorists to actually see or hear anything of any importance had all ended in basically the same way – with Terry being chased by the military.

This night had been no different. As she sped the motorbike up, Paul was screaming in her ear, "Dammit, Terry! I told you hang back out of range of their detectors."

"Yeah, well, I thought by freezing my ass off before they had a chance to get me that I could just sneak in. How did I know they'd change their equipment to motion detectors?"

Her teeth were still chattering even though the suit was now warming her up.

A net was fired from somewhere. It hit her in the chest and ripped her from the seat of the bike. She hit the pavement, skidded across the street and hit the curb, now firmly tangled in the net. But she had drawn her laser and was already cutting through the net as the military boys approached.

"Freeze, lay still and you will not be hurt," the closest one said.

"You freeze, throw down your fucking weapons, and I just might believe you," Terry said. She shook the net free and took off running. She was hurt. Her visor was telling her as much, not that she wouldn't have figured that out when her right leg wanted to buckle under her. "Bike, come to me," Terry ordered. The suit gave her a shot of adrenalin, and she was barely aware of the sound of gunfire as she jumped through the air, landed on the seat and took off again.

"Terry, there's a road block on 47th street and one on Baltimore. Take Curtain to the first alley on your left, this will lead you to Mamouth, which is clear."

"Got you, Control." But when she swung into the alley there was a garbage truck in the way and no room on either side to get around. One of the garbage men was throwing a bag into the truck.

She slid the bike up beside him and he jumped hearing the noise and seeing the strange apparition that was Vigilance. "Dude, the army is after me, could you move this thing the hell out of my way fast?"

"Cool," he said, and yelled at the driver through his walking talkie. "Move this shit can, Bobby, Vigilance needs through."

The truck moved out of the alley just as the army boys rounded the corner, and Terry barely scooted through before the garbage truck backed back into the alley. Terry laughed and took off into the night.

"It's too risky," Paul said, as the doctor looked at Terry's leg. "We can't take any more chances. We're just going to have to stay away and hope the military or whatever the hell they are is actually going to do something."

Terry started to say something, and Owen quickly held up his hand, which was filled with a slice of pizza. "Terry, please don't use the sardine analogy while I'm eating."

"I was just going to agree." Terry made a face as the Doctor poked at a certain spot on her leg.

"Does that hurt?" the doctor asked.

She smacked him in the shoulder, "Does that?"

"Ouch, I'm thinking that's a yes." He turned to Paul. "It's going to bruise really badly, not going to make walking a pleasant experience for awhile, but nothing's dislocated that I can see, nothing's broken, and..."

"Two questions," Terry interrupted. "First, why are you talking to him? It's my leg. Second," she addressed Paul. "If we're so top secret and shit, then how come this guy and half the staff of a hospital know?"

Paul and the doctor both smiled, then Paul answered. "I met them all and they met me in a Survivors of Violent Crimes group."

"We all have a common goal," the doctor said with a smile, "and I was talking to him because most times the patient is in such a state of shock that they don't actually hear what you're saying. Keep the leg elevated for a couple of days. I'll give you some painkillers and you should be fine."

Terry nodded. The hip wasn't the only sore spot. Her back hurt and so did her right arm, but even she had known the injuries were fairly minor compared to her leg, hip, whatever.

When the doctor left she turned to Paul. "So, is trusting the government the best we can do?"

"I'll try to figure out anything that might be a target, try to monitor where our military friends are. You can go back to what you were doing. Let's see if they'll leave the position to look for you or if they stay put. I've had really good luck picking up their bands."

"Wish we were having as good luck picking up the terrorists' conversations," Terry said.

"They must know people are listening. Otherwise even with the half-assed stuff we've been able to collect so far surely they would have said something. I think they're writing everything down, but unfortunately I was never able to get at a good enough angle for even the suit to see what's on the fucking table," Terry said. She rubbed at her leg and then sat up. She groaned. "For once, I'm glad Natalie is going to be gone for a few days. Maybe I'll be healed before she gets back."

Owen handed her pants to her and she started to put them on. She wasn't having a lot of luck, so Owen helped her. Terry looked up to see Paul smiling.

"What?" she demanded.

"You guys just gave me an idea," Paul said.

"Huh?" they both said in confusion.

"Well, things aren't always what they seem are they? I mean just for a minute it looked more like Owen was undressing than dressing you."

They both laughed, and Terry said to Owen, "Admit your secret desire."

"I yearn for you, I burn for you," Owen said dramatically.

"Boys and girls, please," Paul cleared his throat, "terrorists at large, lives hanging in the balance."

They nodded. "What you have in mind, boss?" Terry asked.

"We create a diversion. We let the army boys chase Vigilance, then Vigilance swoops in on the terrorists," Paul said.

"Huh?" Owen and Terry said again.

"We build a third suit and put someone else in it. They get the army boys attention and lure them away," Paul said.

"That's a great idea!" Terry said excitedly.

"Yeah, well where are you two coconuts going to find someone else crazy enough to wear that suit?" Owen asked.

Terry and Paul looked at Owen then each other and shook their heads. Owen looked at them and laughed. "No fucking way." He shook his head no. "You know, Paul, there is just so much that a man will do to get a piece of ass."

"When the army boys go after Owen..." Paul started.

"What part of no fucking way did you not understand?" Owen demanded.

Paul ignored him. "... you go check out the terrorists and try to find out what they're up to."

"Why not just kill them?" Terry said. "Why screw with them? All this speculation about whether they could lead the government to the big shot behind it all is immaterial if they're able to pull off their attack. Especially if our government actually wants their attack to be successful, and you don't know whether they do or not. What if it's a bio weapon? It could wipe out the whole city, the whole coast. I don't think we can take that chance."

"You're right," Paul said. "When the military boys seem more interested in Vigilance than they do keeping an eye on the terrorists. When they go after Owen…"

"Fuck you!" Owen yelled and trotted across the room and up the stairs.

Paul cleared his throat. "When they go after Owen, you go in and kill them all. I'll get the other suit up and running while you're healing."

"Paul, are you sure Owen's going to go along with this?"

"Yeah, all I have to do is try to talk him into it, let him throw a living, screaming, oh my God he finally sounds like a gay boy fit, then I apologize, grovel, and tell him I'll find someone else to do it though I doubt I can find anyone I trust as much or who's as competent. Then he'll apologize for acting like a baby because it isn't all that dangerous, and then he'll agree to do it." Paul shrugged implying it was a done deal.

"You really are a manipulative bitch."

"In and out, right?" Owen said in her ear.

"Right, just go in till you get their attention, then run in on the bike, then make a run for it."

"You're making it sound easy, but the last time you did that you damn near got killed, and I'm not as fast as you are and I sure as hell don't have that fancy butt-kicking Oriental fighting crap." Owen said. "What if they net me like they did you?"

"Don't worry, I'll be watching till I'm sure you're clear. I'll be on the roof. If it looks like you're having any trouble I'll start shooting at the GI Joe bastards from behind. It'll blow the operation, but you'll be able to get away clean."

"Great, so I really am Robin," Owen mumbled. "What about you?"

"Don't worry about me, dude, I'm Vigilance, you're just a guy in a really neat suit."

Owen had no trouble either getting the army guys to chase him or getting away. He might not run as fast, but when it came to the motorbike Owen out-classed her big time.

With the army out of the way, Terry grabbed hold of the bio steel rope she'd secured to a vent pipe in the roof and swung down in an arch. She burst through the closed window, laser at the ready, entering in a shower of glass and windowsill boards that was bound to both surprise the shit out of the terrorists and be impressive as hell.

She landed on the floor expecting all hell to break loose

and was disappointed to find nothing.

There was no one there. Nothing but pizza boxes and other garbage to show that there had ever been anyone there at all.

"God dammit!" Terry hissed.

"If you had just crawled down the rope and looked in the window you would have known they weren't there and you could have saved your energy for something real." Paul said.

"Fuck you! Audio up, audio up," she ordered, but there was nothing. Not a sound. Except for trash and old furniture the room was empty. Beyond the room she could hear the other tenants of the building talking, most of them about the noise, but none of them were speaking Arabic. She started going through the pizza boxes and garbage looking for any clue that might tell them what the terrorist bastards were up to. She was about to give up when she noticed something. She checked another box and another. "You see this?"

"Trash?" Paul said

"These pizza boxes are clean."

"So?"

"So, brain boy, when's the last time you ordered a pizza and the cheese wasn't stuck all over the roof of the box? There were never any pizzas in about half of these boxes."

"Damn, they're getting their instructions – probably their weapons, too – with the pizzas."

Terry looked on the exterior of the box till she found a phone number, address and the name of the pizza parlor. "I'm heading over there."

"I'll see if I can find anything on World of Pizza," Paul said.

Terry climbed back up the rope and reached the roof. She crawled down the fire escape on the far side of the building, the same way she'd gotten up there without being detected. She got on her bike and took off just as Paul announced. "Robin just slid into base."

"Good, I'm heading for the pizza parlor," she took off. "So Control, since the terrorists weren't there anymore..."

"Yeah, that's what I was thinking," Paul said, not letting her finish. "Since the terrorist have left, their only reason for being there was to try and catch you."

"Which means they don't give a diddly shit about the terrorists."

"They could have more than one team in the city," Paul

suggested.

"Maybe, but wouldn't they be on the same frequency, and if you're picking up one cell why wouldn't you pick up the other?"

"Good question."

Terry pulled up in front of the pizza parlor in question, and found the building had been gutted by fire. They weren't leaving a very good trail.

She checked the place out, but charred wood and cinders couldn't tell you much.

She heard something, realized what it was, and got to her bike just as her long distance vision saw the army boys heading her way. They had guessed at her next location. Clever boys. She took off before they knew she was there and headed in.

Owen had changed out of the suit and into his clothes before she pulled into the reinvented storage locker. She popped off her own helmet and smiled at him.

"See now, Owen, wasn't that fun?"

"Only if you also enjoy wrestling alligators and eating crushed glass," Owen shook his head. "I knew you were completely out of your fucking little butch mind, but I had no idea just how completely nutso you were till I was out there in this thing." He swung the case he held, almost hitting Terry in the process. "I'm running for my life, wondering if when they got tired of chasing me they'd just start shooting and if the suit is going to protect me. This whole thing is beyond crazy, it's bizarre. You're risking your neck, we're all risking serious jail time. For what? It's not fun, and I don't think it's doing one damn bit of good. Not when you weigh it all out." He looked at his feet. "I've had it. I'm leaving Paul, Terry."

"You're what! What the hell for?"

"I would never ask him to do something like that, Terry. I couldn't ask him to risk his life like that, and he didn't even blink. Hell... I wouldn't ask you to get in the damn suit, and you're so crazy you think it's a party. How much could he care about me if he doesn't even think twice about using me as a decoy for heavily armed soldiers? In his eyes I'm no different from you. Someone who's easy to use because I want something that only he can give me. It's simple, Terry. I love him, but he doesn't love me. That being the case, I'm not going to risk my life or my freedom for him anymore."

"Owen... you were in the suit, man. Nothing can happen to you..."

"So says the woman who almost got killed in it, has been seriously injured more than once while wearing it, and yet continues to do so. You're not going to be happy till you fart around and get yourself killed, and I don't want to be part of that, either."

"Owen... there are terrorists in the city and the government doesn't care. They aren't doing one damn thing to stop them."

"Let's say you're right, that you and Paul are both right. What the hell do you think you can do about it? Terrorists being backed by huge organizations that want to kill a bunch of people for God and with our own government basically turning a blind eye while they go after you. You can't win!" Owen laughed then, though he obviously wasn't amused. He stopped and looked at her, close to tears. "Don't you get it! No one cares. As long as they have their big screen TV's and all their shots, they just don't care about anyone else. You were part of that world, one of the beautiful people. Hell, you still could be if you put half the effort into your career that you put into jumping around on buildings running around trying to save the world.

"Here's a clue for you. You can't save the world. One person can't make a difference. It's all bullshit. You're going to keep playing at crime fighter till you get yourself killed, and when you're dead nothing you did will matter. Natalie will have to bury the woman she loves, and the Hollywood press corps will hype your death for a few days. Life will go on for everyone but you."

"Maybe I can't save the whole fucking world. I never said I could. Maybe I can't even save this city, but maybe, just maybe, I can save one little piece of it. Paul's right. The most important thing we do is give the people some hope."

"Paul's not right about anything," Owen said, his voice breaking before he got himself back under control. "Didn't you hear a word I said? The woman you say you love is going to be left with a cold, dead body. Don't you get it, Terry? Paul keeps trying to save his family. He's doing all of this trying to save his family, and they're all dead. None of this is ever going to bring them back. None of this is going to fix the part of him that's broken. He's obsessed and so are you. At least I understand what drives him, but what's driving you, Terry? Why are you doing this?"

"I believe in it," she stammered out.

"That's bullshit, and you know it. You're addicted to it because you feel like you're in total control, but you aren't in control, Terry. No one's ever in complete control. You do it because it makes you feel special and important, but why isn't it enough to have a gorgeous woman who loves you and a career most people would die for even in it's current state, a perfect body and a face... My God, Terry, you're a beautiful, talented, intelligent young woman with your whole life ahead of you. Why do you need this?"

"I... I don't know!" Terry yelled back helplessly.

"Yeah... Well, you and Paul have a nice life, because I'm out of here, and it's only a matter of time till Natalie gets tired of playing this game, too... Oh, but wait, maybe not, I mean I can't imagine you putting Natalie in the suit and sending her out as bait." He watched to see if she was going to deny what he said. She finally started to speak, but he held up his hand... "Stop right there. I've known you long enough to know when you're getting ready to act out a part. I know you'd never put her in the suit for any reason, because you can say anything you want, but the truth is that you know how dangerous what you do is, and you actually love her, so you'd never force her to do anything that might put her in danger."

"Owen, think about it. You love Paul, he does love you..."

"I don't think that he does, Terry. You don't know him like I do. I've been with him for five years. He's so obsessed with the whole Vigilance thing that there isn't room for anything else in his life. In order to spend time with him, to become important to him, I had to help him with the project. It's all he thinks about, all he talks about. He lives and breathes it. You take the suit off and go to bed and that's it. Paul never wears the suit, but he never stops playing the game, ever. This seems sudden to you, but it's been building for a long time. This was that proverbial straw that broke the camel's back. This project doesn't mean anything to me, Terry. I'm not getting any younger, and I'm tired of putting my life on hold waiting for Paul to get tired of playing Batman and Robin. Let's face it, Batman really doesn't need Robin. If you're smart,

Terry, you'll start to concentrate on what's important and stop worrying about saving even this little corner of the world. I'll see you later."

"Be careful," Terry said as he got into his car with the box. She watched him drive away, wondering if she should call and tell Paul what to expect when Owen got home, but talked herself out of it. This was something Paul would have to handle on his own. Besides, part of her knew that Owen was right, at least about her. Maybe it was time for her to step back and take a real look at just what she was doing and the real reason she was doing it.

She entered the apartment quietly and looked at the clock. It was one forty-five AM. She cringed; she should have just gone on home. Natalie wasn't expecting her, but after what Owen had told her she felt the need to be with Natalie, to let her know how much she cared.

When she heard the bedroom door open she said, "I didn't mean to wake you," and someone started screaming. She was so startled by the action that she jumped. "Nat!" She started down the hall. "It's just me, Jesus! I didn't mean to scare you."

And it wasn't Natalie at all, but some dishwater blond woman about three inches shorter than herself and a good fifty pounds overweight. "Oh, somebody's gettin' an ass kicking." She grabbed the woman by the throat and pinned her against the wall.

"Terry for God's sake, let her go!" Natalie screamed from behind her. "What... what are you doing here?"

"Well, apparently finding out that I'm being played like a big idiot!" Terry screamed, not letting the other woman go.

"Terry... for God's sake it's my cousin Shirley!"

"That's just sick!" Terry screamed in outrage.

"We aren't sleeping together, you dumb ass."

"Oh, ah... Oh. You have to admit it was an honest mistake." Terry let the woman go. "I'm.. I'm." She started laughing then. "I'm so relieved." Natalie glared at her, and she quickly looked duly chastised. "And I'm sorry." Obviously from the look on Natalie's face that wasn't quite good enough. "I'm incredibly, grovelingly sorry."

"It's all right," Shirley said.

"Are you sure you're all right, Shirl? I know Terry's real

strong."

"I'm fine," Shirley said, rubbing at her throat. "I'm just going to go to the bathroom and go back to bed. It... it was nice meeting you," she lied as she walked into the bathroom.

Terry walked over to the door. "Nice meeting you, too, and again, I'm so very sorry."

"It's all right," she said, and please move away from the door was implied.

Natalie grabbed hold of Terry's arm and dragged her towards her bedroom. "God Terry," she started in an angry whisper, "I can't believe you." They walked into the bedroom. She shut the door and her voice went up a little. "Even if I was having an affair – which, by the way, the fact that you'd jump to that conclusion immediately is actually pretty insulting – but even if I was having an affair, how would kicking her ass help? What purpose would beating someone to a bloody pulp serve?"

"I'd feel better," Terry said with a shrug.

"Why?"

"I don't know. Because they hurt me and I hurt them back."

"Oh, I forgot the Terry North school of justice. They hurt me. I hurt them. Ug." She burped and scratched her ass. Terry must have smiled because the next thing she knew Natalie was in her face hissing in a loud whisper. "It's not funny, Terry. Violence isn't the answer to all the world's problems."

"Here we go again." Terry rolled her eyes, walked over, flopped on the bed, and slipped her boots off. "I'm tired, can't we just go to sleep?"

"Dammit, Terry I'm tired, too. It's two o'clock in the morning. You come marching in here for sex after a night of playing Vigilance – and don't even pretend you just want to sleep, because we both know that after you go out on the street and play God you like to come home and get your rocks off..."

"Ah, come on, Nat..."

"No, you shut up for a minute. You're making me crazy with this shit. I never know where you are, what the hell you're doing, you come and go as you please. You come in here unannounced and damn near kill my cousin..."

"Isn't that a little melodramatic even for you, Nat?"

"Is it?" Natalie asked, staring daggers at her. "I know what you're capable of, both emotionally and physically."

"So now I'm a crazed murderer because I overreacted to finding a strange woman in your apartment. Who's overreacting now?"

"You go out every night now, Terry," Nat said as if suddenly all the wind had been taken out of her sails. "You take the fucking thing everywhere we go. Can't you see what's happening to us? Between my work and this... this crap, we see each other on the run. When we first started dating you couldn't stand to be apart from me, you used to make up excuses to come down here to be with me, or get me up to your place. We were supposed to be working towards living together like a real couple, so we should be gradually spending more and more time together and instead we see each other less and less."

"We could be spending time together right now if you'd quit screaming."

Natalie made a muffled sound that sounded like she was trying to throw up her liver, and then she almost did scream. "Dammit, Terry, I'm not screaming. I want you to quit all this crazy violent shit before you get killed. I want us to have a normal life..."

"We're TV people. We don't have normal lives," Terry countered.

"You know, I'm thinking Regis Philbin doesn't put on a suit and drive around the city on a motor bike beating up crooks for kicks. We could be that normal at least."

"I don't do it for kicks."

Natalie looked at Terry incredulously, and now Terry was pissed off, most probably because Natalie was saying the same thing that Owen had said and she still didn't have a good answer. "You know, Nat... You don't know everything. You ain't exactly that easy to live with yourself. Your schedule's pretty screwed, too. You leave the cap off the toothpaste, you never put a new roll of toilet paper in the bathroom, you drool in your sleep..."

"You dress up like a superhero and run around the city killing people," Natalie hissed in disbelief.

Terry sighed. "So we're back to that again.'

"That's it! I can't take this, get out!"

"What?" Terry asked in shocked disbelief.

"Get out! Get out! Get out!" Natalie got behind her and

shoved on her back till Terry stood up. She kept shoving her towards the bedroom door, stopping only to walk around Terry and open it.

"Come on, baby, can't we talk about it?"

"No," Natalie hissed, all attempts to keep her voice low now forgotten. "No we can't talk." She was crying now. She moved behind Terry and shoved her out the door. "You have to go, because you're a complete nut job, and I'm never going to have any sort of real life with you because you're completely out of your tiny screwed up little mind. I love you, but I just can't keep doing this. It isn't healthy."

"Honey... I'll change..."

"No you won't. You'll say you will, and I'll believe you, and then you'll go right on doing what you want to do because – as I pointed out earlier – you're a fucking nut job. Now get out." She was still pushing on Terry's back, but Terry had stopped. She turned to face Natalie, forcing her to push on her chest.

"Baby, I love you. We can work this out."

"Not tonight." Natalie cried, stopping to wipe her nose on the sleeve of her robe. "I can't handle this tonight. Do you know why Shirley's here?" Natalie didn't give her a chance to answer. "My grandfather died today. I hadn't seen him in six months because of my work and this thing with you and now he's dead. And I tried to call you, but of course I couldn't because duty had called and you were out there being something that isn't quite you. Someone that I don't even know."

"Nat, I'm so sorry." She moved to hold Natalie, but Natalie held up a hand to stop her.

"I want you to go, Terry."

"Honey... I don't think you should be alone."

"I'm not alone; Shirley's here. I have enough shit to deal with right now. I don't want to deal with you tonight." She pointed at the case. "Take that thing with you."

Terry nodded and walked over to get it. She looked down at her bootless feet. Natalie sighed went back to the bedroom and got them. Terry took them and put them on, then she picked up the case. She looked at Natalie. "I do love you, Nat, and I am really, really sorry... for everything. I'll call you tomorrow."

Natalie nodded and then took a step closer and kissed Terry on the check. Terry fought the urge to sigh with relief. "Be careful," she said

"I will. We can work this out, baby."

"I hope so," Natalie said and closed the door.

Terry stood outside the closed door for a long time. What a shitty fucking day she was having.

She sighed, then started walking towards the stairs... with her case. She stopped at the top of the stairs and thought about tossing it down them. Senseless and noisy because it wouldn't do a damn thing to the case much less the suit inside it.

She was standing at the bottom of the stairs before she knew it. She looked back up.

Wait a fucking minute! This isn't the new me, this is the old me. The one that just expects and accepts defeat. This is pure bullshit, if I leave now it's going to put a rift between us and we'll end up like Owen and Paul. I'm going right back up these stair. She needs me tonight, and it isn't my fault I wasn't there for her, because I didn't know that her grandfather had croaked. I can be here now, and she has to realize that.

Someone ran into her, and if it weren't for her quick reflexes they would have both wound up down the stairs. She looked down at the person she had caught in one arm and smiled. "Nat... I couldn't just leave."

"I couldn't let you leave." Natalie wrapped her arms around Terry's neck and started to cry.

"I'm really sorry, baby," Terry said.

"Me, too. I've just been so upset, and you're never home any more, and..."

They had hardly gotten into the apartment when they started heavy petting, then they were doing it on the kitchen counter and in the sink like Glenn Close and Michael Douglas in that movie she could never remember the name of. And it was all good and very hot, and why was the cast of The Andy Griffith Show watching them, and why were they all laughing?

"My God, Terry! Terry, are you all right?" Nat was screaming and there was either a really bad earthquake or someone was shaking her.

Terry opened her eyes and looked through the haze up at Natalie and her cousin. The sun was shining and she must be in Natalie's bedroom except her head was sitting at the wrong angle and there was a knot on the top of it. She had a fleeting memory of something hard hitting the back of her head, then nothing. She rubbed at the knot. Her vision was starting to clear.

"Terry are you all right?" Natalie asked again then, in a high pitched voice. "Shirley, call 911."

Shirley apparently called even as Terry was trying to say that it wasn't necessary, and that she *was* all right. It was like one of those dreams where you were trying to scream but your voice wouldn't work.

"What sort of shitty security does this building have!" Nat screamed. "Terry, can you hear me? Have you been out here all night?"

"I... I think so," Terry said, finally finding her voice.

"Did you fall down the stairs?"

"I don't think so, at least not without help. I think some-one hit me," She put a hand up and rubbed the back of her head again, then moved into a more comfortable position. "From the feel of the shape of the knot I'd say they used a black jack and... Oh my God." She jumped up and almost fell and Natalie rose from her kneeling position to steady her. "The suit," she whispered, looking around. The box was no-where in sight.

"Sit down and be still, Terry. Screw the suit!" Natalie said angrily. "I don't give a damn about the suit. I only care about you."

"Find the case, Nat."

"Fuck the case, Terry, sit down on the stairs. The para-medics will be here in a minute."

Terry did sit down, mostly because if she didn't she was going to fall down. She rested her face in her hands. "Nat, please, check the top of the stairs for the case."

"Some creep probably thought there was something valu-able in the case."

"There is..."

"God dammit, Terry. Look at yourself. You're hurt. I broke up with you last night, and you still only give a damn about the suit."

"You broke up with me?" Terry said, jerking her head up to look at Natalie. She started to cry. "You broke up with me? I thought we were just having a fight." She started sobbing then, her whole body shaking.

Natalie sat on the step beside her and held her. "Calm

down, Terry, I'm not going to break up with you unless you don't forget about that fucking suit for a minute," Natalie said in a whisper.

"Please, Nat, don't leave me. I'll be better," Terry sniffled. "My head hurts and my vision is blurred and... could you just look?"

"I'm not going to leave you alone with God only knows what wrong with you to go look for that fucking case."

"The ambulance is on its way," Shirley announced.

Terry wanted to say she didn't need it, but was feeling more like she did every second. She started to imagine a crack in her skull and bleeding in her brain. She even checked her nose, which was caked with dried blood and didn't help calm her down. One of her ears had blood in it, but the other was clean, so maybe she'd just bloodied her nose in the fall and it had run into her ear from the way she was laying. She hurt everywhere.

"Please, Nat," Terry said. Natalie started crying then and went to check the stairs, when she came back she was crying even harder and Terry could hear the sirens close.

"It's not there, all right? Forget about it. Who gives a fuck? I can't do this, Terry. I can't and I won't. I've got to go to my grandfather's funeral today. If you keep this up, you're going to wind up dead, and I don't want to go to your funeral, too. Please, baby."

Terry tossed a warning look from Nat to Shirley, and Nat blew up. She started stomping around throwing her arms around her head and screaming, "I don't give a fuck about any of it right now. You're leading Terry, you're leading but no one is following. It's just you out there, only you and you aren't really a fucking superhero."

The paramedics showed up then. and between Shirley and the medics she couldn't very well explain to Natalie that what she was most worried about was that someone had known exactly what they were taking and that if they knew that, they also knew the secret identity of the night stalker called Vigilance, who both the police and the military wanted to capture.

They did a number of tests including an MRI and a CT scan, and then told her that her brain was swollen and that she had several contusions and bruises, but no internal bleeding and nothing was broken. They decided to keep her for observation because she had a severe concussion.

Natalie looked down at her. She had quit crying and seemed to have gotten over her mad. "How do you feel?"

"Better. I think mostly I had just convinced myself that I was seriously wounded. I'm sorry, Nat. About everything."

"I can't do this, Terry," she whispered. "I don't want to live with Vigilance any more. I want to live with Terry North. I love you. I want to spend the rest of my life with you. I don't want to bury you. I'd rather say good bye to you now than wrap my whole life around yours and then lose you."

Terry nodded. "I understand. You're right. Everything you're saying is right. I have a lot to think about. I don't want to lose you, Nat. Listen... I'm all right here, why don't you go on to the funeral home, be with your mother and your family today? I'll be fine."

"Are you sure?"

"Yeah." Natalie kissed her, and she knew what her decision had to be.

Natalie hadn't been gone long enough for her to get to sleep when Paul showed up.

"I heard about the 'mugging' on the TV. Now, what really happened?"

"Someone knocked me in the head, let me fall down a flight of steps, and took the case."

"You're fucking kidding me."

"No I'm not. Now either it was just some piddly-assed crook that even if he gets it open isn't going to know what the hell he's found, or... someone knows who I am and now they have the suit."

"Fuck!"

"Doesn't it have a homing beacon on it?" Terry asked.

Paul made a face. "That would have been a good idea," he said with a helpless shrug.

"Fuck!" Terry rubbed at her face, which felt numb. "So... did Owen leave you?"

"It doesn't matter now."

"Then I'm guessing yes. Listen, Paul... it ain't worth it. Any of it. I've been laying here thinking, and I'm... well I'm through..."

"What the hell..."

"Natalie's going to leave me unless I quit, and she would be right to do it. Just like Owen was right to walk out on you.

You may not give a damn whether he leaves you or not, but I don't want to lose Natalie. If I have to choose, it's got to be her. This shit," she pointed at her head, "It ain't so fun. Unless you plan to go find some other ignorant asshole to pour into the suit and another lover who'll put up with your moody shit, I suggest you put this whole thing to rest..."

"Are you forgetting that there is a terrorist cell loose in this city, that hundreds possibly thousands of people may be in danger..."

"Do *you* realize that as it stands now I can think of no way for us to stop them from doing just what they plan to do? Thanks to our own damn government, they got away, we lost them. Someone tried to kill me maybe because they know who I am. Owen left you and Natalie kicked me out just before I was attacked. Her grandfather died yesterday. I should have been there for her, but I wasn't because I was too busy playing superhero."

"The city is depending on us, on you, Terry. They need you, justice has to have a voice..."

"Well it doesn't have to be mine. Paul, in case you haven't figured it out, my reasons for doing this aren't all that idealistic or pure. I mostly like to kick the living shit out of assholes. To tell the truth, if you'll admit it, at least a big part of what motivates you is a power trip, too. We made a difference. I know that, you know that, but with our own government turned against us it's only a matter of time till they shut us down, and while it's been fun. I just ain't into dying for the cause, or even going to jail."

"Don't make any decisions now," Paul said. "Wait till you get to feeling better. Take time to look at the big picture."

Terry sighed. "You think about the big picture. Look at who's running our country. Gay rights have been set back so far that it's not likely now that we'll get those rights in our lifetime. For all intents and purposes the religious right has taken over our fucking country. This idiot is in the White House, and daily they're taking away yet another freedom that everyone's taking for granted, and I don't see any way to stop them. Vigilance can save a body here and a body there, but that same government, the one that doesn't give a damn about you and I as humans, *is hunting us*. They aren't going to be happy till they kill me, take the suit and make hundreds of them. Do you really want to risk the suit falling into the hands of this neo-fascist regime?

"We can't save the world, bud. We tried, but the truth is that soon they're going to shove people like you and me back into the closet. They're going to force us into hiding. And if we... I, have to go into hiding, I don't want to be alone. If you think about it, you don't want to, either. Nat said something and she's right. We're leading but no one's following. Crime's down in the city, but crime's down because the criminals are afraid of Vigilance. Not because people are seeing what we're doing and following our lead, watching out for one another, stepping in, putting themselves in harm's way to save another.

"I love my life, Paul. That wasn't always the truth, but it is now. I could be perfectly happy without being Vigilance. But I can't be happy without Natalie, and I don't want to die. I'm even tired of getting beat up."

Natalie had cried like a baby all through the funeral and very few of her tears were actually for her grandfather, which was doing nothing to help with her guilt. She should be comforting her mother and instead her mother was comforting her. She felt like the world's biggest *shmuck*.

They had gone back to her parents' house to sit *shiva*. She snuck off to her old room, threw herself across her bed, and just bawled.

She hadn't heard anyone come in, but she felt someone sit on the bed, and they started patting her back.

"I'm sorry Mom, really sorry."

"I'm not your mom, and I'm the one who's sorry."

Natalie rolled over, and Terry dried the tears from Natalie's face with her thumb. "Shouldn't you be in the hospital, Terry... your head?"

"It's all right, they gave me some anti-inflammatories and told me not to drive or climb ladders or run heavy equipment for a week, so I called a light, single-storied cab. I'm fine." Terry moved to lie beside Natalie on the bed, propping her head on a pillow so that she could look at her. "I told Paul I'm not doing Vigilance anymore. It's over. Just you and me."

"Are you sure?"

"No doubts. You're right; we aren't changing anything, just prolonging the inevitable. And you're right about the other, too. Eventually, if I keep playing this game I will get killed or go to jail, and then what?"

Natalie hugged her, and she tried to act like it didn't hurt, but she must not have done a very good job because Natalie let go of her and said, "Oh, baby, I'm so sorry. I forgot."

"It's all right. I'm sorry I missed your grandfather's funeral."

"It couldn't be helped. I'm just glad you're all right... That we're going to be all right. I'm sorry, Terry, I know how much you enjoy it, but it's just..."

"It's crazy. I'm beginning to understand that now. A lot of different things happened last night, Nat, and all of them seemed to be pointing a big neon sign at the fact that it's time for me to stop playing this game. I'm kidding myself that I'm making a difference. I'm rationalizing that it's all about saving lives and doing good, because the truth is that I'm only doing it for the rush. I'm putting you through hell, risking my neck, and maybe in the end I'm doing more harm than good, just so I can feel important again."

"You *are* important, Terry. You're important to me."

Terry smiled and ran a hand through Natalie's hair. "I guess that will have to be enough. I'll adapt to being me and only me again, after all it's not the first time I've hung up my superhero costume."

Chapter 10

Terry was sitting in a lawn chair outside her front door drinking a beer and just contemplating nature when Paul drove up.

"Damn," she muttered. She was dreading this.

Paul got out of the car and walked towards her.

She held up her hand. "Don't waste your breath, Paul. I've made up my mind."

Paul laughed, grabbed another lawn chair and pulled it over to sit beside her. "Actually… I came over to tell you that you were right."

Terry looked at him through squinted eyes, "Huh?"

"I got to thinking about what you said, and I had to admit that everything you said was true. Then I started thinking how could we stop them? How could we stomp on the religious right and take our country back? How could we make the voting sheep see the truth behind all the lies? Then I realized that we couldn't. The only thing we could do was cut out the people causing the problems like a cancer, and then I started making a list of who we would have to assassinate, and it all seemed perfectly plausible to me, because after all we're the good guys. That's when a little voice in my head said, "Power corrupts, absolute power corrupts absolutely. And I knew we had to stop.

"It was a good run, but it's time to pull the plug before we start doing what *they're* doing and justifying it the same way – *because we're the good guys*. We're right and they're wrong. Us playing God is no different than them playing God, so… that's it."

"Except we have to get that suit back," Terry said.

"Yes, we have to get the suit back."

It was a lot harder to convince Natalie of the necessity of the endeavor, but she finally relented and admitted that it was important to get the suit back if they were going to get Vigilance out of their life once and for all.

Terry stomped through the front door of Paul's house without knocking.

"I know! I know who's got the suit," she announced.

"So do I. It's the military. They pulled my files up, put two and two together and figured out the connection between us. Then it was as simple as figuring out that you were in every city that Vigilance showed up in. Your sex, your height, your weight..."

"Bullshit! If it was the military they'd already have hauled our asses in. No, it's not them, it's the paparazzi fuck," Terry interrupted Paul. "He had already been to Natalie's apartment, remember? Where I was hit, that would have been the same spot he stood in to take the pictures he blackmailed Natalie with. I beat him up in the parking lot, and then when he blackmailed Nat, Vigilance paid him a visit. He must have just figured it out, and..."

"I knew it," Owen said walking out of the kitchen holding a sandwich, which he threw against the wall just over Paul's head. Owen glared at Paul. "I knew you weren't going to quit. I knew it was all just bullshit. You two are like addicts. Is there a fucking twelve-step program for people who want to be superheroes? A support group... oh but wait! Paul's little support group was part of what started this whole mess in the first place."

"Calm down, Owen, we aren't going to start up again. I told you we'd quit, and we have. But we have to get that suit back," Paul said.

"Damn right," Terry said flopping into a chair. "Either way, that suit links us to Vigilance. Either way, eventually the suit is going to end up in the hands of the fucking government, and we can't afford that. Not while the Republicans are in office."

"You're looking for excuses to play superhero again. He told me he wouldn't, and you told her you wouldn't, but neither of you can just quit. This is your first excuse and then later there will be others. It's like getting a quick fix, and that never works and eventually you'll be doing it all the time. You're fucking junkies!" Owen started to leave the room and Paul got up quickly and grabbed his arm.

"Owen, it's over. I said it and I meant it, but we have to get the other suit back. We have to, for way too many reasons to count."

They tried Terry's hunch first because hers was the easiest to test, and besides she was in the suit and when she was in the suit, she more or less did what she damn well pleased. She easily broke into his apartment and a quick search found the case hidden under some old clothes in a closet. There were scuffmarks all around the latch, and he'd smashed the opening pad with a hammer.

Terry frowned. She didn't have a choice. The guy was scum and he'd definitely brought it on himself, but she still couldn't feel good about what she was about to do. She was able to activate the camouflage on the box with a voice command, so he hadn't been able to damage the box, much less its contents. As she walked into the living room he came in dragging an acetylene torch behind him.

When he had closed the door she said, "That won't open the box, either."

"Oh shit!" The guy dropped the torch.

"You just never learn your lesson, do you?"

"I... I know who you are. I've told other people. I've..."

"No you haven't. I know the press if I don't know anything else. You wouldn't tell anyone. You'd be too afraid someone might scoop you. The sad thing is that you don't even understand what you've done," Terry said, though she doubted the voice synthesizer let the sincere sadness in her voice come through.

"I... you can have your case."

"That isn't enough anymore. You figured out my secret identity. With or without evidence you'll out me. When you do, the government won't be laughing, they'll be investigating, and they're too close as it is. Your story will be all they need to put the pieces together. I can't let that happen. The technology that allows me to be Vigilance can't fall into the wrong hands, and right now the worst hands possible is our own government. So... you have to go."

He knew instantly what she meant. "I... please I'll do anything."

"We've already been down this road, and I already gave you your shot. You either weren't listening or you didn't believe me. It's *way* too late to cut a deal. I gave you lots of opportunities to just leave me and mine alone, but you wouldn't do it. You damn near killed me. I imagine that you wanted me dead, so… there is no telling how far you'd go to uncover me. You don't give a damn about what will happen to me, my friends, my lover, or ultimately the country or the world. You just want a Goddamn story. That one shot that's going to make you a household name. I've been a household name before, and now I am again. Though the name and the face have changed, I really haven't, and I just can't stand loose ends, never could."

She rushed forward and directed the heel of her hand at the bridge of his nose with all the force in her body. "I am the darkness," she whispered to no one in particular.

It was overkill, really. His entire face seemed to implode. But his death was quick and fairly painless, if messy. She went to the sink in his kitchen and washed the blood off her smart fiber covered hand. She walked back into the living room and waited for the body to stop convulsing. When it had she picked up the acetylene bottle and dropped it on his face.

"Well fuck!" she cursed, wiped her feet on a clean spot on the corpse's pants, then went to the bathroom, got in the shower, and washed the blood off the suit. She dried off before stepping out of the shower. She checked all the photos and exposed all the film in the cameras, though she'd found nothing incriminating. The stuff on his computer *was*, so she fragged his hard drive.

Maybe they'd think it was an accident. Maybe the police would check for blood and find residue in the sink and shower and know it was a murder, but either way they wouldn't know that it was her. None of her DNA was at the scene, no fingerprints, no description. No real evidence meant no case. Now the suit – both the suits – were going to be retired. So, even if the police did by some miracle manage to link Vigilance to the crime there would be no chance of them linking Vigilance to Terry. Not after tonight.

She grabbed the case and walked through the window and onto the fire escape. She walked down three stories then dropped the case and climbed to the bottom of the fire escape ladder. At the bottom she let go and dropped to the alley right beside the case. There would be no way for the police to know if anyone had entered at all much less whether they had used the window or the door.

It was in fact the perfect crime.

"The problem with the perfect crime is that there's no one

to brag to," she mumbled, then added, "It's done," Terry told Paul as if he didn't know. She climbed onto the bike – which was all but completely invisible in the dark of night – started it and took off.

"Good, return to base immediately," Paul ordered.

"Like I planned to take a trip around the city!" Terry practically yelled back.

Paul laughed. "Don't even pretend like you didn't at least think about it."

"Actually, no. She wanted me to go to that Actors against... bad stuff awards ceremony tonight..."

Paul laughed again. "Actors take Action," he reminded.

Terry nodded. "Yep, that would be it, any way... I blew that off to do this, so if I do anything besides go straight back to base, take this suit off and pack it in mothballs, my life won't be worth living."

Of course that didn't stop her from taking the long way or weaving in and out of traffic at breakneck speeds, and Paul told her as much.

"Ah crap!" Paul's voice suddenly rang in her ears, loud enough that it hurt.

"What the fuck!" Terry yelled back, hoping his earpiece did at least half the damage to him that her helmet had just done to her.

"Terry, the terrorists. Of all the things happening around Hollywood, what would this government be the least concerned about protecting from terrorists?"

"An entire ballroom full of the most liberal actors in the country," Terry said in a gasp. "Christ on a crutch! It's perfect. The terrorists blow up all these activists who cause this administration nothing but grief and makes them martyrs of his cause. And it makes sense that the terrorists would target it because it will have hundreds of big name stars in attendance and it won't be well guarded. In fact, they probably won't question the terrorist bastards at all because that would be politically incorrect."

"Terry... where the hell are you going?" Paul asked.

"*She's* there, dork, where the hell do you *think* I'm going?"

Chapter 11

Natalie had come with Roxanne and Byron who were now seriously dating to the point of utter nausea. They had gotten to that baby talking/open lust phase in their relationship where at any minute the gurgling could stop and they'd just start necking no matter where they were or who was watching.

She sighed as the cameras flashed, catching her costars in yet another clinch. She felt mostly ignored and knew she wouldn't have been if Terry had been with her. Photographers still strong-armed each other and walked over other stars to get pictures of she and Terry together. Alone? Well, she didn't seem to even be worth noticing.

Then there was the reason that Terry wasn't with her, which did nothing to make her feel better.

Off playing Vigilance, doing an entire list of things that are neither safe nor sane. And I'm just hoping that Owen is wrong and that we're not in for a long period of one excuse after another to dress up and go out on the town until she's gone all the time again and... Don't think about it, Nat, don't borrow trouble. Isn't that what Mother always says? Yes, but then Daddy doesn't dress up in tights and run around the city fighting crime. Oh God! I hope she's really going to quit. I hope she isn't just playing me.

They had just entered the ballroom, her costars had momentarily come up for air, and they were temporarily out of the camera's glare, which she half thought wasn't a coincidence.

"What's with you?" Roxanne asked. "You look like you've swallowed a mouth full of raw eel."

"And I suppose it would have killed you to stop sucking face long enough to tell me that when we were on the red carpet, so I might have done something about it." Natalie said with a sigh. "God alone knows what the tabloids will print. No doubt I'll be in this mood because I have broken up with Terry or caught her humping a buffalo or some damn thing."

"What's wrong, Nat?" Byron asked. "I mean of course besides Terry's bison fixation."

Natalie shrugged. "What else? It's Terry. She's doing something stupid."

Roxanne laughed, "What tells you that Nat? Some wacky sixth sense?"

"No, it's Terry. If you can't see her, she's doing something stupid." Natalie sighed yet again. It was as if she simply couldn't get enough air. She was feeling more uncomfortable by the minute. Oddly enough, Roxanne's crack about a sixth sense wasn't too far off the mark. It was probably just the paranoia that accompanied having a mate who thought she was Superman without a penis, but something just didn't feel right.

A man of Middle Eastern descent whom she didn't recognize pushed past them, and warning bells started to go off. There was a Middle Eastern terrorist cell working in LA, that's what Terry had been working on when she'd given up being Vigilance... Well, almost given up, there was this *just one more thing.*

That man might be one of the terrorists. This would be a perfect target. Terry said the government acted like they cared more about catching her than they did the terrorists, and... She's making me as fucking crazy as she is. He was just a man. Probably not even an Arab, but an Eskimo or Indian or some damn thing. Even if he was an Arab that doesn't mean he's a terrorist. I have friends who are Arabs and they're fine people. Now I'm a bigot. She's turning me into a bigot. Of course ever since the Oklahoma City bombing I don't trust rednecks in camouflage, either, so it's not really a bigot thing.

"Geez, Nat, what's Terry doing anyway?" Byron asked.

"Doing crazy shit." Nat threw her hands around in huge arcs as she all but stomped into the ballroom. "She's completely nuts, and she's making me as crazy as she is, and that's saying a lot."

The man who seated them looked as if he wasn't at all sure that Natalie wasn't going to knock him unconscious with one of her flailing arms as she continued to talk with her hands all the way to the table. "She's got a death wish, you know. I love her, and she's going to fart around and get herself killed."

"I think you're being a little over dramatic, dear," Roxanne said with a laugh. "Come on, honey, just calm down. Sit and enjoy the banquet and presentation."

Natalie nodded and sat in the chair the maitre d' held out for her. "Thanks," she said and he nodded with a smile. A waiter rushed over to take their drink orders, and she wound up ordering a gin and tonic and asking him to go light on the tonic. Her hands were shaking.

"I know you've never presented before, Nat," Roxanne said patting her hand, "but it isn't that big a deal, and if you screw up here, so what? It isn't even televised."

But there were cameras everywhere she looked. Some of it would be televised. Certainly it could be, and wouldn't this be a perfect place for a terrorist attack? There wasn't much security, and there were lots and lots of very public, and therefore very important targets.

"Christ, Nat. Take a Valium," Byron said, and it was clear that he was only half kidding.

Natalie forced a smile and all but gulped down the drink the waiter placed in front of her. She was nervous, that was all, and why shouldn't she be? She was here to present an award, and Terry wasn't with her to support her because she was off playing Vigilance, which never made Natalie very comfortable.

"That's better," Roxanne said, and then she and Byron were baby talking each other, which was promptly followed by the necking and the cameras flashing everywhere.

"Straight people are so gross," Natalie mumbled and finished her drink.

"God dammit, Nat! Turn your fucking cell phone on." But the helmet told her once again that the phone was off. She slid her bike behind the Palace Entertainment Center.

She got off the bike. She knew why Nat's cell phone was off. She hated it when people left their damn phones on at public functions and they rang right in the middle of someone's performance or presentation. It was damn rude.

She wished Natalie had chosen tonight to be just that rude. She could have told her to get her sweet ass the fuck out of the building.

A warning light started to flash on the right hand side of her visor. When she looked at it, it read "suspect number three detected at six o'clock". She swiveled her head, and there he was. "Dammit, Controll!"

"I know. I wish I were wrong, too," he said. "We're here."

"We?"

"Yeah, I'm here, too, shithead, and between you and me I don't think he's a damn bit sorry that he was right," Owen said. "For what good it does I'm in."

"Then let's rock and roll," Terry said. She watched as the terrorist walked to a window at the back of the building, where he stopped and looked around. Seeing nothing he pulled at the bars on the window and they came free. No doubt they'd fixed them and any alarm system attached to them weeks ago. He opened the window and slid through into the building, and Terry followed him. Once inside the building she palmed his head and slammed it into the wall, hard. There was a loud smacking sound as she broke his skull and the plasterboard with the severity of the impact.

"Audio up, up, up," she commanded. "Audio, down, down." She said quickly as the sound of thousands of people whispering assaulted her ears. *Stupid, stupid, way too far, think, you have to quit being scared and just think.* She could hear the sound of approaching footsteps. She looked around, saw a door and hoped it was a service closet. She grabbed the body by its arms, broke the lock on the door and shoved the body in just as two security guards rounded the corner. They looked up and right at where she was standing. She didn't move. She didn't even breathe. The hall wasn't bright, but it was light enough that if she moved they'd see her, or at the very least part of her.

"I heard something," the guy whose patch read Bud said.

"You heard nothing, come on," the one named Jack answered. She thought about how handy this helmet would be at a convention when she could never quite read what the fans' names were on their badges. Of course she could just break down and get the glasses she no doubt needed, but that wasn't likely to happen any time soon.

As soon as they were gone she started to move, and then she stopped.

They made a mistake. If they had come down here just a little bit closer they might have noticed the hole in the wall, the broken doorknob, the open, unbarred window. They would have seen me. I'm making mistakes, too. I was too loud, and now I'm missing something obvious. I'm messing up because this time Natalie's in danger and I can't think straight and because she's in danger I can't afford to fuck this up. Think, I have to think, but... I can't.

"Control, what should I do?" she asked.

"Check the body for weapons, any kind of explosives," Paul said

"Be careful, remember, Vigilance, these are Muslim terrorists. Rigging a bomb that will blow them up is commonplace. Run a scan," Owen said.

See? There's another mistake. He's right. I should have run a scan for explosives before I punched him much less dragged him in the closet. Terry walked back into the room where she'd stowed the body. "Computer, scan for explosive devices."

Her visor told her the computer detected nothing but the gun under his left arm.

Terry reached in the guy's jacket and pulled out the weapon, a thirty-five with a fifteen round clip and two extra clips. Nothing fancy, but more than enough to do some major damage in a room full of people.

She put them all into a mop bucket and set it on a shelf out of sight.

She heard more noise in the hall and then whispered words – in Arabic according to the readout on her visor.

She had to kill them more quietly, and she didn't even think for a moment about not killing them. So maybe she was already too far gone. It didn't matter. Natalie was here. They wouldn't think anything of killing her and a lot of other people, and these weren't just any people. These weren't strangers, these people were her colleagues, and many of them were her friends. People she knew, that she'd worked with, that she loved.

This time it was personal.

When she heard them walk past the closet she stepped out. "Scan for explosives," she ordered.

She didn't wait for the entire readout. The minute she saw the word no, she aimed her weapon.

The two men turned at the sound of the closing door and made a clumsy attempt to pull their weapons. Her visor told her these were suspects six and eight. She raised her laser side arm and put a neat hole right between the eyes of first one and then the other.

She dragged them quickly into the closet, retrieved their

weapons, and put them into the bucket with the other one.

"Dilemma," Terry said.

"What?" Paul asked.

"I want to get to the main ball room, but if I leave the window unwatched more hostiles could come through it. What if the window is to be their main point of entry? They could come in behind me."

Before Paul had a chance to answer, the two security guards rounded the corner at the end of the hall again.

"I'm telling you I heard something," Bud insisted.

Terry moved towards them with deliberation.

"No, Vigilance, don't," Paul ordered.

She ignored him. "Hey, you boys," she said.

The security guards looked in awe at the shimmering shape before them.

"Listen, dudes, I need your help."

"Vigilance?" they both asked.

"You know any other invisible superheroes running around the city?"

"No," they answered.

"Dude, let's go dude," Jack said to Bud.

"You run and I'll have to knock your asses out. Well, maybe not your asses. I don't have time for this shit. Listen, there are terrorists all over this fucking building. Some of them have come in that back window, and I've taken care of them. All I need for you knuckleheads to do is watch that back window and make damn sure no more thugs come through it. Can you do that?"

"Sure thing," Bud said.

"Are you nuts?" Jack asked his partner in a whisper.

"Dude, it's Vigilance. Quit being a fucking panty waist and come on," Bud ordered, and started towards the back window.

"Good man," Terry said as she scooted past them and headed for the main ballroom.

"You want us to call the cops?" Bud asked her departing form.

"God, no. That's what they want – to cause a big scene. You get cops in here and they'll have nowhere to run so they'll just start killing people. Or worse yet the cops will start shooting and they'll kill more people than the terrorists. No, you let me take care of the terrorists, you just make damn sure no one else gets in that window."

"Will do."

Terry started back on her way. "That was stupid," Paul said. "They're going to call the police. That's going to let the military know what's going on and right where you are, and while the government isn't one bit interested in saving a roomful of liberal actors, they'd go through hell and high water to get their hands on you."

"He's not going to call the police, he wants to be a hero," Terry said. "Now shut up, I'm trying to think."

Halfway through her second drink Natalie started to calm down considerably. Janey and her husband Tom had just entered the room and they joined them at their table.

"Where's my slutty friend?" Janey asked as she was seated.

"Off making the world safe for humankind," Natalie laughed out.

"Good, I hate sitting next to her, the bitch always makes me look like an emaciated Boy Scout. It's hell being less feminine looking than the butch dyke," Janey said with a laugh. "But seriously, I was looking forward to seeing the shithead. Where is she?"

"Believe me when I tell you that if I told you, you wouldn't believe me."

"Then she's either dorking some guy or putting on a pink pinafore," Janey said.

Natalie laughed then. "Nothing that drastic. She had some unfinished business to attend to. Of course it simply couldn't wait. You know how Terry gets."

Janey nodded and pointed at the couple necking across the table from her. "What's with them?"

"They're rutting pigs. Could you two fuckers kindly give it a rest so that the fucking cameras will quit flashing? The light's going to give me away," a voice said from out of nowhere.

Natalie snapped quickly around and could easily make out the shimmer of Terry's suit in the flashing light of the cameras as Terry dropped to hide behind her back.

"What the hell are you doing?"

"You all need to get out of the building. You're in danger," the voice whispered.

"Knock it off! You dumb fucks are going to ruin Terry's

cover," Natalie spat at Roxanne and Byron.

"Christ, Honey," the voice cracked at Natalie's shoulder.

"What in hell's name is going on?" Janey demanded.

"Shut the fuck up, Janey. Act normal. You guys are fucking actors. Act like nothing is happening and listen." The voice got lower and harder to hear. "There are terrorists in the building. I don't know what they're up to exactly, but I've already caught three of them. I have no idea how many more there are. You're all going to get up and move very calmly towards the exit. When you're all in the clear get in your cars and go home."

"What about you, Terry?" Natalie asked in a worried tone.

"God dammit, Nat," the voice spit.

"Terry... Terry is Vigilance," Janey said in a shocked whisper.

"Thanks, honey, thanks a whole fucking lot," the voice said. "Now get up and start moving."

They got up and started out of the room, the shimmering form following protectively behind them.

"Terry, you have to come with us, you can't do this, not by yourself," Natalie said and reached back and grabbed Terry's hand.

"Let go of me and quit saying my name."

"This is so whacked," Roxanne said. "You were right, Nat, your old lady is a nut job."

"See?" Natalie said.

"Shut up all of you. Control keeps screaming 'breach' in my head. Everyone just shut up."

"**She just sunk us, Vigilance.** She just sunk us, we're screwed, we are so completely and totally screwed," Paul said

"Shut up Control, I can't think."

"We're all going to jail, Terry."

"You know what, Control? That's the least of my worries right now. So shut the fuck up." Natalie and the others couldn't hear her unless she wanted them to. She pushed Natalie along. She wanted her and the others out of the building – that many less people to worry about. She wanted Natalie to be safe.

They were almost to the exit when the door slammed shut and the terrorists ran out of the crowd. Putting them – of course – in the worst possible spot in the room.

Two terrorists were at the front door, one at each of the back doors, and six made their way to the middle of the room.

People were screaming and crying. One of the terrorists emptied his clip into the ceiling and there was startling silence. Terry realized that she had knocked Natalie to the ground. "Stay down," she ordered in a whisper.

"Turn your cameras on. I want a live feed," the one she presumed was the leader ordered all the camera men scattered around the room. She was sure they would all comply, and that would mean something worse than terrorists would be on the way soon, at least worse for her. The military.

"I'm so sorry, Terry," Natalie whispered.

Terry knelt beside her. "Why?" Terry whispered back in her synthesized voice. "For telling everyone who I am? Don't worry about that now."

"For making you quit, maybe if I hadn't..."

"Nat... don't worry about anything right now except being smart. You're a smart woman, and you've been trained. Concentrate on that, on staying alive. After all, I'm in the suit. Not much can happen to me."

"Then do something," Janey ordered in a whisper.

The asshole was telling the cameras his demands. He wanted the government to release all their people who were currently incarcerated, or they were going to start shooting one hostage every ten minutes until they did. In other words they just wanted to kill a bunch of people, but they wanted it to seem like the government had an option.

"Scan for explosives," she told her computer. She moved from one terrorist to another. No explosives, and so far he wasn't threatening to blow up the building, but they'd been in and out of here possibly for weeks and they could have put a bomb practically anywhere. Still, this made more sense. Guns were easy to get, easy to use, easy to conceal, hard to trace, and in many ways a lot more frightening. A bomb went off, and you just assumed you got killed more or less instantly. And even knowing that Muslim terrorists blew themselves up on a regular basis, it was still hard for the American mind to think that they would. So as long as they were in the building you didn't believe they'd blow it up.

But this thing with the guns... Maybe they'd pick you and maybe not. Maybe they'd just wound you, maybe they'd give you a wound that would make sure you died, but slowly.

Maybe they'd rape the women, and make the men watch.

Yes, this was decidedly scarier, and she was afraid to move. Because as long as Natalie was with her she could protect her, but if she stayed by Natalie she wasn't going to be able to stop them from doing what they wanted to do. She was trying to decide what to do next, and then the leader picked his first victim.

Not unexpectedly he picked the person with the most recognizable face, who because of Terry was standing in the big middle of the damn room. He walked forward, pointed, and two of his bullyboys walked towards Janey. They grabbed her by the arm, Tom moved to try to stop them and wound up with a face full of rifle butt for his trouble. He landed with a thud at her feet. Her visor said he was still alive, which was more than she could say for the two men who'd grabbed Janey. Tom's heroics had been just the distraction she needed. She jumped up and grabbed the guy's rifle from his hand, swung it around and caved his face in with it. Then she swung quickly around and snapped a kick into the chest of the other man. He started to drop to his knees as the air was forced from his lungs, and she brought the rifle butt down on the base of his skull with enough force to separate his spine from his head.

Cameras were flashing everywhere.

"Stop it you morons!" Natalie screamed. "The flash lets them see Vigilance."

Surprisingly the flashing stopped, so it turned out that when it came right down to it the press cared more about their own necks than they did getting footage.

Terry moved from that position anyway, telling Janey, "Run and take cover."

As Terry ran she drew her laser pistol and fired at the leader, hitting him in the chest and bringing him down. Even without the camera flashes the light was too bright in the ballroom, and soon Terry was feeling the sting of bullets as they ricocheted off her body.

"The lights, we have to get rid of the lights. She can see in the dark, but we have to get rid of the lights," Natalie told Byron. She assumed they'd just try to find the switch.

Byron nodded. "Come on." He grabbed a table and knocked it over. Natalie and Roxanne helped him and he moved the table, using it as a shield. He grabbed the rifle of one of the gunmen who had grabbed Janey and had been subsequently killed by Terry, then he moved to a good vantage point and started to take out the lights one by one. Roxanne looked at him in astonishment.

He grinned and said, "BB gun," and continued firing.

Terry didn't know who was helping her, but she was glad for the help. She had taken down another of the terrorists with her laser, but she was hurt. Her visor said she had a cracked rib, and her leg was smarting where she'd been hit. But the suit had shot her full of adrenalin and now she had her camouflage back. People were screaming and running around like idiots. The terrorists were panicking, too, and people were getting hurt.

"Body count, Control," Terry demanded.

"Four, Terry. You killed four, there are six left. Two at the front door."

She saw them. Got a bead on one, fired, and then took the other one out. "And now there are four."

"Get out, the front doors are clear everyone get out," she ordered. People might trample each other, but at least if they were heading in one direction she didn't have to worry as much about where they were. People weren't really cattle. Give them one direction to go in, and they'd all go that way.

She swung quickly, saw a clear shot and took it. "And then there were three," she muttered.

She closed the distance between herself and the remaining terrorists and took out another one. A bullet hit her in the chest, slinging her sideways and breaking the previously cracked rib. Above her the light that had given her away broke. Lying there as the glass rained down on her she saw another one, fired, and he went down. She staggered to her feet...

...and felt something make contact with the back of her helmet. The bullet knocked her already wobbly body off balance and she fell forward. She rolled quickly and saw the terrorist standing over her, a camera in one hand, his gun in the other. She saw the camera flash and the gun go off. She fired her laser into the man's chest as the bullet smashed her visor.

Chapter 12

"How do you think I feel?" Terry asked hotly. "How do I feel!"

"I don't know, that's why I asked," Janey said with agitation. "Why do you have to be such a jerk?"

"Because I feel like hammered dog shit, that's why!"

"Cut, Cut!" the director yelled. "Dammit, Terry, for the tenth time, the line is hammered dog *crap*. You can't say *shit* on a network show in prime time. Let's take ten."

Terry got out of the hospital bed in her gown and followed Janey off the set.

"Hammered dog crap just sounds wrong. Besides what's the big difference between crap and shit?" Terry asked Janey.

"Getting to go home and staying here all night," Janey answered. "Just say it and quit being such a prima donna. I wanted to do a TV show so I'd have more time at home. I'd like to get the scene done so I *can* go home. Wouldn't you like to go home?"

"Not really. Nat's filming on location and I'm just bored at home alone."

"Well, I'm not, so just do your damn line. Go leap over a tall building in a single bound, or make the streets safe for hookers if you're too bored," Janey said.

"Shush, keep it down," Terry ordered.

"Chill out, Terry. Don't get your shorts in a knot. You saved my life. I'm not going to give up your dirty little secret. Besides, we've got a hit TV show and I'd hate for them to have to replace you. The chemistry would just be all wrong."

After what they all liked to call their little night of terror all of them had changed. Nothing quite like staring death in the face with your friends and loved ones to make you realize what really mattered. Janey had decided that she wanted to go back to the day-to-day grind, weekends and evenings off life of TV, and she'd gone to the creators of *Monster Killer* with the idea of creating a show built around the two characters she and Terry had played on the show. They had jumped at the idea. Three months later Terry and Janey were signing contracts, and two months after that they were shooting. Now a year later they had one of the hottest shows on TV.

The country also had a new president and administration. Paul had gathered together all the evidence that he had surrounding the terrorist attack and sent it to every news agency in the country. When news got out that the administration had been more interested in catching the country's hero than in stopping a major terrorist cell, they began to wonder where this president's priorities were. When they learned that the administration thought it was a good idea to let a bunch of Middle Eastern terrorists kill their favorite stars because they didn't like their politics, they began to wonder where they stood in the president's agenda. And when the news got out that a room full of "liberal" actors had stopped a terrorist attack by killing all the terrorists without a single casualty on our side they began to realize that "liberal" was just a label that the ultra right wing put on people who didn't want to send our boys overseas to die in a war over nothing larger than one man's pissing contest.

Voters turned out in record numbers to bury the bum. Things weren't back to normal yet, but they were getting better. For one thing people had hope again.

"What are you thinking?" Janey asked when Terry had been silent too long.

Terry shrugged. "How smug you must have felt when the terrorist picked you to die first."

Janey shuddered. "That's not funny, Terry."

Terry smiled, "However it is true." She started back for the set.

"Well, it does rather tell you how important you are when the terrorist thug picks you out of a crowd of other actors to piss off the capitalist imperialist pig dogs." Janey started following Terry.

"It's hard to believe that such a God awful thing could have turned out to save the country. If it hadn't happened, old numb-nuts would still be president. If he'd been reelected... Well, I'm thinking with the havoc he was able to wreak in four years that if he'd been reelected America would be nothing but a smoking hole by now."

"When you put it that way it almost makes it worth the nightmares. Although I have to say mine have just about stopped."

"Mine haven't."

The visor had stopped the bullet – barely – but it had knocked out her ability to see and communicate with Control. She was dazed and she was hurt, and the police and military had been arriving on the scene as the actors were running out of the building.

Natalie had grabbed her arm and jerked her to her feet with a strength Terry wouldn't have thought she possessed.

"We have to get you out of here," Natalie said as she started pulling her towards the back of the ballroom. How she knew which door Terry had entered through neither one of them had been able to figure out to this day. She'd pulled Terry into the hallway and helped her lean against the wall. "Terry, how bad are you hurt?"

"Not bad, at least I don't think so. My visor's out, though, so I can't be sure, and I might as well be blind because I can't see out of it. I also can't contact Control, but I don't think I'm hurt that bad, all things considered."

"The bike can drive itself right?

"Yes, yes the bike can drive itself, but I can't get to it."

"You don't have to." She grabbed Terry again and pulled her down the hall and into a room. She closed the door. "Take the suit off."

"Honey, I'm hardly in the mood."

"Take the fucking suit off," Natalie ordered, and for some reason Terry obeyed her. She took the helmet off and the suit deactivated. Terry looked around. They were in some sort of pantry. There certainly weren't any clothes there.

"I think I know what you're trying to do. But, honey, if I take the suit off, what am I going to put on?"

"My clothes."

Terry had started taking the suit off.

"Oh my God, Terry," Natalie had said upon seeing her injuries. She took her head in one hand and looked into her eyes. "Your ribs are broken again, and I think you're concussed."

Terry had winked at her. "But I still look damn good for a chick who got shot four times."

"Quit making stupid jokes." The tears were streaming down Natalie's cheeks as she took off her dress. She handed it to Terry who looked at it skeptically.

"I'd never wear this color, and it's like seven sizes too

small."

"It's stretch fabric. Do you think anyone's going to notice? There are injured stars and dead terrorists everywhere, not to mention police and military. It's a mass of confusion. No one's going to know or care what you're wearing," Natalie said. Terry couldn't put the dress on herself, so Natalie helped her, and then helped her into her underwear.

"Now go out there and just lay among the wounded till someone comes to get you."

"What are you going to do, Nat?"

"This time I'm going to play superhero. Which way did you come in?"

Terry told her. "But, Nat, there are two guys there and they are going to see you."

"No, they're going to see Vigilance." Natalie hit the helmet on the floor hard and the rest of the visor fell out so that she could see. Then she put the helmet on.

"But the suit won't work for you, Nat."

"Just go, Terry," Nat ordered. "Trust me. Trust me like I have trusted in you every time you put this stupid assed suit on."

"But you don't trust me, you sit around and worry till I come home."

"Then do that."

So Terry had stumbled out into the chaos to be carted off to the hospital with the rest of the victims, and Natalie had told her how she'd made her escape when she'd come to the hospital to visit her.

She had turned her cell phone on and used it to call Paul. She'd told him that Terry was hurt and what she'd done to hide Terry's identity. She needed Paul to help her find the bike and to have it bring her home. Then they would all be home clear.

As it turned out the two security guards Terry had left to watch the back window had most probably gotten scared when guns started going off and had run away. Whatever the cause, there was no one there when Natalie got there, so then it was just a matter of climbing out the window in the rather heavy suit and making her way to the bike, which Paul had programmed to make a bleeping sound until she found it. She got on the bike just as the first of the military were starting to file into the alley and had barely made a clean getaway.

So, Natalie had protected Terry's secret identity. Except of course that she had inadvertently told Tom and Janey, Roxanne and Byron that Terry was Vigilance. They all seemed more than happy to forget what they knew, except for Janey who liked to talk about it with Terry but wasn't going to tell anyone else.

So life was back to normal.

Mostly.

She said crap instead of shit and they all got to go home for the day.

Terry drove back to their apartment. She smiled. She didn't know exactly when it had become *their* apartment and *their* house instead of *her* house and *Natalie's* apartment. Probably at some point after "their little night of terror."

She walked in, flopped into a chair, and thought seriously about going to sleep and sleeping for about fifteen years. She was that tired.

"So... aren't you even going to say hi?" Natalie asked.

Terry sprang from the chair and ran across the room to embrace Natalie who stood at the end of the hall expectantly. All thoughts of being exhausted suddenly left Terry as she held Natalie. "I thought you weren't going to be back till next week."

"The film wrapped early," she said. "So, anything exciting happen while I was gone?"

"Nothing we can't talk about later." She grabbed Natalie's hand and started pulling her towards the bedroom until Natalie pulled free and ran past her.

They spent the next hour just reacquainting themselves with each other. Finally feeling sufficiently knowledgeable of one another again they rested in each other's arms.

"I missed you," Terry said.

"I missed you, too. So... anything exciting happen while I was gone?" Natalie asked again.

"Nothing too big. Beat up a couple of hoods, stopped a liquor store robbery. Shot the next two episodes of the show. Went to a dinner party at Janey's. You?"

"Well... I beat up a pimp and blew up a crack house, and yes I was very careful."

"It's just not the same working alone is it?"

"Not really," Natalie smiled. "So... does Batman need

Robin?"

"I don't know, but I need you."

The End

About the Author

Selina Rosen has sold several stories to *Marion Zimmer Bradley's Fantasy Magazine,* two of which were reprinted in anthologies. She has also sold stories to *Chicks In Chain Mail: Turn the Other Chick, Thieves' World: Turning Points, Iguana Informer, Cosmic Debris, Distant Journeys, Such A Pretty Face, Personal Demons,* and a few other magazines and anthologies. Four of her novels, *Queen of Denial, Recycled, Chains of Freedom,* and *Chains of Destruction,* were published in 1999, 2001, 2002, and 2003 by Meisha Merlin Publishing. Meisha Merlin will be publishing *Chains of Redemption* (the third and final book in the Chains trilogy) sometime in 2004. She also has several novellas and stories in anthologies that are available through Yard Dog Press (www.yarddogpress.com), and Yard Dog also published her novels, *Fire & Ice* in 2001, and *Hammer Town* in 2003.

Ms. Rosen says, "If you're reading this, then you've already bought one of my books. Come to my website (http://www..selinarosen.com) and let me know how you like it, or just talk – I really *like* to talk!!"

About the Cover Artist

Sherri Dean lives in a small town outside Kansas City, Missouri. A veteran in the field of Animal Health, she spends her quality time enjoying art, writing, costuming and reading comics.

Her artwork is featured in *Bubbas of the Apocalypse: the Card Game* from Yard Dog Press. She enjoys feedback, and her latest works – including a book cover and t-shirt design – can be seen at the Yard Dog Press site at http://www.yarddogpress.com

Yard Dog Press Titles As Of This Print Date

Hammer Town, Selina Rosen

The Happiness Box, Beverly A. Hale

The Host Series: The Host, Fright Eater, Gang Approval, Selina Rosen

Houston, We've Got Bubbas!, Edited by Selina Rosen

How I Spent the Apocolypse, Selina Rosen

I Didn't Quite Make It To Oz, Edited by Selina Rosen

I Should Have Stayed In Oz, Edited by Selina Rosen

Illusions of Sanity, James K. Burk

In the Shadows, Bradley H. Sinor

International House of Bubbas, Edited by Selina Rosen

It's the Great Bumpkin, Cletus Brown!, Katherine A. Turski

The Killswitch Review, Steven-Elliot Altman & Diane DeKelb-Rittenhouse

The Leopard's Daughter, Lee Killough

The Lightning Horse, John Moore

The Logic of Departure, Mark W. Tiedemann

The Long, Cold Walk To Mars, Jeffrey Turner

Marking the Signs and Other Tales Of Mischief, Laura J. Underwood

Material Things, Selina Rosen

Medieval Misfits: Renaissance Rejects, Tracy S. Morris

Mirror Images, Susan Satterfield

More Stories That Won't Make Your Parents Hurl, Edited by Selina Rosen

Music for Four Hands, Louis Antonelli & Edward Morris

My Life with Geeks and Freaks, Claudia Christian

The Necronomicrap: A Guide To Your Horoooscope, Tim Frayser

Playing With Secrets, Bradley H & Sue P. Sinor

Redheads In Love, Linda L. Donahue, Rhonda Eudaly, Julia S. Mandala, & Dusty Rainbolt

Reruns, Selina Rosen

Rock 'n' Roll Universe, Ken Rand

Shadows In Green, Richard Dansky

Some Distant Shore, Dave Creek

Stories That Won't Make Your Parents Hurl, Edited by Selina Rosen

Strange Twists Of Fate, James K. Burk

Tales From the Home for Wayward Spirits and Bar-B-Que Grill, Rie Sheridan

Tales from Keltora, Laura J. Underwood

Tales Of the Lucky Nickel Saloon, Second Ave., Laramie, Wyoming, U S of A, Ken Rand

Texistani: Indo-Pak Food From A Texas Kitchen, Beverly A. Hale

That's All Folks, J. F. Gonzalez

Through Wyoming Eyes, Ken Rand
Turn Left to Tomorrow, Robin Wayne Bailey
Wandering Lark, Laura J. Underwood
Wings of Morning, Katharine Eliska Kimbriel
Zombies In Oz and Other Undead Musings, Robin Wayne Bailey

Double Dog
(A YDP Imprint):

#1:
Of Stars & Shadows,
Mark W. Tiedemann
This Instance Of Me,
Jeffrey Turner

#2:
Gods and Other Children,
Bill D. Allen
Tranquility,
Tracy Morris

#3:
Home Is the Hunter,
James K. Burk
Farstep Station,
Lazette Gifford

#4:
Sabre Dance,
Melanie Fletcher
The Lunari Mask,
Laura J. Underwood

#5:
House of Doors,
Julia Mandala
Jaguar Moon,
Linda A. Donahue

Just Cause
(A YDP Imprint):

Death Under the Crescent Moon
Dusty Rainbolt

The Ghost Writer
Selina Rosen

*It's Not Rocket Science: Spirituality
for the Working-Class Soul*
Selina Rosen

Not My Life
Selina Rosen

The Pit
Selina Rosen

*Plots and Protagonists: A Refer-
ence Guide for Writers*
Mel. White

Vanishing Fame
Selina Rosen

Non-YDP titles we distribute:

Chains of Freedom
Chains of Destruction
Jabone's Sword
Queen of Denial
Recycled
Strange Robby
Sword Masters
Selina Rosen

Three Ways to Order:

1. Write us a letter telling us what you want, then send it along with your check or money order (made payable to Yard Dog Press) to: Yard Dog Press, 710 W. Redbud Lane, Alma, AR 72921-7247

2. Use selinarosen@cox.net or lynnstran@cox.net to contact us and place your order. Then send your check or money order to the address above. *This has the advantage of allowing you to check on the availability of short-stock items such as T-shirts and back-issues of Yard Dog Comics.*

3. Contact us as in #1 or #2 above and pay with a credit card or by debit from your checking account. Either give us the credit card information in your letter/Email/phone call, or go to our website and use our shopping carts. If you send us your information, please include your name as it appears on the card, your credit card number, the expiration date, and the 3 or 4-digit security code after your signature on the back (CVV). Please remember that we will include media rate (minimum $3.00) S/H for mailing in the lower 48 states.

Watch our website at
www.yarddogpress.com
for news of upcoming projects
and new titles!!